With Love from
Bliss

Also by Ruth Glover
A Place Called Bliss

The Saskatchewan Saga

With Love from Bliss

A NOVEL

RUTH GLOVER

Fleming H. Revell
A Division of Baker Book House Co
Grand Rapids, Michigan 49516

© 2001 by Ruth Glover

Published by Fleming H. Revell
a division of Baker Book House Company
P.O. Box 6287, Grand Rapids, MI 49516-6287

Printed in the United States of America

Library of Congress Cataloging-in-Publication Data

Glover, Ruth.
    With love from bliss : a novel / Ruth Glover.
        p.   cm.— (The Saskatchewan saga)
    Sequel to : A place called bliss.
    ISBN 0-8007-5744-0
    1. Frontier and pioneer life—Fiction. 2. Saskatchewan—Fiction.
I. Title.
PS3557.L678 W58 2001
813'.54—dc21   00-067352

Scripture is from the King James Version of the Bible.

For current information about all releases from Baker Book House, visit our web site:
http://www.bakerbooks.com

To Lela,
sister in all but birth

The figure on the bed was scrunched into a ball as tightly as the human body can fold and not be in the womb. Shaken by an occasional sob or hiccup, it seemed the child, though motionless, was awake. If she was asleep, her rest was wracked by bad dreams.

The sound of carriage wheels on the gravel below brought the small girl upright. On her cheeks were the marks of tears; her eyes were filled with something more than misery—something that reminded one of an animal backed into a corner, afraid.

Perhaps the one who entered the room saw and understood both the unhappiness and the fear. Perhaps she also saw the child's pathetic vulnerability quickly cloaked with a pretense at dignity that was as pitiful as it was false. At any rate, Sister Bernadine's voice, when she spoke, held a tinge of compassion along with the usual authority.

"Come now, Kerry, this is no way to go downstairs and greet your aunt, *Mrs. Sebastian Maxwell*, who's come to get you, and on such short notice."

Sister Bernadine was aware that she had emphasized the name of the guest who was even now alighting from the carriage, and a slight flush tinged her face. To think that she would be impressed by the high and mighty! Or perhaps it was the wealth associated with the Maxwell name. And who could blame her, constantly aware as she was of the needs of The Beneficent Sisters of Charity, the order to which she belonged, religiously devoted to the care of the poor. What was it the proverb said? "He that hath mercy on the poor, happy is he." Sister Bernadine, face-to-face with another example of that poverty, supposed she should be the happiest of persons. Instead, her heart ached for the overwhelming needs all around her and this small girl in particular, and she grieved over the little she could do about any of it. Still, her reaction to the wealth of the Maxwells was a worldly attitude and quite shamed her.

The child, huddled on the unmade bed with her mismatched and threadbare clothing askew and her hair tumbled, either did not know or did not care about the wealth and the prestige of her kin, and she looked painfully lost and alone. So alone. Poor, wee mite! She deserved some tender, loving care. Would the esteemed Mrs. Sebastian Maxwell provide it? Certainly the well-to-do woman was well able to lavish comfort and relief wherever she deemed it fitting, but on one small, inconspicuous mortal? Time would tell.

And was the child inconspicuous, after all? Hadn't she, more than once in the last few days, rattled Sister Bernadine herself, as well as every Sister who came in contact with her, and by the very Word of God to which they were committed? If Sister Bernadine were a betting woman, she would have laid odds on Kerry Ferne being a power unto herself in most any situation that life (and Mrs. Sebastian Maxwell) might bring her way.

Now, in accordance with what Sister Bernadine already knew about her, Kerry summoned her considerable courage once again. Though her voice quavered, she looked up at the Sister bending over her and spoke clearly.

"She's come? My Aunt Charlotte's come?"

"Sure, and did you think she wouldn't?" Sister's tone was brisk, perhaps to forestall any repetition of the one and only demonstration of grief Kerry had allowed herself. What a heartrending scene it had been when the child was led—herded—from her father's graveside. It would be best, Sister thought, if she could be brought to accept the finality of her loss, best that she adjust to her new status quickly—that of niece of one of the most affluent and influential women in the province of Ontario. To the aunt's credit, she had promptly responded to the wire informing her of her brother's death, delaying her arrival only until the funeral was over and her brother's mortal remains were committed to the earth. Why the delay, no one knew.

Now her carriage was at the door; surely it was a good sign for the future of the child.

"Come, rise and shine. Get your hair brushed and your face washed," Sister said crisply. But her hands were gentle as she pulled aside the bedding the small fist clutched so defensively—and so inadequately—against what must seem to be a strange and hostile world.

That Kerry did indeed regard it as hostile had been revealed by her words when she was informed that her aunt had been contacted, words that a studied theologian might have come up with, words of a remote Scripture. But what a Scripture! Hearing her aunt's name, the child had quoted darkly, "A man's foes are those of his own household."

Remembering the incident, Sister Bernadine found herself, again, startled and even dismayed by the strange, even dire, words. Where would the child have learned such a bitter attitude toward her father's sister? Was it that Avery Ferne, scholarly gentleman though he was, had been on bad terms with Charlotte Maxwell? But if Avery Ferne's daughter had learned Bible verses of any sort under his tutelage, he was a different man indeed from the image the world saw—that of an intemperate rake with an unsavory reputation, addicted to gambling and with a habit of not paying his bills. But here was his small daughter, spouting Scripture like a vested pontiff.

There was a story back of all this, and Sister Bernadine's curiosity was aroused. But she quelled it in face of the need at hand—and just now that was Kerry's rising from the bed and making herself presentable.

But what a precocious child! There were additional times when she had inserted Scripture into conversations, some of it suitable enough, some of it with a most uncomfortable application.

The night after the dreary burial, for instance, when Sister Claude was putting the drooping child to bed and attempting to comfort her with the assurance that her aunt would soon come for her, Kerry had shaken her head with its dark curls and quoted, "I will set him in safety from him that puffeth at him."

"I was speechless," Sister Claude confessed later to Sister Bernadine and others. "Have any of you ever heard of such a passage from the Bible? I certainly haven't. It was unsettling, to say the least. And what did she mean by it?"

The quirking of a lip here and there—some of the Sisters had personal knowledge of the ready and sometimes guilt-provoking quotations—was quickly replaced by a more decorous expression when Sister Claude frowned and paused.

Seemly order restored, Sister Claude continued. "And then she looked up at me with her great, dark eyes and said, quite earnestly, 'I believe that *her* can be used in place of *him*, don't you? Else it wouldn't be fair, would it? I mean, all the Scriptures seem to be given to men, but they must mean both men and women, don't you think?'"

Nodded heads affirmed that the child had touched on a surprisingly thoughtful truth.

"I was considerably at sea in my thinking by this time," Sister Claude continued, fully appreciative of her attentive audience. "I must have shown my confusion, because she got an anxious look on her face and said, 'What I mean is, like where the Bible says that man is born to trouble, as the sparks fly upward.

It's been my experience'—mind you, this is coming from a nine-year-old—'that women are born to trouble, too, so it must mean *both* men and women when it says man or him.'

"Then she asked me, anxiously again, if I understood her. By this time I wasn't certain of anything, and I guess she saw it; she's a sensitive child. She went on, patiently—and I don't mind telling you, I felt like a dunderhead—'So what that Scripture means is that *she,* meaning me, will be safe from *her,* meaning Aunt Charlotte, that puffeth at me.'"

"Puffeth?" someone repeated.

"How very odd!" exclaimed another, while someone murmured "Dunderhead?"

"It has an element of truth in it!" This was spoken warmly by Sister Vivian, a novitiate and the youngest in the listening group.

When a dozen pairs of eyes were turned on her, Sister Vivian blushed, gathered her courage, and hurried on with her comment.

"I mean about the Bible including woman in its references to man. I think it means *mankind.*"

"Well, of course, Sister—"

"But," Sister Vivian hastened to add, humbly, "I don't understand, not one bit, the *puffeth* part."

"That's all right, dear," someone said kindly, "I'm sure we're all at sea about it."

While Sister Vivian subsided, and needles resumed their mending of the rips and tears and worn places of the castoff clothes being repaired for the poor of the city, someone asked Sister Claude, "Well, what did you say to the child after all this?"

Sister Claude looked around at the expectant faces and took a new lease on the narrative.

"Well, quite naturally I think, I asked, 'Puffeth? What do you mean, puffeth?' It seemed reasonable of me to ask, since she was speaking in riddles, and even though I felt it put her in the place of teacher and me of learner, still—"

Sister Claude was sometimes inclined toward garrulousness. This was known by all and usually borne with long-suffering, but now someone brought her quickly back to the matter at hand.

"Yes, yes, Sister, it was indeed a reasonable reaction on your part. I'm sure I might have thought the same thing in the circumstances. But then what?"

"Well," Sister Claude said, "she gave me more of that same verse, which was, 'The Lord will rise for the oppression of the poor and the sighing of the needy.' Imagine my reaction by this time, if you can. It was the strangest conversation I've almost ever had. Even stranger than when that delivery man asked me if any of us had ever considered—"

"Yes, yes, Sister, we all remember, and how splendidly you answered him. And then what did she say?"

"She said," Sister Claude mimicked warningly, *"And Sister, you better watch out when the Lord rises!"*

Numerous gasps were heard as needles paused, heads were shaken, and voices raised in perplexity, dismay, or amazement.

This child! Didn't she beat all!

"When I asked her—rather crossly, I'm afraid, for I was quite put out by this time—if she also memorized Scripture references, she said 'Psalm 12, verse 5' quick as a wink."

"Psalm 12 . . . hmmm," several voices repeated as the information was stored away for possible confirmation or further study.

Sister Evangeline, who had unpacked the child's meager belongings, spoke next. "She has a Bible. King James, of course—they're Protestants—and it's old and dilapidated, much used by somebody. The name Esther Morley is written on the flyleaf. Does anyone here know if that was her mother, and if so, what happened to her? Dead, I suppose, or we wouldn't be searching out this obscure aunt."

"Not obscure, Sister! Certainly not obscure," Sister Bernadine corrected. "Not by any stretch of the imagination. Definitely not obscure. No one can belong to the Maxwell family, particularly the *Sebastian* Maxwell family, and be obscure. I thought everyone knew that."

Sister Evangeline could have pointed out that she had chosen a life of retreat and self-denial and that she didn't engage her faculties, as a rule, in worldly matters, but she was too sweet-tempered to do so. But for one wild moment, until she drew rein on her emotions, she almost blurted out, much as the child herself might have, *Not minding high things, but consenting to the humble!* Immediate contrition for such retaliatory thoughts kept her on her knees scrubbing the steps most of the afternoon.

Sister Bernadine was placidly continuing, "Yes, the mother of the child is indeed deceased. Esther Morley—now there's an obscure name for you. Being married to that rapscallion didn't elevate her reputation any, I'm sorry to say."

"He wasn't always so dissolute—Avery Ferne, I mean," someone supplied. "It's possible that his wife's death marked a turning point—a downward turning point. It wouldn't be easy to be left alone with the care of a small child."

"It happens all the time," Sister Bernadine responded, "and it doesn't turn men into ne'er-do-wells. It's fortunate indeed, for little Kerry's sake, that the landlady had knowledge of the Maxwell connection, or the child might have ended up on the street among the hordes of children tossed aside to survive or perish as they will. Goodness knows we do our best to rescue them. Or do we? Sometimes I wonder if we are selfless enough . . ."

"Well, the Maxwells are known for their charitable works. Kerry Ferne has fallen on her feet, I'd say."

"Lucky child!"

"Fortunate child, fortunate and blessed." Sister Bernadine folded her mending and slipped away to other tasks, as did her companions, several of them in search of a Bible, only to find the Douay version silent on the subject of puffing.

W hen the child was presentable—washed and combed and straightened—still there was a delay in meeting the important guest. Sister Bernadine thought it wise to collect her charge's possessions and take them down at the same time she presented the child. She couldn't imagine that Mrs. Sebastian Maxwell would spend valuable time in the small receiving room while her niece's baggage was being assembled—especially these particular ragtag items—and be happy about it.

She was right. When at last Sister Bernadine entered the room, with Kerry lagging behind, it was to find Charlotte Maxwell tight-lipped. The reason was plain: Sister Vivian was fumbling, scarlet-faced, at the task of mopping tea from the woman's skirt, which was the handsomest mourning costume imaginable, clearly expensive, made of silk moire, and fittingly black in color.

"You may go, Sister," Sister Bernadine said quietly, and Sister Vivian, with another anguished glance at the guest's stony eyes and flared nostrils—which seemed remarkably at home in the long, handsome face—made her escape, an empty cup tipping in her shaking hand.

Shepherding the small girl forward, Sister Bernadine introduced herself to the woman seated before her, adding, "And this, of course," indicating the child, "is Kerry," and lest there be any question about the woman's responsibility, "the daughter of Avery Ferne, your brother."

With two fingers of one be-ringed hand Charlotte Maxwell held the damaged skirt away from her knee; with the other she blotted the wet spot with a serviette. Long moments passed before she turned her attention to the waiting pair. A mere dip of the flowered, winged, gathered lace and straw creation that seemed to reign supreme on the iron-gray head was the only acknowledgment she accorded Sister. Her gaze was fixed on the small face at Sister Bernadine's elbow.

"So you are Kerry."

"I'm Keren," the child said, and only Sister caught the attempt at bravery in the two words. But Kerry was not through. "Spelled with two e's. K-e-r-e-n."

The sentence hung in the air between them like a protective shield on a field of battle.

To the astonished Sister, it seemed that the child was making a startling effort to keep her identity from being lost in that of the woman, doing it the only way she knew and doing it instinctively. Sister had a momentary vision of a swimmer clinging to a capsized boat, desperately resisting the tug of the current. She clasped with a firm grip the small hand that had somehow made its way into hers.

"K-*e*, K-*a*," the aunt said briskly. "What could it possibly matter? It sounds the same no matter how it's spelled. It has a foreign ring to it," she continued quenchingly, "that certainly isn't Scottish." The Ferne family, into which Charlotte had been born, was Scotch through and through, and though brother Avery had not graced the name, still it should have its honorable recognition, especially by this upstart child, or so it seemed to be implied from the speaker's tone. Keren with an *e* indeed! Charlotte Maxwell hoped that the annoying *e* would not pop into her mind every time she spoke the name.

Kerry was doggedly pursuing the subject. "It's from the Bible, you see. Job had seven sons and three daughters—that was *after* the first set of seven and three died when a great wind came from the wilderness and smote the four corners of the house where they were eating and drinking." Kerry finished the sentence in one breath.

"I always thought it was amazing that the number should be the same the second time around. Don't you, Aunt? Only God could do that, don't you think? He wanted Job to have exactly seven sons and three daughters, I guess. I heard that the number seven is supposed to be lucky. It wasn't lucky for Job though, was it?"

Kerry finally paused, looking at her aunt, who was opening and closing her mouth in a most surprising way. After a gasp or two, Mrs. Maxwell prepared to give some sort of answer to this conversation, which had gotten so quickly out of hand.

But once again Kerry was prepared, and she continued. "Well, anyway, in case you wonder what this has to do with my name and the way it's spelled, the last three daughters were called Jemima, Kezia, and Keren-happuch. I've always been grateful I wasn't named Kezia. There's no way to make Kezia sound soft and pretty is there? It's that *zzzz* in there. My papa always said it sounded like a buzz saw. That's when I said I didn't like the happuch part of my name. Papa said it reminded him of 'happy,' and his little Kerry made him happy."

The child's eyes were enormous and almost purple in color in the late afternoon light. Her face, already pale, was white, and the look of strain on it was frightening.

Sister Bernadine jiggled the hand she held, and said, when the child's face turned up to her, "And he was so right. I'm sure little girls are made to make people happy. So, Keren-happuch, shall we gather your things together so you may start on the first leg of a new adventure?"

The purple-black eyes turned slowly toward Charlotte Maxwell, whose pale eyes blinked, and who couldn't seem to collect herself enough to speak coherently. Her niece spoke again.

"So that's why I'm called Keren with two e's. It's all on account of Job, you see."

Her audience didn't look as though she "saw" at all.

"Poor Job," Kerry continued, as though she were a watch wound tightly and not about to run down, "to lose all those loved ones at one time. I feel ever so grateful that I have only lost one person—two, actually, though my mama died a long time ago. But sometimes it's hard to be grateful, isn't it?"

Kerry at last fell silent, perhaps because Sister Bernadine's hand was, now, pressing her shoulder. She watched her aunt's flaring nostrils with fascination. Sister Bernadine had the fleeting thought that those nostrils and that flare might be a meaningful signal across the years, if Kerry but knew it.

Apparently the taut silence was more than the child could stand. "I find it hard," she said, taking a deep breath, "that though I have her name, I don't look like Keren-happuch. You see," she went on, "in all the land no women were found as fair as the daughters of Job. Wouldn't you just love to be the fairest in all the land, Aunt? I certainly would.

"Do you think *fair* means light complected?" she asked. "I hope it doesn't, 'cause I'm dark. When I asked Mrs. Peabody, our landlady, about it, she didn't know. That's a funny word, isn't it—landlady? Mrs. Peabody was always saying 'My lands!' and she did own the land and the house. But Miss Perley, who had the room next to ours, always said 'My heavens,' and she didn't own any of the heavens, did she? When I talked to Papa about it, he laughed and said Miss Perley *was* a heavenly body—"

Sister appeared to be tongue-tied; Charlotte Maxwell was mopping her brow with the tea-stained serviette. Kerry took a breath and continued.

"I think fair means beautiful, and of course I'm not the fairest in the land, even though Papa said—"

"That's all very interesting, I'm sure," Charlotte Maxwell was finally able to interject. "I trust we are not to be subjected to the patriarch Job's history on a continuing basis."

"But it's a story with a happy ending—I do so love happy endings, don't you? Job ended up with twice as much as he had before, did you know that? Except it was the same amount of sons and daughters . . . well who would want fourteen sons, anyway?"

"Well, Keren with an e—excuse me, *two* e's—we won't dally any longer over names and spelling and fair maidens, be they dark or light complexioned. Stories with happy endings, indeed! It's not a storybook world, my girl." Thus spoke the woman of high degree, with her rings on her fingers, her furs around her shoulders, her carriage at the door, and a mansion full of treasures awaiting her return home.

"Now then," the aunt said, indicating the boxes and bags clumped at her feet, "are these your . . . things?"

For a moment Kerry was downcast. But not for long. Her eyes brightened, she drew in a full breath of air, and responded in true Kerry fashion: "It's a good thing that man's life consisteth not in the abundance of things which he possesseth, isn't it, Aunt?"

Aunt Charlotte's face, to the watching Sister, was a study in aggravation and curiosity.

"Consisteth . . . possesseth?" With some of the abundance of her possessions on full display—modish ensemble, jewels in her ears and on her fingers—Charlotte Maxwell murmured the question faintly.

"She's quoting the Bible," Sister Bernadine supplied quickly. "She seems to know a good portion of it by heart. We've been, er, privileged to hear some of it." No one had ever accused Sister Bernadine of a sense of humor, but one would have wondered now, noting a certain mischievous gleam in her eye and the upward tug of the corner of one lip.

"Gracious me," Charlotte Maxwell murmured and caught herself immediately lest her niece, whose eyes had indeed brightened at the small expletive, should feel led to rate her aunt along with the utterers of "My land" and "My heavens." If truth were told, Charlotte Maxwell wasn't feeling all that gracious at the moment.

This was rectified, however, a little later when she placed a generous check in the hands of Sister Bernadine as the ill-matched pair—small, shabby girl and elegantly gowned woman—made their departure, the carriage driver having been summoned to carry out Kerry's meager possessions.

Sister Bernadine closed the door behind them and turned to find nuns creeping from hiding places, with inquiring faces.

"There goes the most unusual child I've come across in a long time, perhaps ever," Sister commented, and her opinion was confirmed by a dozen nodding heads. Nodding, or shaking, in wordless wonder.

"But—has she met her match in Mrs. Sebastian Maxwell, not to mention the formidable Maxwell clan? Or as Kerry might say, is it possible that a little child shall lead them?"

"Either that," Sister Claude said with a shake of her head, "or they'll hang a millstone about her neck and drown her."

The Scripture-quoting Sisters looked at one another with a certain grim humor mixed with astonishment that they should have found themselves so influenced by one small girl in so short a time.

The last trace of anything familiar was gone, shut forever from her by the closing of the heavy convent door and the finality of Sister Bernadine's encouraging pat. Kerry's small moment of panic faded before the imposing turnout awaiting her on the graveled drive—a pair of matched grays, a shining rig, a uniformed attendant. Her sense of curiosity, well developed though fed thus far on the husks and fish heads of life, caused her eyes to brighten and her unquenchable spirit to surface.

"Is this yours, Aunt? I always dreamed of riding in a surrey. Papa and I walked, mostly, or caught the trolley, which was awfully crowded and smelled bad. I'm small, you see, and shorter than most of the riders, and Papa said it brought my nose direckly in contack with parts of the anatomy that were 'specially arrow-matic.'"

"I don't wish to hear such rubbish repeated, Kerry. Avery Ferne never did have a discerning bone in his body. No, nor a discriminating one, either. Now get into the rig, which is by the way—though why I bother to explain I'll never know—a carriage, not a surrey. I can see," Charlotte Maxwell added with a sigh, "that there's much, so much, you need to learn. Where have you been, child, and what have you been doing, that you know Scripture by the ream and nothing about conveyances?"

"Why," Kerry said, and her sigh almost equaled her aunt's, "Right here in Toronto. All the time. Nine years." It sounded like nine l-o-n-g years, a lifetime of years.

"And where," she asked, with an innocence that could not make it offensive, "have you been, Aunt?"

"First off," that lady said, buttoning her glove carefully, the end of her nose pink, a sure indication, to Kerry, of extreme aggravation and a mighty effort to control it, "don't call me 'Aunt' like that. Charlotte is my name, and it seems I am your aunt, so the glorious result of such an association must be Aunt Charlotte, right?"

"I can tell you're upset, Aunt Charlotte, because your nose is pink. Papa's nose did the same thing. It was a sign to me."

"A sign?" Charlotte couldn't keep from asking, though she looked at the child sharply.

"A sign to beware. And that's when I'd get something to read and go sit on my bed or on the footstool in a corner. That's how come I memorized so much Scripture."

The picture the child conjured up was not a good one; even Charlotte could see that, and for the moment her heart, not really hard but extremely given to vexation, suffered a twinge of sympathy for the small figure at her side. And more than that, the fact that she reminded the child of Avery, whose ways she abhorred, was like a knife point at the throat—threatening and frightening. Was she so much like him after all? Had she really climbed so short a distance up the social scale?

With an unconscious twitch of the telltale nose, Charlotte turned to the liveried man standing at the horses' heads with his eyes fixed on a point somewhere in the far distance, his face impassive.

"Gideon, put Miss Keren—with two e's—into the carriage, please." The tone of her voice was not humorous, but Kerry's eyes smiled, her mouth quickly rejecting the grin that tugged at its corners.

Gideon approached smartly and reached for the youngster at his mistress's side, to hoist her onto the carriage step. He paused as Kerry looked up at him and said brightly, "Gibeon— I love the sound of that name. One of my very most favorite stories is when the Lord delivered up the Amorites—don't you just love the sound of 'delivered up'? It gives me the goose pumps." Kerry's joyous laughter was like a flash of light cleaving the late afternoon sky. "My papa always said goose pumps and goose bimples. Once I saw a naked goose—Mrs. Peabody was going to roast it for Christmas dinner—and it was *very* pimply."

"Keren—" Charlotte Maxwell couldn't have imagined in her wildest dreams that she would ever be conversing, on a public thoroughfare, in front of a servant, about the texture of a goose's skin.

But Kerry, not about to be deflected, stepped back a pace, flung out her arm, pointed dramatically heavenward, and trilled grandly: "'Sun, stand thou still upon Gibeon; and'" here her finger changed its direction, "'thou, Moon, in the valley of Ajalon.'"

Even the usually expressionless Gideon looked startled, and Charlotte Maxwell, caught off guard again, failed to speak quickly enough to stem the drama being enacted before her eyes.

"So," Kerry delivered, with the eyes of a zealot, "'the sun stood still, and the moon stayed, until the people had avenged themselves upon their enemies.'"

Slowly her arm dropped to her side, her gaze lowered from the lofty heights it had been contemplating, and she said, "I tried to get a miracle once. I certainly needed a miracle. Cordelia, that's Mrs. Peabody's daughter, said that her mama would throw us out in the street if we didn't pay up our rent. I kicked her, and even Papa didn't understand, though I explained about Joshua smiting the hindmost of his enemies, and that I was just doing the biblical thing."

"Kerry!" Charlotte Maxwell said in terrible voice. "That will be enough of that! Let it be understood here and now that you are not Joshua. Neither are you David, so don't think about heaving a slingshot at some nonexistent giant. And neither are you Elijah, to run before the chariot. *Now get into the carriage!* And," she added as an afterthought, "the name isn't Gibeon, it's Gideon, so all those histrionics were wasted."

Kerry was encouraged over someone conversing with her about the Scriptures. "Yes, but Aunt," she answered, forgetting the admonition about addressing her relative properly, "don't you just get little thrills all up and down your backbone over the part that says the hand of the Lord was on him? I just love that part. What do you suppose it's like to have the hand of the Lord on you? Once when Miss Perley—"

"She of the heavenly body," Charlotte Maxwell found herself muttering, much to her astonishment and chagrin, and forgetting entirely to chastise her niece for discussing so freely a private and unmentionable part of one's anatomy—thrills up one's backbone, indeed!

"When Miss Perley was in our room and I was told to go to sleep, she put me to bed and patted me. But I think the hand of God would be even more comforting, don't you?"

Mrs. Sebastian Maxwell finally found herself outmaneuvered, outwitted, and outtalked. "Just—get—into—the—carriage," she managed, with more restraint than she could have imagined speaking to any living soul aside from her venerable queen.

Finally, somewhat chastened—either that or dry of further inspiration—Kerry submitted to Gideon's help and stepped up into a carriage so trim and smart that she was immediately tempted to new heights of eloquence.

Running her hand over the tufted seat, she said, "I love this machine-buffed leather, don't you, Aunt? I find it very satisfying to the soul, as well as to the hindmost." And she jounced up and down a few times as her aunt seated herself.

Charlotte Maxwell's sallow face seemed to pale, and her eyes closed. But when she spoke, she said only "buffed?" faintly. "Hindmost" she simply couldn't deal with.

"Yes. And the back and seats are prob'ly built of the best selected yellow poplar panels. Do these look like best selected yellow poplar, Aunt?"

"Yellow . . . poplar . . . panels . . ." Charlotte was half whispering, with a dazed look upon her face.

"The sills are prob'ly second-growth ash. And they're put together in the very best possible manner, screwed and plugged from inside and outside. But what bothers me, Aunt, is that I don't even know what that means. Do you see anything that looks like it's plugged? It's s'posed to be good, though, not bad, like a plugged nickel."

The redoubtable Gideon, in the process of stowing the young person's shabby belongings, seemed to be battling against a change of expression—a most unusual event.

"Including," Kerry was continuing, "full silver-plated hub bands, prop nuts, dash rail, etcetera. That's the way the catalog ended that part—etcetera."

"Et-cet-era? Catalog?" Something was wrong with Charlotte's voice.

"When I wasn't reading the Bible, I was reading the catalog," Kerry explained. "Oh, I could furnish an entire house with everything you would need, from the 'Highest Grade Acme Dining Room Sideboard and Refrigerator Combined' to a 'Planished Coffee Pot,' the same as the Planished Tea Pot, except it has a lip spout. Oh yes, Aunt Charlotte, there's many an hour of good reading in a catalog. Mine, though, was several years old. The fashions have prob'ly changed. I'm not sure," she said doubtfully, "if you're dressed in the latest for spring and summer, but," she hastened on, seeing her aunt's darkening brow, "I think you prob'ly are. Miss Perley kindly gave the catalog to me one day after I guess I had quoted too much Scripture. She knows Scripture, too, Aunt Charlotte. She asked me if I'd ever read the one that said, 'I was dumb, I opened not my mouth.' And then she dug around in her trunk and found the catalog and gave it to me, and said, 'Here, read this.' Wasn't that kind of her?"

"I think I've heard quite enough of the estimable Miss Perley, thank you. Now, if you'll just settle down, we'll start what will be a long journey home." Charlotte Maxwell added with a sigh, "A very, very long journey home."

"But I'm so happy to be riding in a Maythorn & Son carriage! I think this is a Victoria, exhibited at Biggleswade. Don't you just love that word—Biggleswade? Aunt Charlotte, what is pumice?"

"Why, it's a powder," Charlotte found herself saying in spite of herself, "glass, volcanic glass, used for smoothing. But what possible reason could you have for asking?"

"This rig is painted in the 'highest style of the art in thirteen coats, the first coats rubbed out with pumice.' Why would they rub out what they painted?"

"Thirteen coats? My goodness—" Charlotte was speaking faintly again.

"See, you're doing it, too."

"Doing? Doing what, pray tell?"

"What Mrs. Peabody did. My lands, she said, and she was a landlady. Miss Perley said my heavens, and she was a heavenly body. You say my goodness, and you *are* good, Aunt Charlotte, else you'd never come all this way just to get your poor relative." Kerry looked up at her newfound aunt with her dark eyes shy and shining with something that closely resembled tears. If Sister Bernadine had seen and heard, she would never have believed the change—from a fierce, black-browed antagonist, to an eager, chatting companion, Kerry Ferne had come full circle in a few moments.

Charlotte Maxwell did something far, far out of character: With a similar sheen to her own eyes, she put a gloved hand over the little one beside her on the richly tufted, machine-buffed Columbus seat; her grim mouth seemed to cooperate by loosening its disapproving lines, and her rigid posture seemed to settle and soften. In spite of herself and her grudging, reluctant response to the call to do her duty and provide a home to her graceless brother's child, she found herself squeezing the hand. Charlotte Maxwell had come full circle.

I took the remainder of the afternoon and into the long-light evening to cross the city. Toronto was a fast-growing city nearing 86,000 in population, sprawling from the Lunatic Asylum on the west to the Don River on the east. Its fashionable homes were located on Jarvis Street, and toward this highfalutin area the carriage steadily bounced and shook. The first frost, or "roadmaker," was still two months away, and their passage was marked by thick gray dust rising and settling on horses, carriage tufts, people, and all. At one point a distant train was clearly heard. Since Kerry didn't pick up her ears and remark that she "just loved" the comparatively new sound, Charlotte supposed, and rightly so, that her brother and his child had lived where the raucous wonder was a regular part of their hearing—and smelling.

And smell it did, but it was just one more smell among many. Of the cities burgeoning into life all across Canada, only Victoria, on the distant island of Vancouver, had sufficient "couth" to keep well-bred Britishers from shuddering over living conditions in the new land. Most places were considered not only uncivilized but raw, rough, and exceedingly primitive. Villages and cities were ripe with the stink of outdoor privies, horse manure, cow dung, uncovered garbage, and roaming pigs. Added to this was the effluvia of human inhabitants long overdue for bathing and often lavishly pomaded with Bearine, a concoction made from pure bear's grease and guaranteed to "make the hair soft, pliant, and glossy" and promised to be "delightful to use."

Supposedly residing in the most refined part of the country— the East, for which she was profoundly grateful—Charlotte Maxwell was tried to the limit with the lack of proprieties. Just to be proper and orderly didn't seem too much to ask; obviously it was. Certainly if a higher scale of living were possible, the Maxwells would have had it. Money was no object; desire was strong; but there was no spit and polish to be obtained at any price!

Throughout what was to be known as the "Victorian" age, the new nation was largely made up of frontier settlements, developing towns, and farms, farms, farms. Just previously, the census had shown that only 12 percent of the population lived in cities; even now the entire nation numbered only 4,833,239 in total population (Canadian families could expect to bury one child out of five). Of that number, the Sebastian Maxwells shone among the few with money and power. Charlotte had the good sense to realize that it wasn't difficult to be upper crust when competition for status was so limited, and when the hoi polloi were farmers, farmers, farmers.

Unknown and unrealized now, the vast plains, touted far and wide by Clifford Sifton, a lawyer from Brandon, Manitoba, and Minister of the Interior in charge of western settlement, were on the verge of turning into the nation's breadbasket. Very shortly a hundred thousand sod-busters would descend, bachelor by bachelor and family by family, on the world's last free land and some of its most productive. Ontario and the maritime provinces were emptying their immigrants—no longer heading south to the United States but west to the prairie provinces. The West meant opportunity. And when opportunity knocked, countless land-hungry men responded, willing to do what was necessary, though it meant almost unbearable hardship, years of grinding work, and risking one's health and very existence.

Most of them arrived with little or no money. For housing and even for food they had no choice but to make do with what the land had to offer. Their huts were made of sod; they slept under umbrellas or oilcloth when it rained; they papered their shacks with newspaper, existed on oatmeal and rabbit stew, and battled mosquito hordes in summer and fierce blizzards in winter.

Just getting to the area of their choice was a major undertaking. Trails were littered with furniture and equipment abandoned along the way. Sebastian Maxwell grew richer by the day as he and his connections provided goods that would—many of them—prove to be impractical and end up discarded along the trail. But he did it with a good conscience, enjoying the expansive feeling of helping to populate the country he had adopted as his own. He relished the fruits of his labor, living what could be called the good life—or as good as was possible at the time— even as his customers lived like field mice in the earth, bought, at times, with their life's blood.

There was about Sebastian an aura of self-satisfaction that came from the certain knowledge that he was of good stock— the best stock. He was of the Scotch Maxwell clan who boasted connection with one James Clerk Maxwell, educator, scientist, and winner of the coveted Adams prize at Cambridge for his essay, "On the Stability of Motion of Saturn's Rings." His recently published "Theory of Heat" was even more prestigious. Sadly, his fame had made little impact on Canada; Sebastian felt the poorer for it and strove to be recognized personally by philanthropy and good deeds. Consequently, when the call came to take in his wife's profligate brother's only child, he had encouraged her to do so. "After all," he said, "you were willing to take on my sister's child."

And it was so; Frances, orphaned and in poor health, had been a member of the Maxwell household since she was twelve. Now fifteen, a sweet child making no demands, needing only food and clothing, a little education when her health permitted, and a few medicines, her presence at Maxwell Manor barely caused a ripple in Sebastian's well-run household. Could one more child make much difference?

Just how great that difference could be weighed uneasily on Charlotte Maxwell's mind as the carriage brought her, with that child, closer home.

And no wonder; the newest member of her household was spouting some obscure Scripture: "'Heaviness in the heart of man—'" Kerry was quoting, and explaining earnestly, "I think that means women, too, Aunt, and maybe even children, *speshully* children—'Heaviness in the heart of man maketh it stoop.' Did you ever have a stoop-ed heart? I know I did."

"You have a habit, child," Charlotte said a trifle peevishly, growing more uneasy about her husband's reaction all the time, "of asking questions and then hurrying on and giving one no opportunity to answer. You've left me with my mouth open several times today. Now, what do you mean, stupid heart?"

Kerry's merry laugh rang out. The impassive face of Gideon seemed about to crack wide open, but he saved himself from such unacceptable behavior by a coughing fit that kept his mistress waiting, with a pained expression, for the child's answer.

"Not *stupid*, Aunt Charlotte! Stoop-ed, like stoopt. It means bent—"

"I know what it means, for heaven's sake. Why don't you just say stoopt, then?"

"I think prob'ly King James would say stoop-*ed*, and it's his book; it says so right in the front. You don't say belovd, do you? No, you say belov-*ed*." Kerry looked at her aunt, discerning the pink nose even in the dimming light. "But," she added quickly, "I've never been called belovd *or* belov-ed, though I s'pose you have. By your husband maybe, and by your children?" It was a question, and for once Kerry waited for an answer. She hadn't thought of the possibility of children in the household until this moment, and an anxious look touched her piquant face. Kerry's contact with other children had been limited, and she found just talking to them a strange and often unsettling experience. Children seemed so . . . *childish*. And sadly lacking in appreciation of the Scriptures.

Charlotte Maxwell sighed and leaned back tiredly against the carriage's "machine-buffed" cushions. "I have no children," she said, and her tone seemed to give the impression that right now she was very happy about her lack.

Kerry relaxed obviously. "I don't blame you," she piped wisely. "Children can be a terr'ble nuisance."

Again Charlotte Maxwell wondered about the child's life with Avery her guide, teacher, and example. Knowing her brother—thoughtless and careless in the best of times, hurtful and impatient, even harsh, when crossed—didn't conjure up a picture of a normal life for any child. And his drinking? Charlotte sighed again and shook her head slightly as if to clear it of unpleasant recollections.

"No children of my own," she found herself explaining to this unchildlike being sitting at her side and peeping at her nose from time to time. "But there *is* another young person in the household—"

"There is? Who is it, Aunt Charlotte?" There was a quick note of interest in the child's voice. It might be a boy; she might like a boy; she'd never had an opportunity to find out. With all her heart and soul Kerry hoped it wouldn't be a girl, like Cordelia, the landlady's daughter. What a frightening possibility! The very thought of Cordelia sent shudders up Kerry's spine. Cordelia had been overbearing, haughty, and spiteful. Play had always turned ugly when Cordelia didn't get her way; and as for reading together, Kerry's favorite pastime, Cordelia spurned that as wasted time. Kerry's pleasure in it was cause for jealousy and cruel thrusts, and Cordelia ended up calling her "lumpy toad!" or some other ugly conglomeration of strange and terrible words (for an almost illiterate child, Cordelia had an amazing stock of insulting words at her command). Kerry had no idea what was meant, usually, but the tone alone was enough get her hackles up and her blood boiling, and she wanted, fiercely, to slap the offender. But Cordelia, with a flounce and a sniff, ran away, scornfully flinging the final indignity over her shoulder: "church mouse!" Kerry rather liked mice, but she supposed that being a poor one would be a hateful thing.

Now, looking down at the young face obviously fearing her answer, Charlotte found herself strangely moved again, and she answered more gently than she would have otherwise. "Frances is the daughter of Mr. Maxwell's sister."

Mr. Maxwell! Here was another cause for worry. Somehow Kerry hadn't imagined that there would be anyone else to consider—just Aunt Charlotte. Now there was a Mr. Maxwell *and* an unknown girl.

It was all too much. Even the ebullient spirit of Keren-happuch Ferne was overcome. With a sigh she folded up for the day, quite naturally laying her whirling head on the silk moire lap, blending a small tear of self-pity with the tea stain and closing her eyes in sleep.

But not before she felt the gloved hand of her Aunt Charlotte brush the tumbled hair back from her forehead in a gesture as old as motherhood. But it was as new, to Kerry, as the ride in a Maythorn & Son carriage, exhibited at Biggleswade and having the first of its thirteen coats of paint rubbed out with pumice.

Maxwell Manor, reached in full dark, was but a large blur to the sleepy Kerry when Gideon lifted her out of the carriage. Her tousled head on his shoulder, eyes only half-open, she had the distinct feeling of coming out of a dark hole into a welcoming retreat. As long as she lived, she was to have that safe feeling whenever she approached the home of her aunt. Somehow cares and fears were left outside, and comfort and a very different kind of care opened their arms and offered a warm embrace.

Late as it was, the Queen Anne double doors with their handsome glazed glass were flung open. Light beckoned softly from the lamp held high in the hand of another uniformed man, older and more stooped than Gideon. The lamplight on his balding head shone a cheery hello and guided the weary travelers across a wide veranda to the sumptuousness beyond.

In spite of the overdone decorating, which was the current rage, Charlotte Maxwell had managed to create a home. As the century waned, clutter was adored, and anything simple or without ornament was identified with pauperism. Parlors boasted stuffed birds, statues, dried flower and human hair wreaths, cupids, japanned trays, swagged window hangings, enameled clocks, heavily carved picture frames hung on golden tasseled cords, ornately framed, stiff and stilted family photographs, and much more; simply to cross a room was hazardous. But one was impressed, all the same, by the tasteless congestion.

The Maxwell home, due to innate good taste and wealth reaching back many generations, was not as unabashedly ostentatious as those of the newly rich, or even of those who had attained middle-class status; goods were cheap and available to them also.

If it was not possible to shop the stores personally, there was always the catalog and its tens of thousands of items—everything from a rubber hairpin to a plow or piano. Ready-made clothes were finally replacing the homemade vintage. And who could resist the pictured articles of clothing, with their enticing descriptions? A woman of modest means could afford "the Latest Style Foulard Percale day dress [one-piece garment as opposed to skirt and waist] with puff-top sleeves, neat turned-down collar, three rows of fancy serpentine braid across bust and back forming yoke; plaited effect from yoke to waist; butterfly epaulets extending over sleeves," costing only $1.15. As for the massive furniture of the day, a solid oak parlor table cost $1.48, a six-piece parlor "suit,"—sofa, easy rocker, large arm chair, and two parlor chairs—having "easy spring seats with hard edges, the fronts being of plush, handsomely corded; casters free," cost but $11.35 and could be received at the post office of the most remote settler.

Here, in about seven hundred closely printed pages, was reading material enough to keep an isolated household fascinated for weeks. The far-ranging rural clientele pored over the "wish book" so diligently and avidly that it became known as the prairie bible and the bible of the bush. The choices were staggering. To buy simple sugar, for example, required earnest deliberation and serious decision making. One must choose:

Cubes
Cut Loaf
XXXX Powdered
Standard Powdered
Fine Granulated
Standard Granulated
Mould A
Confectioners' A
Off A
White Phoenix Extra
Phoenix C No. 2
Yellow No. 3
Yellow No. 4
Yellow No. 5
Golden Brown No. 6
Cuban Dark No. 7

What an age in which to live! Surely no other generation was as blessed. Or as burdened, for the pictured wares were enticing, and "more is better" was the hue and cry of the day.

When Kerry, in Gideon's arms, was carried across an Axminster rug, she was no more impressed by its richness than by the China straw matting that had graced her landlady's floor for ten cents a yard. Settled by Gideon, at his mistress's command, on an elegant upholstered piece called a Turkish Tete-a-Tete, Kerry was no more impressed by its plush "bands and rolls and heavy worsted fringe" than by Mrs. Peabody's "lounge" upholstered in carpet of questionable age and quality. But it all felt right, good, and blissfully comforting to the poor waif that was Kerry Ferne.

Left alone while her aunt saw to the disposing of her niece's bits and pieces, Kerry shut her eyes in utmost peace and hardly wakened when she was picked up again and carried upstairs. Here, in a quiet, tasteful room that had largely escaped the indulgences of the rest of the house, she was undressed by a round-faced, hefty woman who kept murmuring such things as "scandalous," "burn these," and "poor wee lass." But it felt right, good, and blissfully comforting. When a soft, dainty, white gown was slipped over her head and her senses told her it wasn't her own Fels Naptha-washed nightie, when she was tucked into a bed where the linens had no lye odor but smelled faintly of lavender, Kerry's final thought for the day was: "If Cordelia could see me now." The church mouse slipped away forever as the weary child drifted off to the first sweet and dreamless sleep she had known since her father's death and the beginning of the nightmare.

———

Pulling off her long kid gloves and flexing her fingers before removing the pins that had held her monumental hat solidly on her head all day, Charlotte Maxwell laid these items into the hands of Mrs. Finch. As cook and general housekeeper, Mrs. Finch had the oversight of the great house with the help of Finch, her husband. Finch was general factotum, serving as butler when that was needed, handyman at times, and jack-of-all-trades, turning his hand to most anything. In the morning and evening he was available to act as Sebastian Maxwell's "man." The other regular help was Gladdy, in her teens and supposedly learning the "ropes" for graduation to full maid. Charlotte Maxwell, proud of being an old-fashioned housekeeper, gave the impression that she managed her home with no other assistance when, in truth, there was a gardener who also served as errand boy, delivery man, washer of windows, painter, anything that wasn't covered by Finch's expertise. And of course there was Gideon, always available to take his mistress wherever she might like to go, grooming and caring for the horses, keeping the family rigs in fine and beautiful shape. All were overworked; all were underpaid, and each was a servant, in every sense of the word; it was the way of the times.

"Is my niece settled?" Charlotte asked, leaning toward a gilded mirror and studying her face momentarily, perhaps better satisfied than usual because of the dimness of the lamp light; full sunlight wasn't kind to the rather horse-faced, sallow-skinned, patrician-nosed lady of the manor.

"Yes, mum. She's off to dreamland, that one. Settled down right proper. She'll need a bath tomorrer. I hain't got her things put away, o'course, but there be'nt many of 'em. What she'll put on in the mornin,' I'm sure I don't know—"

"Yes, yes, a bath in the morning, and as for clothes—get some of Frances's outgrown things. Now, please bring up a tray. Something light—an omelet, perhaps. Has Mr. Maxwell dined?"

"Long ago, mum. It's comin' on midnight, y' know." Mrs. Finch slyly pointed out the long day and her personal lengthy contribution, which was not, obviously, about to come to an end any time soon.

Charlotte heard the barely concealed complaint and steeled herself against any unnecessary sympathy (after all, the woman was paid the going wage and was well fed—very well fed, Charlotte thought rather critically as she noted the round face and rotund figure standing before her with guileless eyes. And full of good Maxwell food. Though, goodness knows, *the laborer is worthy of his hire*).

Catching herself in the middle of quoting a Scripture where she had never done so previously, Charlotte Maxwell paused, dumbfounded, chagrined beyond imagining. To be so influenced by one small person! The plan was to *be* an influence. Had she, Charlotte, even in one day, made any impact at all on a child who was almost totally lacking in social skills? Or had that child, blithely and casually, *made* an impact? Charlotte squirmed and flushed hotly just thinking about it. The laborer is worthy of his hire, indeed! Where had the thought come from, and why? Weren't the Maxwells lenient with their help, didn't they pay wages promptly, and didn't they give out new uniforms each Christmas? What more could they do? Charlotte turned a cold and fishy eye on the woman beaming with satisfaction over a thrust well delivered and added with a sigh, "You may go to bed as soon as the kitchen is tidied. You can pick up the tray in the morning. And on your way down, please stop in at the library and tell Mr. Maxwell I should be happy for an opportunity to see him before he retires."

Below stairs, in his dark-paneled, comfortable "study," Sebastian Maxwell turned reluctantly from his desk and the spread of blueprints and papers, removed the much-chewed cheroot stub from his mouth, pulled his vest down over his generous paunch, and prepared to go upstairs to meet his wife. Apt to cushion himself away from the toils of everyday life in the great house, he presumed that, by now, Charlotte would be settling herself for a night's rest, all reference to mundane matters of the house wisely put aside lest it be upsetting to the head of the home who, above all, relished his quiet and privacy. And just now he had the burden of obtaining property for a summer place, as so many of his contemporaries were doing.

The cost of land for the erection of summer residences had rocketed. Lake Simcoe and Muskoka Lakes were choice areas, and Sebastian felt a glow of satisfaction in having obtained one of the last available sites. Land that had gone for fifty cents an acre could now command over eleven dollars. Cottage life was quickly becoming anything but rustic as the competition to excel spread from society home to society home. Magnificent gingerbreaded palaces were built, some of them with room for as many as fifty guests. To be invited to such a "cottage" was a high honor; to be able to issue such an invitation even more honorable.

Thank goodness, Sebastian thought fleetingly as he laid aside the plans for his new summer residence. Lotte, as he fondly called his wife, with her naturally supercilious nose and stern-featured face, created an aura of respectability and position that was not always meant nor deserved, but that served Sebastian's purpose:

Never, never give the slightest hint of being in any way socially inferior to the Kirkpatricks.

Lady Kirkpatrick, wife of Ontario's lieutenant governor, was the haughtiest of the haughty in Toronto society. She had chosen Wednesday as her day for an "at home," leaving the remaining times available for the anxious ladies of the city as they strove to avoid the social insult of being called "provincial"—one who didn't know the rules of proper etiquette. Pity the man who laughed too loudly, used slang, or failed to stand slightly to one side or behind his chair, never in front, or in other ways showed ignorance of good and acceptable manners—he was labeled a boor. Good manners mattered intensely. Naturally the best-selling book of the day was Emily Holt's *Encyclopaedia of Etiquette: What to Write, What to Wear, What to Do, What to Say, A Book of Manners for Everyday Use.*

Beatrice Fairfax and Dorothy Dix had columns in the daily newspapers doling out advice to the uninformed: When a woman rises to leave, every man in the room gets to his feet. When calling, a woman does not remove her gloves or wraps; she shakes hands with her hostess, accepts a cup of tea (one only, never more), and does it all without removing her gloves. To do otherwise was to prove oneself gauche, lacking in good breeding, ill-mannered and unfit for genteel circles.

Many a "comer"—that is, one working diligently at being accepted—burned with shame as she pored over the columns and realized that she had been wearing gloves of the improper length to tea or that she had overstayed by five minutes the acceptable half hour allowed for the formal call! Such humiliation.

Sebastian Maxwell, "to the manner (and manor) born" in Scotland, schooled and taught and trained until the proper thing to do was part and parcel of his very being, was correctly suave and polished in all ways. His wife, coming from an excellent though impoverished Scottish family, was a model of propriety. Though no beauty even when young, there had been a glow of health and vigor about her that was attractive. And she had the good breeding necessary for a Maxwell.

Entering his wife's room, finding her sitting at her dressing table brushing her hair and preparing to braid it for the night, Sebastian moved ponderously across the room and stood behind her. Putting his sausage-fingered hands on her shoulders, he bent and kissed her cheek.

"Home safe and sound, I see. Get the child?" Sebastian spoke in small bursts, whether from preference or because physical effort shortened his breath and reddened his apple-like cheeks. To say more when less would do, to Sebastian, seemed totally unnecessary.

Though his wife knew his aversion to scenes or undue emotion of any sort, her eyes raised, met his in the mirror and, with rare passion she burst forth with, "Child? However Avery raised his daughter, it hasn't prepared her for a life other than that of a preacher of the gospel! The child is a fountain of admonitions, dire warnings, and predictions. It will take a firm hand and an iron will to make a silk purse out of this . . . sow's ear!"

Knowing her as he did, studying her in the mirror, noting her face with its heightened color, the sparkle in her rather colorless eyes, and the small touch of energy and even renewed youth about her, Sebastian said, "You do love a challenge, my dear. Are you sure this one isn't more than you want to tackle?" Unspoken, but delicately hinted at, was her age (and his), and the threat to the peace and quiet of the home; Sebastian felt a small frisson of disquiet in his spirit. But Charlotte, usually sensitive to his moods, flung her braid over her shoulder, squared her shoulders, leaned forward, looked herself in the eye, and said, "I believe I'm up to it!"

M orning came, as mornings always do, and with it and her awakening, Kerry's peace and contentment of the previous night were replaced by anxiety. Surely this present happiness would vanish away, and she would find herself back with the nuns, uncertain and afraid. Or back in Mrs. Peabody's rooming house with Papa snoring across the room, sleeping off a night's carousing—long hours during which she, Kerry, had nothing to do but peruse the Bible or the outdated catalog once again. A familiar pattern; not one she longed to return to. It was the familiarity she clung to, the stability of something known, something of her own. Though it might be marked with a certain misery, it was misery accustomed to and thus her own. And miserable she had been, and lonely, with an unchallenged mind that craved learning and knowledge and an empty heart that cried for affection and attention.

Once, alone and desperate for something to do, she had cut paper dolls from the catalog—a father and mother and baby. Garments for them were cut from the clothing pages, with little tabs to hang them upon the shoulders of the figures. When that was done, she cut furniture for the dolls' home, furnishing it room by room with selections from the big book. Thereafter, she played "house." This game kept her entertained through many a lonely day and long evening. When not playing with the cutouts, the pieces were carefully gathered up and saved between the catalog's pages, to be lifted out and brought to life again and again. One cold day, to start a fire, her father had carelessly wrenched a handful of paper from the catalog, held a match to it, and tossed it into the fireplace. Kerry, suddenly sick and stricken dumb, had watched the little play family curl and catch fire and burn away to ashes. Her own father's funeral, not long afterwards, was not cause for any more anguish than the moment her paper friends were taken from her.

That day and many others, alone, and with the fire dying down and the room too cold for comfort, Kerry pulled a quilt around her, sat on the window ledge in the only light there was, and entertained herself as best she could—by reading. And reading the Bible, one of the only two items available, the other being the desecrated catalog.

The Psalms were favorites, and she turned to them. Rather than finding comfort from the beautiful, singing words such as "Keep me as the apple of the eye; hide me under the shadow of thy wings" and other passages equally promising, she brooded over, "My bones are vexed, my soul is also sore vexed," and, "I am weary with my groaning; all the night make I my bed to swim; I water my couch with my tears." And she did; far too often, she did.

❧━━━━❧

Coming awake in a downy, comfortable bed in a graciously appointed room in Maxwell Manor, an ordinary child would have looked around and exclaimed, "Oh, how pretty, how nice!" One would hope that Kerry, with her Scripture-saturated mind, would find her heart overflowing with something like, "The lines are fallen unto me in pleasant places; yea, I have a goodly heritage."

But Kerry's reaction—perhaps a natural one in view of the disappointments she had experienced all her life—was cautious: "He raiseth up the poor out of the dust," came to mind. This was followed after a long moment by a hesitant "Alleluia."

It was this alleluia Gladdy, the maid, heard when she entered the room, a congregation of one for Kerry's faint praise. It's hard to say who was the most startled—the praiser or the congregation. Seeing the maid for the first time, Kerry clutched the blankets around her, raising her head from the pillow and staring at the apparition that was Gladys McBean.

Gladdy was a broomstick of a girl with unmanageable hair of a strawberry color, impressive in its wildness. This mop of hair stood out from her head like an explosion of last year's straw stack, making her head appear to be as wide as her narrow shoulders. She was properly uniformed, however, and this allayed somewhat Kerry's sudden spurt of anxiety.

"Was yer prayin'?" Gladdy questioned, stepping to the side of the bed. "Or singin', maybe?"

Kerry's imagination was immediately captured; young as she was, she recognized in Gladdy one of a kind; her kind.

With her eyebrows almost disappearing into her hair, her hands red and rough, her face untroubled by the worries of the world, Gladdy (her nickname suited her disposition) was unlike anyone Kerry had ever met. Granted, her circle of acquaintances was limited; but anyone with a lick of discernment would see the little maid as a person in her own right. Though Gladdy was learning the rules and would usually adhere to them, one never knew just when she would burst asunder the bands of decorum and be herself.

Just now she was apparently uncertain how to handle this particular situation; never before had she welcomed a stranger to the household by standing at the bedside. In all things, she strove to do what Mrs. Finch, her mentor, would do. In Gladdy's opinion Mrs. Finch was a fount of knowledge, the final authority, and to be emulated closely. But this was one situation that hadn't been covered in Mrs. Finch's training sessions; she had simply directed Gladdy to "the new missy's room" to awaken her, prepare her for a bath and breakfast, and hurry about it. Gladdy was, quite literally, aquiver with the magnitude of her obligation. But first off, she had faced this surprising comment and was caught untrained for it and unprepared.

"I was just saying alleluia." Kerry answered Gladdy's spontaneous question defensively, as if ejaculations of praise were common occurrences and beyond notice.

"Hallelujah," Gladdy repeated, savoring the word. "I never heard anybody say it before. That's why—"

It was all Kerry needed. Sitting up abruptly, drawing up her knees and clasping them in her arms, she said earnestly, "Not *hal*-le-lu-jah—alleluia. King James says alleluia. But," she added kindly, noting the confusion on the face of the little maid, "I think it means the same thing."

"King James?" Gladdy repeated, that being the part of Kerry's explanation she understood best. "We haven't got a King James," she said scornfully, for once superior to somebody in her knowledge. "We've got a queen—Queen Victoria. God bless the queen!" she finished, as Mrs. Finch herself might have.

"God bless the queen," Kerry responded properly and automatically, adding, "Well, I know, silly. But she didn't write the Bible, did she?"

Gladdy was nonplussed, and her quick defense of the good queen stuck in her throat. "She could of," she said feebly, "if she wanted to. She can do anyfing she wants to. You can, when you're queen, you know. Anyway, why was you sayin' alleluia, all alone, and early in the morning like this, not even in church?"

It didn't make sense to Gladdy. And Gladdy, unlike the "new missy," was not given to flights of fancy; nothing in her neglected life had encouraged it.

"It's a shout of praise," Kerry explained.

"Well, yours was more of a whisper. So, did somefing good happen? Or was you just practicing—in hopes of somefing good

44

happening?" Hope, Gladdy could understand, being of an unquenchably optimistic nature. It didn't take much for Gladdy to skip and rejoice, in her own way. She was, after all, not much older than the new missy and was no stranger to deprivation, disappointment, even abuse. Gladdy McBean was a survivor.

Not knowing whether this strange girl resembled the despised Cordelia and would hear her confidences and make fun of them, Kerry grew stubborn about revealing the feelings that had prompted her experiment with praise. As usual, when backed into a corner or when uncomfortable or when words simply failed her, Kerry resorted to Scripture, though, if she were questioned about it, oftentimes she didn't half understand what she was quoting.

Quoting Scripture, Kerry had found, usually resulted in setting the opponent at a disadvantage, perhaps giving Kerry an opportunity to gather her wits about her. Sometimes, she had noted, it tended to infuriate the other party. Once, taking Miss Perley's combs back to her, which she had somehow left in the Ferne room, Kerry had looked around at the clothes scattered everywhere, the bed unmade, the soiled dishes on the table, and said, innocently enough, "Where no oxen are, the crib is clean." Miss Perley's ordinary treatment of Kerry—at least in the presence of her father—was fawning and petting, but in this instance she had flushed an ugly red, snatched up her combs, and said, "You're too lippy by far, Miss Smarty!"

Now again, Scripture came readily to Kerry's defense: "A prudent man concealeth knowledge," she quoted primly, thus confusing Gladdy more than ever.

"Man? What man?" the little maid asked, momentarily forgetting the bath preparations Mrs. Finch had instructed her to make.

Kerry sighed, sorry she'd brought it up. "It says *man*, but it means women, too, see?"

Gladdy moved across the room to the windows, gave the drapes a yank, and said saucily, suddenly quite sure she had nothing to fear from this newcomer, "No, I don't see. And now maybe you can see a little better. It's a sunny day out there, *see?*"

Kerry slid her legs from under the covers, stretched to reach the floor, and stood up. Her attention was drawn first to the dainty nightgown that fell around her ankles in soft luxury, unlike anything she had seen, and certainly like nothing she had worn.

"Who put me to bed?" she asked, half-memories coming to mind.

"Mrs. Finch, I guess," Gladdy answered. "Now if you'll just take it orf, we'll give you the baff you shoulda had last night. I'm Gladys, but I'm called Gladdy, and I'm Mrs. Finch's helper." Associating herself with the all-powerful Mrs. Finch seemed more important, somehow, than maid. "Now then, here comes the baffwater—"

Mrs. Finch's helper turned importantly to the door and ushered in an elderly man. His hair was thinning on top of his head, he was long and thin of body and had a sharp, red nose that twitched from time to time—he was Finch, butler, valet, runner of the household, and now bearer of a container of hot water. He was followed by a nondescript man of indeterminate age, of lack-luster color and appearance—Biddle, gardener, handyman, and just now bearer of a zinc tub.

At their appearance Kerry had quickly pulled the corner of the bedding around her nightgown-sheathed form, but the two men seemed not to see her. The tub was set in front of the fire-place, the water poured into it, and Biddle and Finch departed with never a word spoken. But the twitch of Finch's nose seemed to indicate the guest's inferiority.

"All right, orf wiff it," Gladdy commanded, and, when Kerry hesitated, "Take it orf so's you can baff."

Gladdy was lately come from the slums of London, gathered up in a sweep that culled the streets for likely candidates for positions in the new world. Some would become wives for bachelors advertising for them; others, like Gladdy, too odd to catch even the most lonely settler's eye, to go into service. It had seemed an excellent opportunity to the street urchin and to the parents who were overburdened and overwhelmed with a large family of children usually left to their own devices, roaming at will, picking up a few cents when possible, and keeping from underfoot at the same time.

Though reluctant, Kerry obeyed, having been "baffed" from time to time by Mrs. Peabody or Miss Perley. But never before had her surroundings been so pleasant, never had the soap been so fragrant nor the room so cozily warm. The towel had always been thin and harsh; the clothes held out to her had always been her own faded, outgrown garments, sometimes the very ones she had removed.

"I'll have you know," Gladdy was saying proudly, "that this house has a baffroom just for baffing. Missus Maxwell thought you'd ravver have one in your own room this time. Snuglike, in front of the fire." Just when the fire in the fireplace had been lit and fed, the sleeping Kerry had not known. But it was warm, and it was inviting, and Kerry submitted happily enough.

Ablutions over, she was bundled into a luxurious towel while Gladdy struggled to brush her dark curls, curls that had never known proper cutting and that now, encouraged by the soft water, good sudsing, and sufficient rinsing, curled riotously around her face, over her shoulders, and down her back.

"Coo," Gladdy said admiringly, "it's pretty. But," she added quickly, "it needs cuttin' orfly bad. Didn't no one never give yer a hair cut?"

What made Gladdy an expert on hair care was questionable, seeing as how her own wild and frizzy mop totally defied control.

The clothes Gladdy offered were secondhand, being outgrown by "Miss Frances" according to the maid, whose voice softened as she spoke of the other young person under the Maxwell roof.

"Well, where is she? Tell me about her!" Kerry demanded, eager yet hesitant to meet the girl mentioned first by her aunt, now by the maid, and always with a certain tenderness. Her experience with friendships had not been encouraging, but in spite of that, she was finding herself excited at the prospect. To date her new acquaintances had been limited to her aunt, a fat, barely remembered someone undressing her, and this wild-haired creature who was giving her a "baff" and remarking on her uncut tresses.

"She's waitin' to meet yer," Gladdy said in reference to Miss Frances. "She won't have her brefuss until you get there. Most times you'll go downstairs to eat, but Miss Frances always has her brefuss in her room. Unless you're sick. You're not sick, are yer?"

"I'm perfectly well," Kerry answered rather huffily. "I'm just small." This eating in her room—rather a strange practice, Kerry thought, but a nice one. She and her papa had eaten at Mrs. Peabody's boarding house table . . . most of the time. When Papa didn't have enough "blunt," as he called it, they sneaked food into their room, food purchased at the shop on the corner—pasties, usually, and not bad. When Miss Perley joined them it became a picnic, with the added excitement of keeping it from the landlady; they carefully picked up every crumb and hid all signs of their lawlessness. Once, when she was sick with a putrid throat, Mrs. Peabody had brought soup in to her and hadn't even scolded when some of it slopped on the bedding. No, Mrs. Peabody hadn't been mean; it was her daughter, Cordelia, who was a snitch and who gladly told her ma whenever she found signs of food in the Ferne room. Kerry had always been afraid Papa would refuse entrance to Cordelia, who was the only playmate, albeit an undependable friend, Kerry had.

But here, in this house, somewhere under the spreading roof, was Miss Frances, surely much nicer than Cordelia, if tones of voice meant anything.

"How come," Kerry asked curiously, "Miss Frances eats her brefuss . . . *breakfast* in her room? Is *she* sick?"

"Miss Frances ain't—isn't in good helf," the London waif explained. "Some days she feels better than ovvers, and Gideon takes her for a drive, or somefing like that."

"How is she today?"

"I don't know, maybe good, cause Mrs. Finch said to take you to her room as soon as you was baffed and dressed."

Walking down the hall in Gladdy's wake, clad in sweet-smelling clothing of unknown material and style but making her feel pretty just to be in it, Kerry felt as if she were in a dream. Was this real? Would it . . . could it . . . last?

But the portraits that graced the halls were heavy, imposing, substantial. Stiffly posed, the Maxwell ancestors gazed conde-scendingly on the humble passersby from gilded frames, secure in their exalted position, unshaken from their eternal imper-turbability.

Down this hallway trod the two small beneficiaries of Maxwell largess: the maid who was nobody in her own right but who felt herself wonderfully superior to underprivileged maids serving a household of less consequence; the orphan, dependent upon Maxwell bounty for her very existence, but who would forever resist all efforts to restrain or constrain her uniqueness.

Each girl watched the tips of her shoes as she walked, as first one and then the other peeped from below the hem of her skirt. The girls' satisfaction dimmed their regard for the rich carpet that glowed underfoot and closed their eyes to the intimidating stare of generations of Maxwells, who certainly must have sniffed in disdain at the insignificant parade: Gladdy, reveling in serge-topped boots laced halfway up her leg, and costing, as she was occasionally reminded by Mrs. Finch, *sixty cents;* Kerry, with a satisfying tingle up her backbone, reveling in chocolate-colored, nine-button shoes of the best kangaroo stock, only a little too large and costing, had she known it, $1.65, a grand sum indeed.

"How beautiful are thy feet with shoes, O prince's daughter!" Kerry half-whispered; Gladdy's kinship was established when she neither mocked nor questioned a comment she must have found unusual if not incomprehensible.

Down the hall and around the corner they marched, an odd couple similar in many ways. Each in her own way a misfit and blissfully unaware of the protocol that shackled society to prescribed ways and made them slaves of fashion and propriety.

In the land of the free, only those souls were free that had a vision of a new life and the courage to seek it out. One immigrant—Robert Service, self-styled God's Vagabond—said it clearly for all those who scorned the easy, familiar way and doggedly forsook the known for the unknown:

> A passion to be free
> Has ever mastered me;
> To none beneath the sun
> Will I bow down,—not one
> Shall leash my liberty.

Kerry and Gladdy had no knowledge of the poet and his viewpoints but were, nevertheless, caretakers of the same spirit. Only their age kept them from being among the bold ones who surged on past the settled areas to the vast plains and deep woods that were beckoning those with a dream and the fortitude to see it through. For many of them it was more costly than they reckoned on, and in the end they paid the ultimate price. As the prairie provinces claimed them (or as they claimed the prairie provinces), some would die of hunger, some of injuries for which there was no hospital, no doctor. Others went mad from the loneliness of it all; most of them submitted to hardship beyond their ability to imagine or to describe and did it with a dedication that did not count the cost but doggedly awaited the gain that must surely follow such devotion, such determination, such investment.

In their prized footwear—Gladdy's purchased for her at the cheapest price possible, Kerry's purchased for someone else and cast off to her—they proudly marched toward their future. Certainly no one watching would have recognized that within the small bosoms a spark burned, which would—given the proper moment—flame into that devotion, that determination, that investment.

"'Ere," Gladdy said eventually, "this is Miss Franny's room."

I t was love at first sight.

Entering another strange room, feeling once again at a disadvantage and about to strike out from that uncomfortable position much as a fighter would throw a hat into the ring, Kerry's challenging "Our soul is exceedingly filled with the scorning of those that are at ease" died on her lips.

For here was no Cordelia Peabody.

Lying in a big bed, surrounded by pillows of frothy white that served to emphasize the paleness of the one propped against them, Frances was an ephemeral being, perhaps even a fairy! Slight of build, making only a small mound of the covers, her only color the faint pink that tinged her thin cheeks and the fair hair that spread around her like a cloud, she seemed an otherworldly being to the wide-eyed Kerry. Prepared for another like the rambunctious, undependable Cordelia of the boarding house, and primed to stiff-arm her verbally, Kerry's protective scriptural greeting, put on like a cloak, fizzled and faded.

Silenced for perhaps the first time in her memory, Kerry found a meaning never understood before in "Let my tongue cleave to the roof of my mouth." Because of that very cleaving, Kerry was dumbstruck.

Not so with the scrap of femininity in the bed. Holding out a blue-veined, white hand toward the newcomer, Frances smiled as sweetly, surely, as an angel. Woe and betide if this promise of purity and perfection should slip and fall from the pedestal upon which Kerry immediately enthroned her!

It was good that Frances was unaware of either the pedestal or the enthroning, so that when she spoke, it was in the gentle tone that was her usual manner.

It was the one word, "Kerry." But the wealth of meaning! The warmth of the gray eyes! The unspoken promise of the outstretched hand!

The little sparrow that was Keren Ferne, displaced, lost, "as a wandering bird cast out of the nest," recognized the mooring when it beckoned. In her borrowed slippers, as on a magic carpet, the sparrow "escaped as a bird out of the snare of the fowler" and flew to the dainty "nest." Without a moment's hesitation she reached out, to have her hand taken and held in a soft grip that was as an iron fist for security.

Kerry was speechless, caught up in the spell that was woven, unconsciously but surely, by the vision that was Franny. But not speechless for long. Mesmerized, she rallied. "Behold, thou art fair; thou hast doves' eyes," she managed, but in a whisper. Never had Kerry been better served by her multitude of Scriptures, for the gray eyes were oval in shape, soulful in expression. Now their quiet depths changed, as a still pond when it is moved by a frolicsome breeze.

Franny's laugh was a tinkle of pure joy, not a shred of it skeptical or scornful. "Oh, I just know we are going to be the best of friends! I think, little Kerry, that you are just what the doctor ordered!"

Kerry's smile was small, tentative, almost as if she were blind for the moment and proceeding by touch alone.

"Come, sit beside me," Frances invited and patted the coverlet. Still blindly, Kerry climbed up by means of a stool onto the white froth that seemed a veritable magic conveyance but was called bed.

"Now, Gladdy," Frances lilted, "we'll have breakfast."

Gladdy, half mesmerized by the pretty scenario, came to with a start. "Yes, Miss Franny, you'll have it d'reckly."

Gladdy spoke in as proper a tone as Mrs. Finch herself might have used. The moment was, for Gladdy, as glorious as it was for Kerry, and she played her role with a lifted heart. *Coo,* she thought, *if me mum could see me now—all grand, and as important as the queen's own maidens.* And Gladdy's hair seemed to vibrate into life as though set aquiver with static generated by her excitement. Her sixty-cent shoes quite literally danced their way to the side of the fireplace mantel. Her red, chapped hands touched for the first time the bell pull that the gentry used so casually to summon lackeys from below to their elevated position, and she gave it a magnificent yank. The opportunity might never come again, and so she lived the moment fully, eking from it every scrap of feeling possible: the responsibility! the power! the satisfaction!

Sure enough, as certainly as though the mistress herself had issued the command, in a few minutes the door opened and Finch appeared, a snowy cloth over one arm, gloved hands bearing a silver tray, chin in the air. Gladdy watched, fascinated, wondering if he could possibly make his way across the room without stumbling against some impediment and slightly disappointed when he didn't. *It would be so consoling to see someone else spill something for once! But Finch performed to perfection. And that's why he's the butler and I'm a maid* . . . nearly, Gladdy's half-formed thoughts ran. And then she ran, quite literally, when Finch's eyes slid in her direction, and his head bobbed bed-ward, indicating, Gladdy supposed, that she get herself over there. Finch's sallow, pinched face took on a long-suffering look as Gladdy helped Franny sit up straight, arranged a place in front of her for the tray, and stepped back, looking at Finch questioningly.

"The towel, Gladys," Finch said in a patient tone. And Gladdy reached cautiously, lest she be the one to upset the tray and face the ultimate humiliation—disapproval in the eyes of Franny and Kerry—to remove the cloth from Finch's black-garbed arm and, at his nodded directions, spread it over the knees of Frances.

With things, finally, to his approval, Finch carefully lowered the tray, righted its first tendency to tip, and said, "If the little Missy will turn slightly, she can reach things quite satisfactorily, I do believe."

Gladdy bit her lip as she concentrated on this maneuver by Kerry. In fact, so intent was she that she tensed her muscles, squirmed her hips, and flexed her fingers in sympathy with the child's movements. Finally, with Finch's help, Kerry's attention, and Gladdy's absorbed but useless convolutions, all was settled to Finch's approval, and he backed away, bowed slightly, and turned to the door. Only when he realized that he wasn't followed by Gladdy did he pause, fix the little maid with his eye, and bob his head—door-ward, this time. Gladdy, till then lost in the fascinating ceremony of breakfast in bed, gave a start, turned, and followed. *Some day,* she promised herself silently, fiercely, *it'll be me havin' brefuss in me nightshirt.*

Gladdy returned to polishing the silver, daydreams coloring her vivid imagination. Just how and when any of it would come to pass, she didn't know, nor care. For now, it was enough to dream. But for the first time there was another figure in her fanciful future: Kerry. Somehow, and dimly, their fate was to be together. Kerry leading, of course, and she, Gladdy, always there to follow through, to accompany, to assist.

Funny, but even in imagination, Gladdy could not conceive of herself as instigator, leader, controller. Too many generations of poverty and subjection had gone into her makeup for Gladdy to even approach the thought of total independence. But the seed was there, planted by the courier who had found her and persuaded her to seek something better for herself, and nourished by the very freedom that she breathed in the new land. It was in the air; men breathed free, many of them for the first time in their lives. Life would be what they made it; free enterprise was everywhere.

Mr. and Mrs. Finch, if they so desired, Gladdy realized, could just up and leave their employers and find work somewhere else. And sometimes they threatened to do so, with an immediate raise in pay forthcoming. You could know your value in a free land. It was incredible to the half-child, half-woman who had known nothing but poverty and suppression in the slums of London. And so now in imagination she soared, but always at the heels of Kerry. So neglected, so alone, so adrift from all things the world counts dear, Gladdy McBean had fixed her wagon to a star that was Kerry Ferne. Where, oh where, would it take her? The sky, that vast, blue bowl so typical of Canada and so endless, was the limit.

⸻

Finch turned in at the kitchen where Olga, his wife, was trussing a bird for the oven.

"Well, did yer see her? What do yer think of her—some little missy, issen she? Now we've got two of 'em. I have a feelin', Finch, this'n issen goin' to be as easy to have around as Miss Frances. Other than takin' Miss Frances her meals now and then, and a few things like that, you'd hardly know her was around, the darlin'."

Finch picked at a thread on his black uniform, found it hard to do with gloves, and turned to Olga for assistance, bobbing his head downward. Olga dutifully wiped her hands on her apron, plucked off the annoying thread, moved to the range, removed a lid, and dropped it in; Mrs. Finch kept an immaculate kitchen. Finch nodded approval. Careless her grammar might be, trying his patience at times, but her rotund form pleased him mightily and the cooking that made her thus. Casting a quick glance at the doors—leading outside, to the hall and the front of the house, and to the pantry where Gladdy worked—he lovingly smacked his wife's considerable back quarters but found the experience lacking its usual satisfaction. *Gloves!*

"This one, though quiet right now, was mighty big-eyed," he answered his wife's summation of the "new missy." "I've an idea she's just biding her time. We'll see what she's like before the week's over, I have no doubt. You know, pet, we'll have to approach the mistress again about extra help. You and I and this little waif Gladdy can't run the place alone, with only occasional help from Biddle and none at all, it seems, from Mr. High and Mighty Gideon. He sits like a king in that carriage and feels himself overworked if he so much as whistles at the horses. It isn't fair, nor right!" Finch was getting himself all worked up, a sure sign that he would approach his employer about either more help or, as usually happened, a raise in pay.

"You're right, as usual," Olga said, nodding her head with its bun of thin hair fastened securely on top. "You're the one to face 'em about it. Tell 'em the Oswalds down the street are in desp'rate need o'help and have been lookin' our way."

"I'd sooner be put in my grave than work for those upstarts. Think they're mighty grand, what with all that new money from the hides of those poor little animals—beaver, mostly, now that the buffalo is as good as gone. Work for them? Never!" Finch turned his sliver of a nose ceiling-ward and looked righteously indignant.

"Well, it's true, o'course, that the mister and missus are superior in every way." There was satisfaction in Olga's voice as she basked in her secondhand importance. Not entirely free from the old ways, Olga, and at times Finch himself, aligned themselves with the family they worked for. The Maxwells being "quality" and their wealth considered "old money" commanded a certain degree of respect from Finch and Olga simply on that account. Because of the Maxwells, the Finches considered themselves superior. In other words, the Finches were snobs.

"I wouldn't set foot in that mausoleum of theirs," said Finch, with another sniff. "But there! I don't need to say that when I talk to the mister." Finch had come far enough so that, in his thoughts, Sebastian was *mister* not *master*.

"Yes, talk to him. If you talk to her, she'll just think of ways to economize or add more jobs for me to do. That little Gladdy's got so much to learn, her's not the greatest help." Olga opened the warming oven and checked the bread rising there.

"She's a willing little thing; don't forget that," Finch cautioned. "We mustn't let them Oswalds get their hands on her, for heaven's sake, or she might jump at the chance to work in a gilded palace. And they'd probably give her more money, just to get her away from the mister and missus. Yes, I'll approach them about additional help. I think," Finch said, his sallow face turning thoughtful, "dinner will be late today. It's just too hard, you understand, for you to get it on the table alone, and with only me to serve. Gladdy spilled gravy on the mister's cuff the last time she helped. Yes, we'll soon have it a little easier around here, or my name isn't Newton Finch."

Olga turned fond eyes on her husband. "Of course it is," she said, "and of course we will. Now, if you'll just skedaddle on up and see what the missus wants for dinner, I'll get started on it. Slowly."

Dinner was indeed delayed. Seated at the long table in the formal dining room, Sebastian Maxwell looked down its length, frowned, and said, "Whatever can be the matter. I have a meeting to attend this evening."

Charlotte sighed. It was about time for Finch to expect a raise in pay. And that meant a devious route to draw it to Sebastian's attention.

"Patience, my dear," she said calmly, more calmly than she felt. It was too much, really, the way Finch manipulated! She had half a mind to turn him over to the Oswalds. She'd noted and understood the gleam in Sophie Oswald's eyes the last time she had come to an "at home." Sophie had followed the impeccable Finch's movements carefully, and Charlotte could almost see the idea taking shape: Get him! Hire him! Take him away from the Maxwells. Pay whatever is necessary.

As if Finch, who knew quality when he saw it, would ever consider such an offer! Still, Charlotte recognized later, it had been used as a lever. But Finch was not the man she thought if he were tempted by all that new wealth. There would be no prestige at all in working for the ostentatious house down the street.

Charlotte well remembered the first time Sophie Oswald had come to call. She had shaken hands with her hostess as was right and proper, but then she had casually removed her veils, gloves, and wrap, and handed them to Finch. Even he, in fact he *particularly*, had been haughtily scornful of this embarrassing error in protocol. She had seen the disapproval in his eyes as Sophie Oswald had then proceeded around the room, shaking hands with the other ladies—a horrible gaffe! It would serve Finch right, she thought now, if she threatened to turn him over to the Oswalds.

On the other hand, if Finch once again declared himself overworked, it might be wise to consider additional help rather than another raise in pay for the existing staff. Yes, that might be the way to go. Franny's health precluded being sent away to school, and her lessons, though sketchy, had been cared for by a visiting tutor. Now, with Kerry as well to educate, a live-in tutor might be the very thing. Perhaps a governess—someone who could instill in the astonishing Kerry a semblance of common sense along with book learning.

Therefore she was able to turn to Finch when he finally appeared behind a dinner cart and say casually, "I can see that your tasks seem too heavy, Finch. I believe it's only right and proper that we relieve you of some of the work, particularly the care of the young ladies, and set about looking for a governess. The Oswalds, I understand, have a governess for their girls *and* a tutor for their boys."

Foiled! the dismayed flash in Finch's eye seemed to say. One more person to tend to had not been what he had in mind. A governess! A new missy, and now a governess! The gloom on Finch's long face put somewhat of a damper on the meal, and Charlotte was relieved when he disappeared at last.

"You know, my dear," she said to her husband, who was all unaware of the current swirling around his dinner table, "we're going to have to see to a governess for the girls."

"Where are they, by the way? I thought they'd grace the dinner table tonight."

"They've talked and laughed all day long, though I did insist on a rest for each of them this afternoon. Frances is quite worn out tonight, so I deemed it wise to send their dinner on up to them." Charlotte sighed. "I'm sure that's back of this new pressure from Finch concerning more money. Did you hear what I said, Sebastian, about a governess? Doesn't it seem the sensible way to go, now that we have two female young people to train and bring up properly?"

Sebastian, replete with a good English boiled dinner complete with Yorkshire pudding and topped off with blancmange, his favorite pudding, mundane though it was, patted his lips and said expansively, "Whatever you think best, my love." And so it was settled.

Gladdy having managed to cut her finger on a knife she was washing, Mrs. Finch herself had appeared in the room where the girls were finishing their dinner, to gather up their dishes and see for herself how the new missy and the established missy were hitting it off, if indeed they were. She too took note of the happy faces and the unending stream of conversation between the young lady and the child.

When Olga Finch had turned toward the hall and was out of hearing range, Kerry, watching with awe the waddling, generous proportions of cook's anatomy, murmured her last verse of the day, changing only the gender (after all, she had concluded that *him* could just as well refer to *her*): "She covereth her face with her fatness, and maketh collops of fat on her flanks."

"Brumley's Elixir may be the answer," Della Baldwin mused aloud, her head, tidily bound with thin brown braids, bent over a newspaper. It was an outdated paper, sent to the Baldwin home by Della's brother, who worked on the *Winnipeg Free Press* and often bundled up a dozen papers at a time and sent them off to the bush family.

"Huh?" Dudley said and stopped chewing momentarily. The sound of his own toast crunching in his ears had caused his mother's words to be indistinct.

"Don't say 'huh,' Dudley," Della corrected automatically, without looking up at the child-man sitting across the table from her. Gangly of leg and arm, awkward of movement, and always hungry, Dudley was concentrating on his breakfast and the effort to bring toast to his mouth without suffering the indignity of its thick layer of golden syrup dripping on his hand, or worse, his Sunday shirt.

His mother looked around the edge of the paper, eyes sorrowful, first of all over the rudeness of his "huh" and then his attention to other, less important details such as food, when his mother had spoken to him.

"Uh, pardon, Mum." Having seen her look, Dudley hastened to make the expected corrections.

Isolated, backwoodsy, in the heart of the Canadian bush the Baldwins might be, but there would be no carelessness of speech or manners in Della's house, thank you!

"That's better, dear. Now then, this that I'm reading should be of interest to you. I was saying that Brumley's Elixir could be the answer."

"The answer, Mum?" Dudley gave a surreptitious lick to one side of the toast where a drop of syrup was in imminent danger of falling.

"The answer to your problem, Dudley."

"My problem?" Dudley, now attentive, asked cautiously. There were numerous things that he wasn't anxious for his mother to know—smoking occasionally behind the barn, for instance.

"Yes, Dudley, your problem." Della sighed and continued patiently, "Your pimples."

At least she didn't know about the smoking. Dudley was both relieved and embarrassed—relieved that his mother apparently didn't know—yet—about the smoking, embarrassed that such a personal thing as his "problem" should be so frankly and ruthlessly exposed. His skin problem, endured by many young people his age, was a constant source of concern to his mother. He would have been happy to forget it; one glance in the mirror in the morning as he combed his hair, and the youthful ailment could be ignored for the remainder of the day.

Dudley was an only child. He often wished for a brother or sister, if only to keep his mother's attention focused somewhere else once in a while! Now he poured himself some milk, missing the glass and slopping a few drops. About to swipe at it with his cuff, he caught his mother's reproachful eye. She laid the paper aside with another sigh, reached for a dish towel, and mopped up the small mess. At the same time Henley, Della's husband and

Dudley's father, closed the kitchen door behind him, set down a pail of milk, took off his hat, and grinned at the familiar scene— Dudley spilling something, Della wiping it up.

"Boys will be boys, eh?" he said with good humor.

At least he hadn't said huh. Nevertheless, "Like father, like son," Della reminded.

As Dudley moved on to his third piece of toast and a second serving of fried eggs, Henley bent over the washstand located in the corner of a room that was the main living quarters for this family of three. Another section of the log house was divided into two small bedrooms. Home life, for homesteaders who braved the hazards of the primitive bush, was necessarily close quarters. For eight or nine months of the year, heat was a problem to be reckoned with, and large areas were hard to keep warm. Freezing to death was as threatening as starvation. More than one loner had been found frozen in his own bed, having been too sick or disoriented to keep his fire going, gradually falling asleep and never waking.

Della laid the paper aside, obviously not finished with it or her thought, poured her husband a mug of coffee, brought another plate of eggs and toast from the range's warming oven, and resumed her place.

Henley took a seat at the round, oak table. His dark hair was touched at the temples with gray, his warm eyes were surrounded by what people called "laugh lines." Henley was a good-natured, good-looking man.

Henley Baldwin had a loving heart, a faithful heart, never wavering in kindness toward his choice of a wife—Della of the sharp tongue and quick temper. On those rare occasions when Della's conscience was pricked by her unreasonableness and she sought absolution, Henley would say, kindly, "Why, hon, you keep a man on his toes, that's all. I'd probably be a poor stick of a fellow without you." Nevertheless, to all and sundry who knew the couple and often felt sorry for the long-suffering husband, Henley deserved better.

"I was just saying that this," and she tapped the paper with her finger, "may be the answer to Dudley's problem."

Like his son before him, Henley was puzzled. Surely she didn't know about the smoking . . . but you never could tell about Della. She knew how to keep things to herself until the strategic moment when her triumph would be complete and the errant person proved guilty beyond a shadow of a doubt. In all such matters, one thing was as sure and as certain as winter—Della would, sooner or later, face the guilty party head-on.

Like his son before him, Henley prompted, "his problem?"

"Henley," she said impatiently, "his pimples, of course." And the eyes of both parents turned on the pinking face of their son. Mouth full of breakfast, Dudley stopped chewing momentarily and looked guiltily at his parents as though sorry to have brought this problem upon them. Della studied the young face critically; Henley more casually. It was a thin face, unformed now, with only a promise of what the man would look like. Lank brown hair fell over a high forehead; the teeth, at this age, appeared too large for the narrow face; a faint fuzz sprouted from the long upper lip; and—yes indeed, numerous eruptions blossomed from ear to large ear and hairline to sensitive, tender mouth and chin.

"He's no worse than I was at his age," the man offered. "He'll outgrow the skin problems; kids always do."

"Still, if there is something that can be done—"

"It don't bother me none, Ma," Dudley said mildly and resumed his chewing.

"I despair of your grammar," Della lamented, sidetracked for the moment. "Not *don't*, and not *Ma*, for heaven's sake! You sound just like the Jurgensons! Perhaps Scandinavians don't know better, but you are English, Dudley, pure English. Now, what were you saying—correctly, if you please."

"It doesn't bother me, Mum," Dudley said meekly, but not too meekly to refuse to say Mummy.

"Now, hon," Henley interjected smoothly, as though from long practice, "what is this about pimples?"

"Impure blood. They're caused by impure blood," Della said with the air of one unearthing a gold mine. "Doesn't that sound reasonable?"

"Impure blood?" Henley repeated, peppering his eggs. "With all this good farm food, milk, and all? I find that hard to believe. It's probably some blockage of the pores, probably too much oil. It's just an overabundance of youthful, er—" Henley hesitated, ignorant of the word *hormones* and at a loss to acceptably explain the masculine tides rising in the young man's system—"vigor," he finished inadequately.

"Vigor! The only vigor I see is in his eating." Della watched a final bite of toast disappear into her son's mouth, noted the working of the prominent Adam's apple in the thin throat, sighed, and turned to the paper and her original thought.

"Yes, impure blood," she repeated, "and these people should know what they're talking about much more than you do, Henley. 'Pimples and sores,'" she read, "'are all positive signs of impure blood. No matter how it became so, it must be purified in order to obtain good health.'"

"He has excellent health," Henley observed. "He's just growing fast, is all. Here, let me see that."

Della turned the paper over to her husband grudgingly. "Why can't you just believe what I say, for heaven's sake?"

Henley located the proper place and said, "This lists additional signs of impure blood as 'dull headache, pains in various parts of the body, sinking at the pit of the stomach'—say, I had sinking in the stomach just before I sat down here. Do you suppose that means I have impure blood?" Henley laughed, and Dudley with him. Henley was the picture of health.

"Pet," Della said in a certain tight tone, and both man and boy knew to beware; "Pet" spoken in this way and in this tone was not an affectionate name. She proceeded in her most gentle voice, "I have great confidence in your wisdom, Henley; you know that. But shall we consider whether, by some chance, this company— trained and practiced in the art of identifying and curing bodily ills—may be better qualified to judge such matters." Then, gentling her tone even more until it was a soft purr, she finished with the knockout punch: "Wouldn't you agree, . . . *Hen?*"

With "Hen," a shortening of his name meant to equate his brains with those of a barnyard chicken and only used in contempt, Henley seemed to deflate like a pricked balloon. He gave his wife one sober glance and then turned his attention to his breakfast. One had the idea that the food was not only cold but tasteless in his mouth.

"It says," Della continued smoothly, "that it is a wonderful remedy and every bottle is sold with a positive guarantee. Now, isn't it worth a few cents to give your one and only son a beautiful complexion?"

"Of course, hon. Whatever you say."

Dudley could never understand his father's quiet compliance, his capitulation in every confrontation. Too young to understand the strength it took to do it, and not fully appreciating the peace that invariably followed, Dudley raged over his father's humiliation and his mother's cruelty. Whether to feel more anger at his mother or his father, he couldn't decide.

Rising, Della kissed her husband's cheek, ruffled his hair, and said, "There's a dear. I was sure you wouldn't object to my ordering a bottle."

Folding the paper, laying it aside, and beginning to gather up the breakfast dishes, she directed, "You men go and get ready for church while I take care of the dishes and get a chicken in the oven. First, Henley my dear, I know you'll take care of straining the milk. Dudley, you seem to have gotten a smidgen of syrup on your shirt front; wipe it off, dear. That's my boy. Do you think you can keep yourself clean while you hitch up? Your shoes, particularly—watch where you step. I'll be ready in two shakes of a lamb's tail. I do so look forward to Sunday service and the inspiration of Parker Jones's sermon. Now you pay attention this morning, Dudley, and don't sit in the back with the Jurgenson boys. Don't you think that's a good suggestion, Henley?" She turned to her husband with a brilliant smile.

Henley swallowed a last gulp of coffee, heard his name, turned toward his wife, and said apologetically, "Sorry, hon, but I was swallowing. What was it?"

"Henley, Henley, that wool gathering will surely get you in trouble someday," Della said lightly. "Time to stop daydreaming, Pet. I said I thought the Jurgenson boys were a bad influence. Would you agree?"

"I'm sure you're right, hon."

Beyond Dudley's remembrance were the early days when Henley's submissive responses—"Whatever you say," and "You're probably right, hon"—had greatly irked his bride. Confrontations, even the smallest difference of opinion, had thrown Della into such a miserable mood that the young husband, to keep the peace, had begun using the terms. At first, he only succeeded in angering her further. But eventually, as Della became convinced that Henley was not being sarcastic, her annoyance ceased, and she took his answers as confirmation that her opinion was correct, her way best. Never had she understood that Henley was avoiding the scenes that had so marred their first weeks of marriage and so shocked him. And since he never spoke in anything but a peaceable tone, Dudley, too, usually heard without reaction. His father's words, after all, were the words that set everything right.

But as he grew older, things didn't seem right. Dudley had a natural rebellion toward his mother's overbearing ways and his father's knuckling under. Once, in the barn, after a particularly strained encounter between his parents, ending with the accustomed giving in by his father, Dudley had burst out, "*Why*, Pa . . . why don't you stick up for yourself? You know you were right in there. I know it; I think Ma knew it, too. Why do you give in like you do?"

Henley had rested on the handle of the pitchfork he was using to clean the stalls and said, reasonably, "She means well, son.

Some people have this nature, you see, where they need to be right. I think your mother may be threatened in some way when anyone opposes her. It doesn't hurt me to let her have her way, to give in, to bite back an angry response. It would only make for considerably more trouble if I didn't.

"And I don't like trouble, son." Henley spoke with a certain grimness. "I guess that's your whole answer. I'm just grateful it's me and not you. You're the apple of your mother's eye. Everything she does for you is out of love, I'm sure. I pray you'll be allowed to grow up to be a real man. That's what I want for you." Then, with unexpected passion, he said, "I'd lay down and die for that."

His usual calm restored, Henley resumed his work.

Eventually Dudley was to conclude that his father sometimes took abuse in order to keep his son from facing it. It made him uncomfortable, even guilty at times. And, at times, he felt like a miserable milksop—the very thing he criticized in his father—hiding behind his father rather than facing up to his mother's unreasonableness. But it was so much more peaceful that way . . . he was, he guessed, more like his father than he had realized.

Buggy was the preferred mode of travel on Sunday, which meant that Dudley rode alongside, the one-seater buggy not accommodating more than two unless a person stood behind the seat. The weather being pleasant, numerous rigs could be seen making their way toward the hamlet called Bliss and the schoolhouse, which also served as the place of worship for the community. Here, people were alighting—some gracefully, some awkwardly; women holding skirts away from the rig's wheels, children jumping over; men greeting one another with hearty handshakes; women, at times, planting a kiss on a proffered cheek. Bibles and quarterlies were gathered up, and the adults made their way into the small white building to look for seats that would accommodate their bulk. Children lingered outside as long as they could.

Pulling up to the fence, Henley brought the buggy to a halt. Jumping out, he moved to the mare's head, looking back to see if Della had gotten safely out of the rig. Dudley waited alongside, still mounted.

Immediately both Henley and Dudley realized that Della was stiffly upright on the buggy's seat, her reproachful eyes on her husband.

As many times as Henley had been called upon to help her alight, it seemed he still managed to forget. And always in a public place, because it was only in public places Della insisted on the gentlemanly gesture. At home she leaped out by herself, with no hesitation, and this made it difficult for Henley to remember to offer aid at other times. He realized he was sorely at fault this morning for his oversight.

"*Hen,* dear," she caroled brightly, "I'm waiting," and only her husband and son heard the unspoken, "Dolt!"

"Watch the mare, son," Henley said quietly, for the horse was skittish amid the noise and confusion of the moment and needed to be checked. Henley made his way back to the side of the buggy.

"Sorry, hon, I should have been more thoughtful," he murmured apologetically, taking her outstretched hand and helping her down.

Not only was Della seething at his oversight, but she was highly embarrassed, for several people had noted the little interchange and were obviously hiding grins. And an embarrassed Della was a fount of fury. The brightness of her smile and the coldness of her eyes sent chills down Dudley's spine.

She spoke far, far too sweetly: "Thank you, *Hen.*"

The Sabbath as a day of rest was strictly observed in back-woods Canada, and nowhere was this more true than in the community of Bliss in the Saskatchewan Territory. The few places of business in the small hamlet—blacksmith shop, general store and post office, grain elevator—closed for the day. Almost without exception entire farm families, in direct obedience of the commandment "Remember the Sabbath day to keep it holy" made the seventh day a time of rest. Of course there was always the "ox in the pit" clause that allowed for necessary labor.

Physical bodies, weary of their labors, attested to the necessity of a day of rest; souls, though as needy, sometimes ignored the Bible's additional injunction of "not forsaking the assembling of ourselves together." Church attendance, however, was the practice of most, and this day was a fine example. The little schoolhouse was packed.

Just inside the entrance was the cloakroom area where the children's lunch pails were kept in a closet, where the water pail sat on a shelf, the communal dipper hanging alongside, and where, on both walls, wraps were hung. Below these hooks were long supply cupboards; with the lids down they made excellent seating. It was here the young people of the community sat during church services. Beyond, and divided from the cloakroom by a big heater that roared red-hot most of the school year, was the schoolroom proper. In front of the smallest desks was the teacher's battered desk, and behind, the blackboard stretched from wall to wall. Above the blackboard hung two large, oak-framed pictures. One depicted a child walking on the edge of a dangerous precipice through the gloom of a storm, with an angel hovering above, wings outspread protectively. The second pictured a huge dog beside a seething sea, a childish form crumpled on the sand at his feet as though just dropped from his open jaws. In each, it seemed clear that protection and rescue were available for children, but Dudley, who had studied them countless times across the years, never could decide whether to put his trust in angels or dogs.

Now, settling himself on the side bench with the youthful males of the community, Dudley—out of school several years and no longer concerned with the mishaps of children, whether pictured or real—focused his attention on the bright gaggle of girls seating themselves, with much flouncing, whispering, and giggling, on the opposite bench. And on one girl in particular.

Fair hair done in braids and wound around her head, face prim and proper, Matilda Hooper's blue eyes were less severely under control and, for a moment, flickered across the room to the watching Dudley. Both young faces colored brightly, and anyone watching would be quite certain there was more than casual friendship between the two.

Both Matilda and Dudley had gone through the Bliss school. Dudley was now verging on eighteen, Matilda on seventeen, and both considered themselves old enough to think seriously of their future. That it might be together was not an impossibility. In fact, since last night, it looked like a distinct possibility. Obviously, from the attention each now fixed on the other, things had progressed to a tentatively serious plateau. While Dudley was young, for a man, to be considering marriage, not so for Matilda; girls married at fourteen and fifteen in this land that was fast filling with bachelors and widowers. Marriageable women were at a premium; no female had to settle for second best when, with a little patience, another prospect would be along with another proposal.

Just last evening, Dudley and Matilda, walking out together, had found the courage to share the private thoughts each had hidden thus far. Even so, plans were in that dreamy, nebulous stage where anything could be considered and all things were possible. Dudley, very manly in Matilda's presence, felt old enough and capable enough to register for a homestead of his own; Matilda, feeling equally grown up, was thrilled by the challenge—pioneer days were by no means over!—and confident she could do her share in making such a venture a success. Though they were penniless, their dreams could see a way. Their future, after all, lay here in the north, with other homesteaders no better prepared than they were.

The first settlers to dare the western wilderness had hugged the wooded areas commonly called "the bush." One immediate problem was easily solved—material for a home. It grew right on the property and in abundance: trees. By law, land had to be cleared almost immediately to prove up a claim, and felling logs for a home was a good place to begin. Caulked with clay or mud, with hand-hewn shingles for the roof—or sod if one were in a hurry—a log house could be ready for occupancy. Hopefully one could afford the extravagance of doors and windows brought in by cart or steamboat; inside, mud-plastered walls were white-washed. A rug, if it was available, was placed over the packed-dirt floor, a few treasured items were hung on walls or placed on shelves, and home took on a certain comfort and familiarity.

Though all this had been accomplished on his father's homestead before his memory, Dudley was certain that he, too, could make a home out of almost nothing. And he dared to believe he would be happy in it—a great incentive. Away from his mother's eyes and tongue, Dudley was a different person, less gauche, more self-assured, even standing more erect and speaking with more confidence.

Yes, he could accomplish all they planned but not in Bliss, for a couple of reasons. Della was one of them. Secondly, though still considered the far-flung frontier, Bliss was, to its second generation, well established and lacking the spirit of the pioneer.

Daringly Matilda and Dudley considered their options: strike out on their own or move in with one set of parents or the other. Moving in with parents was ruled out immediately.

"I don't want to be anybody's man . . . or boy, if you know what I mean." Dudley had expressed himself bravely. "I want to stand on my own two feet. Dad says, when we've talked about the future for me, that I have all the gumption he had and says it'll be enough. I want to make it on my own."

"Your mum? What does she say, you being the only child?" a cautious Matilda asked.

"Well," he had said, more uncertainly, "I haven't mentioned it to her. But," he added, "if I go, I go, and that's that. It's not like it isn't happening all the time—children leaving to start their own lives. Ma and Pa, in their day, came from the east coast and were among the first to settle here. Things were rough for them—"

"And for my folks as well," Matilda said. "But I don't know, Dudley; I'm still very uncertain about all this, and I haven't agreed for sure, you understand."

"Well, of course I understand. I haven't asked for sure either, have I?" Dudley was full of bravado on the outside, very uncertain on the inside, especially where girls were concerned. It was a marvel and a miracle that Matilda had responded as she had, the very first time they talked about it. Well, he admitted, groundwork had been laid for several months, ever since he had noticed her particularly at the Sunday school picnic and dared to eat his picnic dinner with her. That Matilda would so much as consider a poor fellow like him for a life's partner! It was almost too much to hope for.

"*If* I say yes," she had continued primly, "and *if* we do get . . . married—"

"*If* I ask," Dudley had answered, surer of himself suddenly and more independent.

"Yes, all that. If we do, where would we go? What do you have in mind?"

"Oh, I dunno," Dudley had answered airily, unsure again but determined to be a man and knowing some decisions were up to him. "Perhaps the Peace River country."

Matilda had looked doubtful. "That's a long ways away. And it's terribly primitive there, isn't it? I just don't know—"

"But you'll think about it, Tilda?" Dudley had asked, his thin face earnest and his eyes filled with hope and dreams.

Looking into her eyes, lost in them, drowning in them, it was then Dudley determined to be a man indeed. He leaned forward, pursed his lips, closed his eyes, and kissed her lips, already half raised to his. In accordance with her proper training regarding young men and their passions, it could not be said that Matilda fully responded. Neither did she refuse him. Nor did she back away as she surely would have done if she had truly objected. And there was no slap, the reaction that all young men feared! One brief moment and she had pulled back, looking up at Dudley with startled, surprised eyes. Startled, Dudley supposed, because she hadn't thought him capable of such a momentous act, and surprised (he hoped) because she had found the experience to be pleasurable, as he certainly had.

After that, it was with swirling head and mind filled with plans Dudley had made his way homeward to help with the chores, evade his mother's keen eyes at the supper table, and go to bed. Here, daydreams turned to nightmares where his mother's scornful lashing stripped away every dream as surely as winter stripped the trees bare of every leaf.

Waking in a sweat, his heart pounding, Dudley vowed, silently and fiercely, that whatever the cost, his dreams would come true. He dreaded the morning light and reality.

That it had started with his mother reprimanding him for syrup on his Sunday shirt should have been laughable; instead, it plunged him into a gloom of despair and hopelessness that lingered all through preparations and the horseback ride to church. And so it had been with sweet relief and a lift to his spirits—in the schoolhouse that Sunday morning—that he met Matilda's glance and found himself ready to dream again and believe that, after all, all things were possible.

When the first song was announced and the congregation rose to its feet, Dudley was able to sing "The Glorious Hope" with zest, if not with harmony:

> A land of corn, and wine, and oil;
> Favored with God's peculiar smile,
> With ev'ry blessing blest;
> There dwells the Lord, our Righteousness,
> And keeps His own in perfect peace,
> And everlasting rest,
> And everlasting rest.

All mistakenly Dudley equated the peace and rest with the fulfilling of his own plans; that it would take divine intervention for them to come to pass, he understood not at all.

Parker Jones was at his serious best. A young man with a mission, Parker Jones was bent and intent on winning for the kingdom the good (and bad) people of Bliss. But even his sermon, intended to bring an unbelieving heart to trust in God and a rich fulfilling of His blessings, was misinterpreted by at least one young hearer.

"'Go thy way,'" the preacher read from the open Bible on the stand before him, and Dudley's heart lifted and he silently responded, *My way! It's a sign to go my way!*

"'. . . and as thou has believed, so be it done unto thee.'" Parker Jones concluded the day's Scripture reading, and an exalted Dudley, eager for his own way and knowing little or nothing of God's, believed. But believed in his own strength and way and counted it done according to God's Word.

Caught up in dreams as he was, catching Matilda's eyes occasionally, even winking once to her confusion and his enjoyment, he was startled when, slicing through the reverent atmosphere of the service, a woman shrieked, and shrieked again.

Ma!

10

"Behold, my belly is as wine which hath no vent; it is ready to burst like new bottles,'" Kerry quoted, totally happy in her misery. This having plenty to eat, three times a day, had never ceased being a marvel.

No matter how many times she did it—speak out of turn, that is—her uncle and aunt appeared to be shocked. Now Sebastian frowned and looked at his wife to rectify the present situation.

"Kerry!" Charlotte said, and her tone of voice conveyed her reprimand very clearly.

"I was just saying, Aunt," Kerry explained reasonably, "that I'm full. Elihu said it, in the Bible, you know," and she looked hopefully at her aunt, trusting that her defense would make a difference.

It didn't strengthen her defense any that Frances, seated across the table, was stifling laughter in her serviette, her eyes dancing over the edge of it, her face red against its snowy whiteness.

"Never repeat that verse again!" Charlotte continued. "Your body parts are your own personal and private business. And never,

never inform your dinner companions that you are full, for heaven's sake. It just isn't done!"

Kerry was silent; not mutinously so, but, as often happened, truly puzzled.

"Do you understand, Kerry?" Aunt Charlotte's voice wobbled a little, as if she weren't quite as adamant as she might be.

Still Kerry was silent, staring down at her empty dinner plate.

"Kerry? Why don't you answer me?"

"'I am young,'" Kerry said dolorously, her face long, "'and ye are very old; wherefore I was afraid, and durst not show you mine opinion.'"

"Does the child have a Scripture for everything?" Aunt Charlotte cried, to no one in particular and to all in general, throwing up her hands in despair. "You may be excused, Kerry! Frances, go with her. Try . . . again . . . to reason with the child. I certainly don't seem to be getting any results."

Frances laid aside her serviette and, barely managing to keep a straight face, said, "Come, Kerry, we'll go upstairs. Excuse me, and good night, Aunt Charlotte. Good night, Uncle Sebastian."

Kerry, looking properly chastened, excused herself and said her good nights, and the girls slipped away from the table.

When Charlotte dared look at her husband, it was to find Sebastian in a reflective mood. "Hmmm," he said. "I'm beginning to see what you mean, my dear. This blatant Bible quoting is one thing when we're here in the privacy of the family; it'll be another thing if she comes out with some such . . . er . . . tarradiddle when guests are present."

Charlotte, having just reprimanded Kerry, now felt a perverse need to defend her. "She's really doing better, Sebastian. When the governess arrives—"

"La," Sebastian put in, rolling eyes like raisins in a puffy bun, "what will *she* have to say about all this?"

"I was saying," Charlotte continued, with dignity, "that when the governess arrives and has the teaching of the child every day, some of the responsibility will be on her shoulders. No doubt we shall see a vast improvement then. As to what she'll think about it—she's paid not to think, isn't she?"

Having made this confounding summation of the situation, Charlotte looked a little confused herself. Sebastian seemed to be having trouble with the whole concept and blinked slowly a few times as he thought out the problem.

"I do hope so," he said finally, though he didn't seem to be sure just what he was hoping for. There was silence while Sebastian stirred cream into his coffee. Finally, the plump cheeks spread in a hint of a smile. "But it certainly does liven up the meals, doesn't it?"

It was all Charlotte needed. Gasping, Charlotte's full-bodied figure shook with her attempt to stifle an eruption of mirth. Soon she was joined by Sebastian in the best laugh they had had together in many years. Only when Finch appeared to remove their dessert dishes did they drop their eyes and fiddle with their fingers, while their nostrils flared and their faces pinked.

Outside the door Finch paused, his ear to the crack, his long face taking on a knowing look at the sounds of laughter that burst forth behind him and which, he could tell, could not totally be muffled, though the mister and missus made a mighty effort.

"You'll never believe it, Olga," he said in the kitchen. "They're laughing together."

"Well, it's laugh or cry, with that'n," Olga said, smiling, too, and remembering the time she had been making plum duff and Kerry had sat at the kitchen table watching. With dark eyes aglow at the mystery of the production and in anticipation of the sweet, Kerry had half-whispered, "Thy paths drop fatness!" It was a high compliment to the cook who spent her days preparing food for others to consume and who, oftentimes, went unthanked and, she felt, unappreciated.

"Did I tell you what she said to me the other day when I served lunch? Something about me giving them their 'meat in due season.' Did you ever hear the like? Perfectly serious, she were, the little lamb." Olga, too, had come under the spell of the "little lamb."

Olga and Finch had progressed to the point where no one had better criticize the "little missy" in their hearing! Laughable, unsettling, pointed, her quotations might be, but there was no meanness in her.

∘———∘

Upstairs, Frances leaned back on the pillows of her bed, exhausted from the climb; reaching a hand for Kerry's, she searched for words on a subject she had plumbed to its depths before now, as several times requested by Aunt Charlotte, who professed to be at her wit's end.

"You know what I'm trying to say, don't you, wee Kerry? You know Aunt Charlotte was distressed. But how can I scold! You mean so well—"

Kerry's sorrowful face looked up, a ray of hope lighting her eyes. "'As vinegar upon nitre, so is he that singeth songs to a heavy heart,'" she said. "And Franny, *he* means *she,* too, did you know that? So *he,* that is, *she,* meaning *you,* singeth songs to my heavy heart. Oh, Franny, that's so good of you!"

Frances shook her head helplessly.

"What is *nit-er?*" Kerry asked now. "Or is it *nit-ree?* I don't know how to pronounce it, and I don't know what it means. Do you, Franny?"

"Maybe, Kerry, it's time to stop saying words you don't understand. Not for my sake, you understand, but for Uncle Sebastian and Aunt Charlotte. They are so good to us. I'm sure you want to please them, don't you?"

"Yes," Kerry said, her eyes downcast now and her voice muffled. "I truly b'lieve I love Aunt Charlotte and maybe even Uncle Sebastian a little." The smallest tear appeared on her rosy cheek, a cheek filling out beautifully from all the "meat in due season" and other good things that were available in abundance in this house of Maxwell.

"You know, Kerry, there are so many other words, good words, that are there for us all to use, if we want to, and if we know them.

79

Why don't we start right now and look up the meaning and the pronunciation of *nitre*. Would you like that? Then you can substitute another word for it, a word you understand. Now, there's a good girl; run and get the dictionary."

And so Frances, lovingly and patiently, directed her dear companion toward the use of alternate words and phrases, thoughts that Kerry could put together herself, expressing herself in her own words and not always in the words of others, biblical though they might be.

There was a great eruption in kind approach, however, with the arrival of the governess. Miss Beery was scandalized by the free-thinking and outspoken Kerry, and her methods were not always wise. The beleaguered and harassed Kerry, trying to express herself when alone with Frances, could come up with no better description of her feelings for the governess than through the use of the familiar Scriptures. In her thinking they were perfectly suitable for the occasion, and nothing else would do.

"'I hate her with perfect hatred,'" she said to Frances one day.

"But you mustn't hate, Kerry," Frances, who had never hated anyone, said gently. "And I don't think hatred is perfect. Can you think of another way to express yourself?"

It had sent Kerry in search of the dictionary—again.

"I feel great an-im-osity and hos-til-ity," she reported happily afterward, "though I don't really know what they mean. Why can't I just say *hate* if that's what I mean?" Her face fell when Frances sighed and took her hand, a sure sign that teaching was needed—again.

But from her beloved Franny, Kerry took every correction. To be like Franny—that was the highest goal she could reach. Therefore Kerry gave herself to the lessons the governess laid out, with a minimum of complaint and, eventually, the use of Scriptures—never mind that they were apropos—abated. At least they were seldom spoken aloud, and when they were, it was under her breath and in the company of Franny alone, or Gladdy.

As Kerry adored Frances, so Gladdy adored Kerry. Older and more worldly wise, still Gladdy found fascination in the child who was so different from anyone she had ever known, who was kind, happy, playful and, perhaps best of all, totally without class consciousness. That Gladdy wore uniforms mattered not a whit; that Gladdy had little or no education did.

"Aunt Charlotte," Kerry brought up one day with her new small layer of polish and propriety in evidence, "Gladdy needs help more than I do."

"Whatever do you mean?" Charlotte asked, laying aside her book and giving her niece her attention, more absorbed with her niece's proper clothing and shining, well-trimmed hair than with her words.

"I mean her grammar, Aunt Charlotte. And she can't read!" Not reading was a shame of massive proportions to Kerry.

"Does she need to?" Charlotte asked. "Olga reads, and Finch, and they are quite capable of directing her in all things."

"But, Aunt! Think of all the things she's missing!" Throwing caution to the winds, Kerry burst forth with, "She was ahungered, and you gave her no meat!" Only a child herself and lacking in words, Kerry couldn't adequately express herself aside from a portion of Scripture.

"Ahungered? Why, though she's thin, she's very well fed!"

"Not food hunger, Aunt Charlotte! She's hungry to learn. I know, because she hangs around when lessons are going on, if she possibly can. And once I found her trying to sound out some word . . . from the Bible," she finished lamely.

Charlotte was made uncomfortable by the little that was said and the much that was hinted at, and Gladdy, to her happiness and Kerry's joy, was included in the study time for one hour each day.

As the years passed and Kerry "grew in favor" with the adults in the family, Aunt Charlotte trusted her with certain errands and responsibilities that called for excursions into the city, always a time of excitement and pleasure. On all such outings she was accompanied—at first by Miss Beery, then by Gladdy, who was judged a fit companion by this time. If Charlotte Maxwell had known the adventures they experienced together, she would have shriveled up and slunk away from proper society, never to be seen or heard from again. If occasionally during "at homes" she noted certain ladies lowering their voices, looking her direction, hiding behind their fans, and gesturing strangely, she failed to make the connection with her niece who was growing up, it seemed, into a biddable, polite, even discreet young woman.

Only Franny knew the true Kerry and, at times, sighed to find her so little changed from the waif who had first come to live among them. Unchanged at heart where the true Kerry dwelt, Kerry went through all the intricacies and niceties of proper decorum as expected of young women just before the end of the century and learned to do it very well. Eventually even the ladies at the society functions ceased their pointing and whispering and head shaking.

And so the outings abroad increased, until Kerry and Gladdy felt themselves to indeed be women of the world.

And what a world it was! What a time in which to live! Something called the motion picture had been patented; a hydroelectric plant opened at Niagara Falls; L.C. Rivard became Montreal's first owner of a motor car—a Locomobile; and a Dr. Henri Casgrain of Quebec became the first known Canadian to drive a motor car—top speed, 18 mph; vaccination of school children was compulsory (setting off a storm of protest); the Imperial Penny Postage (2 cents) was inaugurated throughout the British Commonwealth; gold was discovered in the Klondike by George Carmack, Skookum Jim, and Tagish Charlie; and immigration to the Canadian West began to boom in earnest.

Though still honored and perhaps revered, the 1890s witnessed the sunset of the good queen's influence. "Britishness" reached its peak with Queen Victoria's Diamond Jubilee and began its decline. Something new, something different emerged: As the swarm of immigrants tasted freedom and grew accustomed to the heady diet, they were to become confident, ambitious, expectant of even better things. They were, to put it into one word, silently but real-ly becoming *Canadian*.

The freedom that Gladdy and Kerry experienced—Kerry in her mid-teen years and Gladdy nearing nineteen—was not shared by Frances except on rare occasions when she was deemed strong enough to go along—usually in the carriage—for an outing in the fresh air. But slowly it became obvious to the two younger girls, to the governess, and to her aunt and uncle, that Frances was showing better color, was even "sparkling" on occasion, and was, in general, exhibiting more of an interest in life. Frances seemed, at last, in her mid-twenties, on the verge of enjoying life as a normal young woman. "She's like a rose in the fall that has decided to bloom," fanciful Kerry described her, then adding, "and she's all the sweeter for the wait."

It was true, Frances was a new person. Frances was in love.

At first not discerned by anyone—for, after all, no one expected invalids to enjoy the ordinary experiences of life—the secret eventually came to light.

A dancing master came twice weekly to teach Kerry (with Gladdy watching and secretly humming and going through the steps all alone at first, then with Kerry as her teacher and partner). These sessions were chaperoned by Frances, and no one—not the spinster Miss Beery, not the chaste Kerry or the innocent Gladdy—was experienced enough in love to see what was happening before their very eyes.

Frances, being stronger, had hinted that she too might like a discreet dance step or two with Señor Garibaldi, he of the swimming dark eyes, the small mustache, and the graceful hands and feet. Kerry, stepping back and allowing Franny to step within the circle of the dancing master's arm, noted Franny's heightened color, which was natural. But the tremulous lips? The starry eyes?

When the first short session was over and Señor Garibaldi bowed gracefully over Franny's hand, it did seem, to Kerry, that he held her hand longer than was necessary. Never could Kerry recall having seen eyes looked into as soulfully; never had Franny lingered—light as a bird and as fragile—so long a time on weary feet. Untaught in love, still Kerry's breath caught for a moment as she recognized the chemistry—as old as time and as new as the moment—that passed between the two. Of its own volition, it seemed, a Scripture sang itself into her heart: "I found him whom my soul loveth: I held him, and would not let him go." Never had Scripture seemed more appropriate. The Song of Solomon, always a puzzle to Kerry, suddenly made sense, beautiful sense.

Still, Franny turned back to Kerry, back to everyday life, and said nothing. But it was not necessary—the secret was out.

"Gladdy," Kerry whispered later, "have you noticed . . . anything unusual about Franny?"

"You mean," Gladdy, more worldly-wise and therefore more observant, said straightaway, "about Señor Garibaldi? I didn't fink . . . *think* you saw, and I didn't know whether to say somefing or not." At times of stress or excitement, Gladdy tended to revert to her old, natural way of speaking. Her speech showed improvement, but to her everlasting sorrow her hair, more like a porcupine with hackles up than anything else when not forcibly restrained, was not as tractable. Now it crouched, as it were, atop her head like a live thing, ready to spring forth at the least excuse; the vibrant color remained as undimmed as ever.

Not certain how Aunt Charlotte and Uncle Sebastian would feel about such an alliance, Kerry said nothing to them of her suspicions concerning Franny and Señor Garibaldi. But even Charlotte and Sebastian noticed the improvement in Frances's health and outlook. Always gentle, kind, soft of speech, and slow to show annoyance—Franny seemed sweeter than ever. Franny glowed. Franny glowed for about six weeks.

There came a day when Señor Garibaldi did not arrive at the scheduled time. Though Kerry waited in the room they called the classroom, he did not come. Neither did Franny, as chaperone. With a sense of something wrong Kerry made her way to Franny's room, to find the drapes closed and the room in semi-darkness though it was mid-afternoon. Franny's low voice had responded to Kerry's knock: "Who is it?"

"It's Kerry. What's wrong? May I come in?"

After a long silence Franny's muffled voice gave permission. She was prostrate on her bed, face white in the gloom, eyes puffed.

Kerry flew to her side. "Franny! Whatever is wrong? What is it?"

"You mustn't be concerned, Kerry. I'm just ill today. That's all—ill."

"But you've been so well, so . . . happy."

Franny was silent, too silent; it was an agonizing silence.

"Shall I get Auntie?" Kerry asked, worried and perplexed.

Franny gave a short laugh; one would have called it a bitter laugh if one didn't know Frances any better than that. "My heavens, no. Above all people, don't call Aunt Charlotte. Just leave me be, Kerry. I'll be all right. Please, dear."

Kerry crept away with the first real unhappiness she had felt in her aunt's home. That it touched her beloved Franny was worse, she believed, than if she herself were the one suffering.

At the dinner table that evening, Sebastian being absent and only Kerry and Charlotte present, an empty chair gaped loudly of Frances's absence; she had so often, of late, been present, adding her special cheer to the occasion. It was a quiet, gloomy affair.

Finally Charlotte, with a sigh, laid aside her serviette, and said, "There is a problem, a very real problem to be faced, Kerry. Particularly by Frances, and we must help her face it and bear the pain."

"What, Aunt? What's wrong? Oh, I can hardly stand it . . . I hurt so."

"Frances hurts far more. Yes, I'll tell you about it, my dear. You are old enough to be treated as an adult, and we mustn't ignore that. You'll need to be an adult, certainly, to help Frances."

"Anything!" Kerry promised.

"It seems Señor Garibaldi," Charlotte said in a strained voice, "has been enticing Frances to fall in love with him. By little actions, soft gripping of her hands, looking into her eyes and, finally, declaring her to be his true love."

"But, Aunt . . . is that so bad? It's made Franny come alive. She's been feeling so much better, and I think it's all because she has hope, now, of a normal future—"

"She has hope of nothing!" Charlotte said in a hard voice. "That man is a blackguard . . . an unprincipled wretch—"

Charlotte's wrath caused her voice to rise, but her vocabulary was inadequate to express her feelings, and she stumbled now with various descriptions of the dancing master, all of them insulting: shameless fortune hunter, traitor, knave, mercenary.

Kerry's face must have shown her bewilderment, for Charlotte ceased her tirade, brought her serviette to her face for a moment, and spoke more calmly. Garibaldi (he no longer rated the "Señor") was a snake in the grass who had inveigled himself into Frances's affections, very soon urging marriage upon her, which was to be a fleeing away in the night, a private ceremony, then and only then making an announcement to the family. A romantic escapade, he had termed it.

"But, Aunt Charlotte—I still don't see—"

"The man is a charlatan, Kerry! A mountebank! With the lowest of purposes!"

"How do we know—"

"From Gideon, that's how."

Gideon, it seemed, while driving the dancing master back and forth, had become a confidant. From the beginning, Señor Garibaldi had been interested in the family's wealth. He had assumed that Miss Frances, being the oldest, was heiress to it all. And he had, forthwith, "pressed his suit." Poor, dear Frances—

gullible, taken in by his protestations of love, yearning for some-one to love, had been easy prey.

Somewhere along the way Garibaldi had brought up to Franny the subject of her parentage—her mother and father, where were they? Abroad, perhaps? Frances had quickly explained that her parents were dead, that she had been taken in by dear Aunt Charlotte and Uncle Sebastian, and that she was, in fact, a penniless orphan, dependent on their love and provision.

"The change in him was instantaneous, I understand," Charlotte said with pity. "In fact, his whole expression revealed his dismay. He turned cold, stepped away from her, with condemnation in his eyes for her as though she had betrayed him. Not understanding . . . perhaps not daring to, Frances cried out . . . asking why it mattered, telling him she never had any expectations of living in wealth . . . that she was a simple woman, with simple desires—"

"Poor Franny!" To so belittle herself! And all for nothing! "Did he . . . spurn her?" Kerry stumbled over the word.

"Worse. He accused her of toying with his affections, of leading him on. Franny fainted, totally overcome, and Garibaldi left her lying there and made his escape. How do I know these details? Gladdy was there, behind the door, hearing it all. She had gone up, hoping to get in on the lesson, but slipped behind the door and listened when she realized something most unnatural was going on. It was she who helped Frances up and got her to her room. Then of course she came for me. Frances, trembling and broken, couldn't explain much. So between what Gideon, Gladdy, and the little Frances said, I pieced together the sordid story. Oh, the cad!"

Recalling Franny's white face and her dead eyes, a great fear welled up in Kerry's heart. What, oh what, did darling Franny have to live for now? Having poor health—for even now she appeared sick, terribly sick, a sickness for which there was no pill, no potion; nothing to occupy her days from now on out; no hope of independence—the future, for Franny, appeared to be a vast wasteland of emptiness.

Strange, that when thrown into a desperate crisis, there was no life-giving, hope-building, faith-strengthening Scripture; among the many Kerry knew, none sprang to mind. If she'd been a little older, a little wiser, and better taught, Kerry might have wondered at this. As it was, she carried her heartache alone, never knowing there was a Friend who surpassed Franny for gentleness, a Burden-bearer who surpassed Aunt Charlotte for comfort, a Father who was more faithful than she could comprehend.

"Oh, Aunt," she cried, devastated, "whatever will happen to her?"

With the sound of the shriek still echoing through the schoolroom, everyone seemed to freeze momentarily in place. When the echoes died out the silence was as thunderous, in its way, as the blood-curdling scream. Parker Jones's sermon notes drooped in his hand; a fussy baby, startled out of its small whimper, stared wide-eyed at it knew not what.

Dudley was the first to move. Galvanized into action, he jumped over the outstretched legs of his companions, curveted around the heater, leaped the short aisle in two strides, and turned toward the couple seated at a desk in the center of the room.

Della's mouth was stretched in a soundless scream, her eyes staring, fixed on her husband. At her side, Henley was slumped forward, his face pressed onto a much-marked desk, just below the initials JB and RM, which were twined together for perpetuity by some forgotten childish swain and more enduring perhaps than the one who carved it. Certainly the desk's present occupant—face on its marred surface, hands hanging at his side—appeared to have fled this "vale of tears."

Now there was a shifting of the congregation; a tide moved the crowd as though some giant finger stirred in their midst; all eyes were centered on the scene being enacted in the middle of the room. Parker Jones dropped his notes and hurried forward. From the benches at the side of the room two men leaped into action, one to lift Henley's head and attempt to look into his eyes, the other to take a wrist and feel for a pulse. They were homesteaders in the Bliss area—Connor Dougal and Gregor Slovinski, each tall, powerful, supremely masculine. As they joined Dudley over the form of his father, none of them knew the bonds this day's business would make between the three of them and the trouble.

Callused but caring hands were moving Della out of the crowded space, comforting arms were placed around her as the women of the congregation, shocked and pale, reached out with the only help they could give at the moment.

"Clear a bench," Connor Dougal directed, and its occupants scattered, to stand against the wall, eyes staring from their heads, lips moving soundlessly, perhaps in prayer.

"Help us move him," Connor continued, and willing hands grasped the dangling legs, the limp arms, and heaved Henley from his crouched position in the childish seat to the narrow bench running down the side of the schoolroom. Here he was laid, one hand and arm falling helplessly toward the floor. Gregor Slovinski's big fingers fumbled with Henley's shirt collar and tie, loosening them and unbuttoning the front of his shirt.

Beyond that there seemed little anyone could do. The crowd looked on helplessly as Connor Dougal began chafing Henley's hands. Gregor Slovinski put an ear to Henley's chest—his too-motionless chest. The crowd against the wall and in the other seats looked questioningly toward the big Slav as he raised his cinnamon-colored head and spoke through his cinnamon-colored beard the words they dreaded to hear: "Notting, I hear notting. You give a lissen," and he beckoned forward one figure in the group—Gramma Jurgenson. Bliss's midwife, and probably the best prepared of anyone in Bliss to deal with sickness and trauma, as well as childbirth, Gramma went through the same procedures as had Connor and Gregor. She too shook a head, having checked the pulse and breath and finding neither.

"Gone," she said briefly. "Probably apoplexy."

Della sobbed aloud; Dudley, standing off to the side, felt as though the world were reeling and put out a hand to the nearest elbow for support. It was Matilda's, and for a moment they held onto each other; then, even then, remembering the proper thing, they stepped apart.

Face-to-face with his first death as a pastor, Parker Jones called for attention and prayer. Whether Della heard him is questionable; her face told the story: disbelief, struggling with panic.

Between his mother's stricken countenance and his father's still face, Dudley felt as though he were in a bad dream. Or a nightmare that was worse, if such could be, than the one of the previous night, a night that now seemed a long time ago and a million miles away. At least he had awakened from that one; there would be no awakening from the horror of this one.

Connor Dougal was quietly seeing to the removal of the body of Henley Baldwin. "Do you have a wagon?" he asked Gregor. "I rode, myself."

"Yah, I got vagon," Gregor answered, nodding. "And I'll bring it to d' gate. Somebody," and his gaze circled the room, "help wit' the Baldwin rig, a'right?"

Parker Jones was administering what solace he could to the colorless Della. Two of the women were rubbing her hands, one on either side; another was wrapping a shawl around her shoulders. Though the day was warm and bright with sunshine, Della was shivering, and the shawl would help.

Blankets were collected from someone's wagon and placed on the bottom of Gregor's wagon, with one reserved to cover the staring face of the dead man. One of the Jurgenson boys held the horses, and someone brought around the Baldwin buggy and horse, with Dudley's horse tied behind.

Though Connor Dougal was prepared to lift the lifeless form of his neighbor and carry it to the wagon, Gregor was the likely one for the job, and he knew it. Making his way back through the crowd and shouldering the younger man aside with a grunt, Gregor bent his mighty frame, gathered Henley into his arms as a child would cradle a rag doll, and made his way through the stunned crowd to the wagon.

The congregation followed silently as Della was half led, half carried by Parker Jones and Connor Dougal, helped into the buggy (no foolish babble now about assistance—without it the half-fainting woman would never make it home).

"Will you drive, son, or shall I?" Connor asked Dudley. Not that he was of an age to be a father figure to the younger man, but the gentle term was offered as a measure of comfort. Indeed, Connor Dougal was only in his mid-twenties, but he was a vigorous, hardened man of the soil, one of Bliss's best advertisements.

Having come from Scotland and homesteaded next to the Baldwins as soon as he was old enough to stake a claim, Connor Dougal had carved his small domain from the thick bush as they all had and were still doing. Only a "bee" at the time of the raising of his buildings—cabin and barn—had given assistance. In turn, that same help was offered readily to other settlers in their time of need. It was a system that threaded the frontier with strong bonds—they needed each other, and no one knew when that need would arise. Here was one example: Henley Baldwin, alive and singing a hymn one moment, stone-cold dead the next. Shivers of fear touched the good folk of Bliss—how quickly, how unexpectedly tragedy could happen. If Parker Jones were smart, the deacons thought to a man, he would strike while the iron was hot and, next Sunday, warn sinners that they were in imminent danger of facing their Maker. Religion was serious business on the frontier.

But Parker Jones, too compassionate for devious tactics, walked back to his small log parsonage with heaviness of heart.

Had he been—to the dead man—all that a pastor should be? Ordinarily taking Sunday dinner with Molly Morrison and her family, he had made his excuses and walked alone to face his responsibility or the lack of it. Feeling the call of God on his young life, preparing himself at Bible school in the east, answering the call of this small rural congregation in the northern reaches of Saskatchewan, Parker quaked at the accountability that was his. Needing a wife, wanting a wife, still he hesitated, wondering how he might divide his attention and feeling that God might come off second best. It was a decision of mammoth proportions, to Parker Jones.

"You're too serious about this, Parker," Molly was to tell him later that day as they walked together in the evening's coolness. "Death is a matter of course. And especially here among so many who have spent themselves and their strength just to get a home started and gather together a few bits and pieces. They literally wear themselves out."

"But I have the feeling that Henley Baldwin was not a happy man," Parker said heavily. "And did I ever talk to him about it? No, I let it lie, trusting my sermons would be a help, I guess. I'm going to have to be more involved than this, Molly. Jesus said, 'They that be whole need not a physician, but they that are sick.' I have a feeling that was one sick man. And I did little or nothing about it!" Parker's eyes were dark with the pain of self-flagellation.

"Is God whipping you like this, Parker, or are you whipping yourself? Surely you can do your best and leave it there."

"But that's the point," Parker responded. "Did I do my best?"

In his heart of hearts Parker Jones had a feeling that he had been intimidated by Della Baldwin. Perhaps he was afraid that any interference, no matter how well intentioned, would be seen as meddling and would result in making life harder for Henley, as Della retaliated.

Parker sighed. It was hard to be "wise as serpents, and harmless as doves."

Molly slipped her hand in his and, uncharacteristically, said no more. Waiting, hoping, longing to be Parker Jones's "help-meet," Molly often curbed her tendency to impatience, willing to learn the lessons she needed to do the job and do it right. She wanted to say now, "He's well out of it, Parker! Everyone knew he was miserable. Can't you see God's good hand in this—for him?"

But Parker Jones was grieving over the family members left behind, and their misery. What had been an unhappy home, would it—now that Della's apparent reason for complaint was out of the picture—be one of contentment at last? With all his heart Parker Jones hoped and prayed so, for her sake as well as for the young man Dudley. To be as miserable as Della was—there must be some reason for it. Parker felt himself ignorant and inexperienced and despaired that prayer, by itself, wasn't enough. *Faith without works is dead,* he reminded himself grimly.

"God 'hath given to us,'" he quoted, "'the ministry of reconciliation.' Could that mean bringing about peace and harmony in that home? I wonder."

"Everyone feels sure that with Henley's passing, Della's source of irritation is out of the way," Molly said.

"I wonder."

G ramma Jurgenson laid out the corpse. Della could barely
face laying out the necessary clothing.

Della's initial near-collapse passed, and she went doggedly
about her household duties. But she was so uncharacteristically
restrained and quiet that Dudley, coming and going—with milk,
chicken feed, and the responsibilities of the working farm heavy
on his young shoulders—felt uneasy. There was, in the home's
atmosphere, a sense of calm before the storm.

"I'm just tired," he excused himself later to an anxious Matilda.

The Baldwin quarter-section backed on Hooper land; to the
left of Baldwin land was the homestead of Connor Dougal, and
the Dougal land backed on the quarter-section of Gregor Slovinski. In other words, the section's four quarters were homesteaded
by the Hoopers, Baldwins, Connor Dougal, and Gregor Slovinski. Of them all, Gregor was the most lately arrived, having emi-
grated from Waldeck—an almost unheard of area lying between
Westphalia and Hess-Nassau, eventually to be absorbed by Prus-
sia—and purchasing the homestead of a homesteader who, at his
wife's insistence, was returning to "civilization."

No one knew much yet about Gregor, excepting that he was a hard worker, honest in all his dealings, and willing to be neighborly; this was the general opinion, and it was enough for now. It was rumored that he had been married, lost his wife and son in a bitter European winter, and was not interested in female companionship now. The sad story only served to melt the hearts of several young females. But he was a little overage, concerned parents pointed out, and that was a bit sobering. No girl wanted to be a bride who would, all too soon, become a widow left with a passel of children and no man's strong back to make a living for them. It happened more times than anyone liked to think about. Just look now, they pointed out to one another—here's another widow, and with a crop in the ground and unharvested. Ah but, someone was quick to say, there is a son, fully grown if not matured, and he can carry on.

Matilda knew all this when she met Dudley. And Dudley certainly looked burdened; "carrying on" was obviously not an easy task. "I'm sure you're tired," Matilda soothed the tense Dudley, so different from the usual care-less boy she knew. Matilda's red lips and milk-white throat had been offered temptingly and distractingly, but even those could not arouse a flicker of manhood in the woebegone Dudley. Something ... *someone?* ... was making him extremely uneasy.

"Matilda," he said tightly, "will you wait? What if I should be ... delayed in carrying out our plans?"

"Delayed?" Matilda's tone was not reassuring. "What do you mean delayed? Naturally we'll wait a reasonable time because of your father's death. Is that what you mean?"

"Never mind," Dudley said. "Everything will be fine; you'll see."

"Surely, Dudley," she said thoughtfully, "your mum will go back east to her family now. Won't she? The homestead is yours, isn't it? After all, you're eighteen. If you're man enough to farm, you're man enough to get married, it seems to me."

Apparently unsure of anything, Dudley hesitated, and they parted with him more tense and troubled than before and with Matilda nourishing a touch of impatience.

At bedtime, Della called Dudley from his room to the table where she was sitting, certain papers spread before her. The coal oil lamp had been lit, casting flickering shadows over the room and adding a touch of fantasy to the proceedings, making them seem unreal. It *was* unreal! It was a bad dream! And surely, the boy part of the man struggled to believe, he would wake in his own bed, with another night and another nightmare behind him.

"It was your father's wish that the homestead be yours and mine, together," Della began. "I suppose that means half of it is yours, and half is mine. Since it really can't be divided—eighty acres each would be silly—it means we share and share alike in all of it. I could have managed it very well by myself.

"It'll mean a lot of hard work, and I trust you are up to it. We can't afford a hired man, and to have someone work it on shares would simply eke away any proceeds we might have. Both options are unthinkable. No, it will have to be your responsibility, and mine. We have the summer to work at the idea; by fall you'll have fit into the harness fine, I'm sure. You're at the age where you are ready to muscle out . . . there'll be no more boyhood days; it's time to grow up and grow up all the way. Now, do you have any questions?"

"Selling, Ma . . . Mum. It is possible to sell—either of us, say, wanting to? Sell our half, maybe to the other one?" Faint hope flickered desperately, before being snuffed out.

"Why on earth would we want to do that? Think straight, Dudley. This is your father's legacy to you and to me. We must do our best, and we must do it in a united way. I need you for the outside work; you need me for the homemaking part and for the wisdom and experience I can bring to the union. Pick up and go on—that's all we can do."

Della pulled a large handkerchief from her apron pocket and buried her face in it. With a shuddering sigh she seemed to put grief aside, even as she had apparently put away the condemnations and self-recriminations—those horrid feelings—that had plagued her earlier immediately following Henley's collapse. Why, she consoled herself, she could clearly remember Henley telling her that he would be a poor stick of a man without her. Well, here sat another—Henley's son. It was a challenge.

With his homestead next to theirs and his house not more than a half mile away, it fell to Connor Dougal to stand by the bereaved mother and son until the time of the funeral. Bodies could not be kept more than a day or two, depending on the weather. The preferred day for funerals was Sunday; that way, no one lost any work time. But Henley having died on a Sunday, a week's wait was impossible. Tuesday was the day settled on. Monday Connor took Della to the homestead of Jack Sweeney, carpenter by trade, who augmented his meager farm income by the making and selling of certain hand-crafted items, coffins among them. Here she made her purchase, and it was trundled back to the Henley home in the back of Connor's wagon. Gramma Jurgenson and others lined it with treasured bits of cloth from their trunks and made a small pillow.

But it was Gregor Slovinski who showed up to put the body in the box. Once again his mighty arms came into play, rippling through the tight shirt sleeves as he lifted Henley's remains and laid them in the coffin, straightening and smoothing the Sunday suit that Henley would wear for the final time. He should not meet his Maker in rough farmer garb, and all involved nodded agreement to the arrangement.

At the appointed time rigs began assembling in the Henley yard, carrying the faithful folks of Bliss, brothers and sisters in this another tragedy in the populating and taming of the frontier. Some brought flowers, probably gathered along the way from the side of the road. Mason jars were filled with water from the trough, the blossoms and greenery were thrust in, and the simple arrangements took their places beside and around the rude catafalque.

The coffin sat on sawhorses under a poplar tree, a kindly acquaintance standing alongside the entire time, keeping flies from the deceased's face with a rolled-up newspaper. Della and Dudley sat before it on kitchen chairs that had been brought out for that purpose. Others sat on the ground or stood in a ragged semicircle around the coffin, and the minister.

The solemnity of the occasion was not lessened by the fact that Mik Loricz was, discreetly but obviously, recording the occasion on camera, his aim being to sell pictures to any who would buy, and satisfying a frontier craving for likenesses to send loved ones "back home." His Baby Hawkeye turned out pictures only two by two and a half, often too small to make out features well, but with care, decent pictures were obtained, and Mik made himself a little extra cash.

Parker Jones took his place at the side of the coffin and looked at the stalwart figures of the bush grouped before him; all seemed resigned in the face of this newest tragedy—a man struck down in his prime, a widow left defenseless, a son bowed too soon with responsibility—and did his best.

Standing in a small area cleared from the penetrating bush, beside a rude log home made with a man's two hands, Parker Jones spoke of a mansion prepared by Jesus himself, awaiting the faithful. He spoke of a rest where man has ceased from his own works. Many an eye misted and many a heart determined to do more about laboring to enter into that rest and being less occupied with the weary body's rest after a day of toil here on earth.

The coffin was nailed shut; caring neighbors hefted it to their shoulders and deposited it in Gregor Slovinski's wagon. Pulling out of the yard, Gregor led the dusty cortege down the road to Bliss's cemetery, where the faithful gathered once more around the coffin settled beside a gaping hole. The black earth that was spilled lavishly at their weary feet was bread and butter to all of them, and a portion of it rested under the fingernails of every man present; it demanded their strength while alive, it claimed their bodies when they died.

"Ashes to ashes . . ." Parker Jones intoned and, with a prayer, the sad day's business was accomplished. As one man they turned back to their rigs, their chores, their lives. Most of them trekked back to the Baldwin home, to tie up in the yard again and partake of the bounty the good women of Bliss had provided.

Lingering over their final good-bye to their loved one, Dudley and Della were the last to leave the cemetery, the last to pull into their yard; a place had been made for them among the dozen or so rigs there. Pulling up in the buggy, Dudley got out and went to the horse's head, holding her steady and the buggy still. But Della made no move to descend. Fixing her son with a straight gaze, she caroled sweetly, "Dudley?"

Dudley, red in the face before the undivided attention of all of Bliss, hastened to his mother's side, reaching a hand to help her down. Though Della's mouth smiled for the benefit of her onlookers, one didn't have to look closely to see that it was a tight smile. Della's eyes, under the edge of her hat and the veil that had been fastened back, were cold, cold.

Reaching her gloved hand for her son's outstretched hand, she said sweetly, "Thank you, *Dud.*"

"How long wilt thou sleep, O sluggard?'" Kerry spoke the words in as merry a tone as she could muster, hoping Franny would be amused.

Usually greatly entertained by Kerry, laughing her delicious tinkly laugh at her pranks and her so-often apropos Scriptures, today Frances turned her head from the light that streamed in as Kerry went around the room opening drapes and letting the midday sun stream into the bedchamber.

Following on Kerry's heels was Gladdy, now a tall and slim young lady; still clothed, however, in her maid's uniform. Gladdy had indeed made good, being promoted to the status of maid several years ago. But in reality she was so much more. Mrs. Finch, older now and fatter, depended on the quick hands and feet and quick mind of the bright and blossoming girl; Charlotte Maxwell found herself using Gladdy as secretary at times, and—to Gladdy's supreme satisfaction—accompanying her on numerous outings. The vibrant hair had not dimmed over the years, but its tendency to wildness was subdued somewhat by valiant attempts at taming. Gladdy herself declared that it went *boing* at the slightest loosening of a pin or slipping of a ribbon. Just now she carried a tray temptingly set with breakfast for two.

"Wake up, Ishbosheth," Kerry caroled, standing at the side of the bed and gently tugging at the coverlet that Franny was using as a shield.

That Frances's case was not totally hopeless—or perhaps as a sign that she was over the worst of her despair—seemed proven when one gray eye peeped out of the covers, and the hint of a smile played at the corner of her mouth.

Señor Garibaldi's cruel desertion had indeed plunged the sensitive Frances to the very depths of despondency. Having glimpsed a better life for herself, with better health and true purpose, her descent into hopelessness was dark and deep. Added to this was a sense of foolishness that she should have, for one moment, thought any man might find, in her pale person, the attractions necessary for love. Yes, Franny suffered.

Many times Kerry had tried to help, first by sympathy, holding the wounded Franny in her arms, then by words—scorning the dastardly dancing master, expressing gratitude that his falseness had come to light before it was too late, verbally recognizing Franny's worth as a treasure to all those—the miserable Garibaldi excepting—who knew her.

"I've come to accept his baseness," Frances had wept eventually, on her long road to healing. "But to have gained such a wonderful measure of strength and health and then to have it snatched from me—I find that more painful than I can say. I was so happy, Kerry! You don't know what it's been like, all these years—housebound, unwell, bored!"

"Shh," Kerry had crooned, smoothing back the fair hair from the pale face. "You'll find it all and more, any day now. Now you know the way to happiness—get up and get out, Franny. It can't hurt to give it a try."

But it had been weeks, and Franny remained, for the most part, huddled in bed.

Kerry, at first desperately worried, then angry, then worried again, was trying a new approach. Or perhaps it was an old approach, for she recalled the many times Franny had found Kerry's unusual quotations refreshing, and had enjoyed many a good laugh at the youngster's frank use of Scripture. Older, wiser, educated, Kerry had found other ways by which to express herself, and the use of Scripture had largely disappeared from her conversation.

This morning, determined to wake, and shake, the injured Frances, she had searched her mind and her memory and had come up with Solomon's warning against idleness. That it had pierced Frances's defenses seemed proven by the peeping eye and the smiling mouth. And sure enough, the use of the name "Ishbosheth" had the desired effect. Throwing back the covers under which she had nurtured her pain, she giggled.

"Ish . . . who?" she managed.

"Ishbosheth. The son of Saul, 'who lay on a bed at noon.' It was deadly for him, and it's deadly for you. So awake, thou that sleepest!"

"Oh, Kerry! You were good for me when you came to me seven . . . or is it eight years ago, and you are good for me now! Have I been a great trial these past weeks?"

"Never!" the loving Kerry proclaimed. "I just want you to see that . . . that a twirling, dipping, skipping, dancing man is not the man for you."

"But," Franny mourned, "will there ever be another? I don't want to lie in Aunt Charlotte's bed all my life! Even I have a natural longing for a home of my own and somebody to love me, and to love." Franny seemed on the verge of tears again.

"First things first," Kerry said, whisking the bedding into order and beckoning forth the waiting Gladdy. "And that's food. Now you eat, you hear?"

"You eat with me," Franny demanded, and Kerry did so, having planned it that way. As they ate their toast and delicately coddled eggs and drank their cocoa, Kerry managed to win more than one smile and several more laughs from Franny, whose color, at the end of the meal, showed a dainty tinge of pink and whose eyes, once again, were full of life.

When breakfast was finished, and the small talk that went with it, Kerry gathered up the tray, placing the current issue of *Canadian Magazine* in Franny's hands.

"You're going to get up and get going," Kerry said firmly. "Now check out that advertisement for the gramophone. Why in the world we shouldn't have one, I don't know. I may be as poor as a church mouse—" Kerry hadn't forgotten the thrusts of earlier, poorer, days by the naughty Cordelia—"but you aren't. How are you going to spend that glorious inheritance if you don't get up and get out?"

Poor Garibaldi—his timing had been poor. Just a few days after his departure, a distant aunt had passed away leaving her not inconsiderable funds to Frances.

"Let's see this marvelous machine," Franny said, and Kerry folded the magazine and pointed. "'It will entertain every member of the family, from grandmother down to baby,'" she read, looking over Franny's shoulder.

"And only fifteen dollars for the large one. And with three free records."

"It comes with a guarantee; you can't get better than that. You love music, Franny! Think what a treat this would be—and how much fun you'd have hunting it up, checking it out, and purchasing it."

"It would be wonderful to get out again," Franny said wistfully.

"You go ahead and read the magazine. You'll notice that The Rambler's Wheel Club has an engagement soon; think how healthy you could get out in the air on the newest Bantam with pneumatic tires—"

"Whatever those are," Franny laughed, already feeling much better and greatly relieved because of it.

That Franny found much more of interest in the magazine than gramophones and bicycles was not to come to light for some time. But it seemed obvious, to Kerry and Gladdy and eventually to Aunt Charlotte, that some magic potion or other was working a miracle, once again, in their Franny.

Could it be love—a second time? And if so, would Franny be any wiser this time?

Sick at heart, Dudley waited at the pasture fence running between the Baldwin and Hooper homesteads. He was always unhappy with himself to some degree or other, and his present circumstances had him feeling particularly unworthy. Not only did he have no beauty of face or form, being as ungainly and unsure as a newborn colt, but he felt he had nothing appealing about his inner man either.

Inner man! He gritted, thinking about it. *Inner boy, more like!*

Man or boy, that inner person was not only sick at heart but angry as well. Angry at his father for leaving him and for the situation it had put him in; angry at his mother for the bonds she—willingly and knowingly, perhaps purposely—twined around him, binding him to her and to the place.

It was not a good binding; they were not bonds of passion for the soil as had bound his father. They were not bonds made before a preacher, pledging to stand by another person for better or for worse. No—and Dudley ground his teeth helplessly—they were the bonds of weakness. He simply had not, he felt, the *guts* to stand up to his mother.

Even *thinking* the word brought forth an eruption of guilty feelings; it was a word his mother never would have countenanced in the mouth of her son. That he thought it rather than speaking it aloud caused him to see his bondage in a more hateful light than ever.

Leaning on a fence post in utmost dejection, waiting for Matilda, remembering his mother branding him *Dud* before the people of the community and recalling his feeling of humiliation brought him very near to tears. And tears were an even more hateful sign of weakness. Dudley's hand came up—not to wipe his eyes but to form a fist in an unfamiliar gesture of defiance. But it was the fence post he slammed, and that futilely, for he felt no better afterwards than before. Like everything he did— it was ineffectual.

Across the fence, in the Hooper pasture, also coming to fetch the cows for milking, Matilda saw him and came to meet him, as often happened at this time of day.

Watching her come, skirts swinging freely with her movements, hair blowing back from her face, Dudley wondered with an ache in his throat whether she would be willing to trade that freedom for the existence he had to offer and feared not. His only hope was that she would wait. Present conditions would not—could not— last. Just what would change, he didn't know. He was long past the age for fairy tales, yet still some faint hope struggled in his despairing heart in a dream as old as childhood and as fragile.

A truer affection than Matilda's would have settled his every fear with a few simple words. A smile, a squeeze of a hand would have done it. Perhaps Matilda's love hadn't ripened sufficiently, perhaps she wasn't capable of the kind of understanding that was needed, perhaps she needed to grow up a little more. Whatever the reason, Dudley despaired of happiness before she spoke.

"How could you let her humiliate you like that?" was the first thing that burst from her.

How to tell her his mother had taken him by surprise; how to explain he was still Della's son and owed her the courtesy due her as his mother; how to say that he had never, in all his life, spoken rudely to her or to any adult?

How to pour out his misery? How to plead for her patience, her understanding? How to offer her marriage and a home, when that home wasn't fully his? How to ask her to wait?

Instead, he was silent, his head down, his boot scuffing the ground at his feet. Realizing how childish that seemed, he stopped abruptly. He felt his cause was lost before he spoke.

Nevertheless, he tried. "Tilda—what she said, what she called me, doesn't mean that's what I am."

"A dud, you mean? I certainly hope not. But how in the world are you going to face everyone now, Dudley? That moment, right then, was the time to say . . . to do something."

Dudley gathered a little courage. "What, Tilda? Slap down my own mother?"

"Of course not that. But surely . . ." Matilda's voice faded away in the face of the impossible situation.

Into the heavy silence came the faint sound of cowbells. Matilda fidgeted a moment, looked toward the other end of the pasture, and said, "Look, I've got to go. Dad and the boys are waiting for the cows. I'll see you Sunday." And she turned and walked—striding free and standing tall—away from him and toward her future.

Hunched and miserable, Dudley stumbled toward his.

When the chores were done, the cows turned out, and the milk strained, Dudley went outside and stood beneath the porch's small overhang, restless and uncertain. With sudden determination he stepped down and turned his steps toward the road.

"Dudley? Where in the world are you going this time of evening? *Dudley*—" Dudley was rather proud of himself—that he plodded on, ignoring the demanding call. Della's voice faded behind him as he turned his steps in the direction of the homestead next to theirs—Connor Dougal's.

Here was a man who had started out, independently, when he was not much older than Dudley. Just a boy himself at the time,

Dudley could recall something of those days—his father's offered friendship and help and the good relationship that had developed. He had seen the young Connor strengthen and mature until he became a man of stature, not only physically but in other ways that counted, ways that couldn't be spelled out but that made him a man in the eyes of the community. No doubt, Dudley supposed now, half bitterly, Connor was a man in his own eyes. And that's where it counts most, Dudley thought with a burst of insight into his own sad self-evaluation. *Weighed in the balances and found wanting!*

"Come on in, Dudley."

Connor's voice greeted Dudley as he stepped up onto the small porch outside the screen door of the lean-to that was Connor's kitchen. The original log house, at first serving as front room, bedroom, and kitchen combined, had been enlarged by the addition of the lean-to; the main room, now divided, with a small bedroom at one end, made comfortable living quarters for the bachelor.

How Connor Dougal had stayed single was a mystery. Thick, brown hair hanging rather boyishly over clear hazel eyes, generous nose, and square-cut, good-humored face made for a very attractive package. Add to this his homestead proved up as required and his farm well stocked, he lacked only—according to the community—a wife.

But Dudley was far from any thoughts concerning the bachelor state of his neighbor. He had found, in the last few days, a level of friendship from this man that he hadn't known before. Now, instinctively, as a chick would seek refuge under a wing, Dudley turned toward Connor. There was something that drew him—just what, he couldn't put a name to. He wasn't long in finding out.

Dudley had known that Connor attended church regularly. He knew Connor was a man of principle. He now knew him to be a man of compassion. He would almost immediately know him to be a man of God.

Connor had been drinking a cup of coffee over a late supper. "Sit down, man," he said right off to the young man who seemed to stand so awkwardly inside his door. "Sorry the flapjacks are all gone, but there's coffee."

Dudley took the mug, added the cream and sugar that were proffered, and took a seat opposite Connor at the table. Leaning an elbow comfortably on the white oilcloth, Connor said, "It's good to see you. I was hoping you'd come by." At Dudley's raised eyebrow he added, "I hadn't had an opportunity to talk with you, to tell you how sorry I am for the loss of your father. A good man—Henley Baldwin. You're a lot like him, I think, and," with a smile, "that's a compliment."

"Yeah . . . I guess," Dudley murmured in a low tone of voice, looking down into the mix of coffee and cream. "That's what everyone says. Even Ma." Dudley didn't add that when Della said it, it was no compliment.

"How're you making out?"

"All right, I guess." Dudley, it seemed, wasn't certain of anything.

Connor studied the young, defenseless, rather doleful countenance of his visitor. "If not, Dudley, and there's some way I can help, you've only to ask."

"I know."

Dudley continued to stare into his cup; Connor stirred his coffee thoughtfully. This was something more than a casual visit, he surmised. Just how to approach an unspoken problem was a problem in itself.

Perhaps he offered up a silent prayer for guidance. At any rate, his next words were inspired, though they obviously pained the young man opposite.

"And how is it with Matilda? If I'm not mistaken, you two are something more than friends."

Dudley shifted in his chair. Dudley cleared his throat. Dudley, after all, could only nod and mutter, "Yeah, well, I guess maybe that's over." There—he'd faced it! Said it!

"I see. Well, a bachelor's life isn't so bad, you know." Connor smiled. Then, with no answering sign of amusement from Dudley, he added thoughtfully, "But if you're unhappy, I could help you pray. I always find comfort that way."

"Yeah, I guess that'd be all right," the younger man said but without enthusiasm.

Connor set down his cup, bowed his head, cleared his throat, and prayed. To Dudley, staring down at a crack in the white oilcloth on the table, it was obvious the pray-er knew what he was doing. His words, though simple, were straightforward and earnest.

Connor prayed that Dudley, having lost his earthly father, might find comfort in the care of the heavenly Father; he prayed that, for the days ahead, Dudley might have the loving hand of the Father leading, guiding, and directing. He prayed that, as the Scripture promised, all things would work together for good.

If his keen eyes failed to find solace in the face of the object of his prayers when he concluded, he was wise enough to say only, "I'll continue to pray for you, Dudley. I'm sure that God has a future for you, a good future, and that He'll see you through to that fulfillment. Now, how about a warm-up on the coffee?"

Walking home through the thick night, Dudley was as much in the dark spiritually as physically. But he left behind one praying, believing man, and even then the first rays of promise were gathering. There would be a sunrise.

❧

But there was no glimmer of it the following Sunday.

There was no staying home from church. Della, as rigid in her religious convictions as in all else, determined they should be there this first Sunday after Henley's grim death. But even she avoided the double desk with the youthful lovers' initials and took a place on the side bench.

As always, Dudley sat in the cloakroom, rather too silent and quiet, self-conscious under the quick, curious glances of his friends. He couldn't blame them; tragedy and trauma made for difficult conversation. It would pass, with time, and his former relationship with the young folk of the community would go on as usual. Except in one instance.

Just before the opening hymn, while the pump organ was being played heartily and vigorously by Sally Dewhurst, through the open door came Bert Felker and Matilda Hooper. They were obviously in the final throes of a good laugh, shoving each other playfully as they separated, Bert to sit on the male side, Matilda to sit with the young women.

Matilda shot one straight and meaningful look at Dudley, which said as plain as words, "It's over, see!" Thereafter, her eyes avoided meeting his stunned gaze.

It hadn't taken Dudley completely by surprise; he had been half prepared for Matilda to explain, hopefully sadly and reluctantly, that they must part company . . . for the time being. But to flaunt Bert Felker in his face—it was rejection with a slap.

When Sunday dinner was over, Dudley picked up the latest pile of newspapers recently arrived from his uncle and, in spite of the disapproval on his mother's face ("Remember the sabbath day, to keep it holy"), made his way deliberately to the porch and the ancient rocking chair. There had to be an opening . . . an opportunity . . . *something . . . somewhere.* . . .

15

"A re you doing your yawning exercises faithfully?" Aunt Charlotte asked, stopping by Franny's room.

"Yes, but I think it's a lot of . . . bunkum," the usually gentle Frances said with uncharacteristic emphasis.

At the sound of a word that she considered coarse, Aunt Charlotte felt called upon to issue a reproachful reprimand, though she seemed halfhearted about it. So even though Franny was twenty-four years old and a model of propriety most of the time, Aunt Charlotte said automatically, "That's not a word a lady would use." Just the saying of it seemed to lift the aunt's spirits, restoring, in a way, a semblance of normalcy where the frail young woman was concerned, and whom they so often treated as an invalid.

Aside from the pills and potions that had been prescribed for Franny by their doctor, friends and family came up with certain remedies from time to time, and most of them were tried, at Charlotte's insistence. "This malingering must be halted," she had said firmly, "and it will, just as soon as we locate the proper restorative."

Consequently, Franny had suffered through:

Blood Pills, designed to cure nervous despondency, loss of memory, irritability of temper, locomotor ataxia, and much more;

Orange Wine Stomach Bitters, guaranteed to be "from the fruits of the Seville orange tree in combination with seventeen different roots and herbs," and treating gastric ailments, want of appetite, low spirits and nervousness, general derangements, and purifying the blood, bones, muscles, and restoring vigor;

Microbe Killer, "one of the grandest remedies known to the present age," for preventing la grippe, catarrh, consumption, malaria, blood poison, rheumatism, and killing the germs that are the cause of the disease.

In spite of these assurances and more, Franny continued wan and peaked, without energy or interest. It was Kerry, desperate for something to lift her dear friend out of the doldrums—mental, physical, emotional—into which she had sunk, who had come up with "Yawning for Exercise."

"According to the results of late investigations," she had reported one day, having just read all about it, "yawning is the most natural form of respiratory exercise. An eminent authority—unfortunately it doesn't give his name—advances the theory that," and Kerry found her place in *The Youth's Companion,* and read, "'everyone should have a good yawn, with stretching of the limbs, morning and evening, for the purpose of ventilating the lungs and strengthening the muscles of respiration.'"

"When I was a child," said a doubtful Aunt Charlotte, ever the stickler for proper protocol, "children were taught that yawning was a breach of good behavior. Now, if this medical testimony may be credited, it is incumbent upon parents—and guardians!—to see that the youthful members of their flock," and she smiled at Franny and Kerry indulgently, having come a great deal along the path of tolerance in the last years, "not only yawn, but practice what may be called the art of yawning. Isn't that the heart of the article, Kerry?"

"That's it," Kerry affirmed, looking at the invalid for her reaction.

"Wait a minute," Franny objected, "you can't just decide to yawn, can you? Don't you have to be sleepy, or tired, or bored?"

"Apparently yawning can be practiced," Kerry declared, "and therefore perfected." And she fell to giving a demonstration.

"At least," Aunt Charlotte said firmly, "cover your mouth when you do it."

"'I will lay mine hand upon my mouth,'" Kerry said, but under her breath so that Aunt Charlotte barely heard, but having heard, awaited the end of the quotation, the tip of her nose pinking only a little. "'Once have I spoken; but I will not answer: yea, twice; but I will proceed no further.'"

"The day hasn't dawned," Aunt Charlotte proclaimed, "when you will not answer. What a day that will be!"

Kerry subsided, as she had learned to do long ago, only breaking over occasionally when Scripture seemed the only way to respond.

And so regular sessions of yawning and stretching had been instigated. "I can't see any advantage to it," Franny finally said fretfully. "And the only thing being stretched is my mouth!"

This called for a critical assessment of yawn therapy by Aunt Charlotte, who then advised, "One must yawn with one's mouth strictly less than fully agape. The muscles it takes to *refrain* from the full-gape position should help affect the cure, I should think."

But another week's yawn experiments failed to lift the invalid from the malaise into which she had sunk.

Not to be defeated in her efforts to bring health and happiness back to Franny, Kerry brought in another magazine, reporting, "Here's an endorsement for Ayer's Sarsaparilla. 'I was unable to sleep,' this woman says. 'I had serious trouble with my kidneys, and suffered greatly with pains in my back. I was also afflicted with headache, loss of appetite and indigestion. A friend persuaded me to use Ayer's Sarsaparilla, and my troubles all disappeared.' What do you say to that, Franny? You don't sleep well, you don't eat well, you have pains—"

"Only since I began the yawning cure!" Franny declared in no uncertain terms.

"Here, then," Kerry said with a discouraged sigh, "you look these cures over and read the endorsements . . . maybe there'll be something that will get your attention." And Kerry left to go about other duties.

Something did get Franny's attention. Something brought a gleam into her lackluster eyes. Something brought a faint pink into her colorless cheeks. Something quickened her breath. Finally, lying back with the paper clutched to her, Franny thought seriously and for a long time. When Gladdy brought lunch in and attempted to remove the paper, Franny let it go with these instructions, "Put it right here on the bedside table. And, Gladdy, when you come back for the tray, please bring pen and ink and paper."

Franny spent a good part of the afternoon on the project. Her composition was covered over when anyone came into the room, and she waited politely until the room was her own again, and then resumed writing. It seemed to take a while—several pages were crumpled and discarded. At last a satisfactory document was completed. Reading it over, with eyes aglow and cheeks flushed, Franny signed and folded it and inserted it into an envelope. When it was addressed and ready to go, she sealed it and slipped it under her pillow.

"Gladdy," she said later when the maid was replenishing the wood in the fireplace, "please send Gideon up to me. And, Gladdy, don't say anything to anyone. All right?"

What could she do? As devoted to Frances as was Kerry, Gladdy promised.

It was Gladdy, many days later, who secretly brought an envelope to Franny, noting as a matter of course that it was addressed to Miss Frances Bentley in care of B. Gideon; this was not surprising, since it was Gideon himself who had handed it to her, rather slyly, as though he too had his instructions not to "tell." Franny clutched the envelope to her, waiting to open it until Gladdy was gone and she was alone. This scenario was repeated numerous times, and each time it was accomplished in secret, with no one else in the family aware of what was happening under their very noses.

Gladdy wasn't the only one to notice that Franny's cheeks blossomed like a rose, that her eyes regained their sparkle, and that she resumed her yawning exercises with new zest. One and all were amazed when she forsook her bed to begin twirling, bending, stretching, performing many more movements than the yawn exercise called for. And thriving on it.

Soon she was rising and dressing immediately after she finished eating her breakfast, followed by occasions when she appeared at the table in the dining room, her presence adding to the feeling of relief and happiness in the household. Miss Frances was well again!

At first Kerry felt extremely gratified—her efforts had paid off. Either Franny was responding to the health regimen in a marvelous way or a miracle had been performed.

There came a day when Franny, with Kerry accompanying her, made a foray into Toronto's shopping district, a bold experiment indeed. She survived it very well, and was, moreover, exhilarated past all explaining.

When caution was urged upon her, "I'm fine, just fine," she insisted, flourishing a list of "things" she needed to purchase, and arranging another shopping trip.

The girls had a delightful time together, like nothing that had marked their relationship previously. Once Gladdy accompanied them, and it seemed like an outing for pleasure.

"I've needed times like this," Franny said. "I promise we'll have more of them."

"'Why,'" a smiling Kerry quoted, prompted to the use of Scripture by the jovial mood that was upon them, "'gaddest thou about so much to change thy ways?'"

Little did she know just how much Franny's ways were changing and would change.

Franny's inheritance, until now, had meant little or nothing to her, accepted with supreme casualness. Now she spent money freely. But on what? The latest in couture? Not at all.

It was because of the unsuitability of her purchases that Kerry began to suspect something was not quite right. Franny's choices were far from the rich, fancy, or fashionable. Rather, they were basic, plain, serviceable. And when Gideon had deposited them in her room, Franny laid them carefully into a trunk that Finch toted down from the attic for her.

"You'd think she were going on the Grand Tour," Olga reported to Finch, having been in Franny's room and had a glimpse into the open trunk. "Except no self-respectin' crayture would step foot in the auld country wiff such a wardrobe as she's accumulatin', the lamb. Looks like she were plannin' a trip to the north pole, it does! And how long do you fink our Miss Franny would survive at the north pole, the precious!"

Kerry had some of the same dark thoughts. When Franny ordered a "bicycle suit," it was more than she could stand and not burst with curiosity. The bloomers, in particular, were startling.

"A bicycle suit! Franny, whatever for? You've never ridden a bicycle in your life! Are you about to start now? And if so, why haven't you ordered—of all things—the machine itself?"

Franny's delicious, tinkly laugh, once again ringing musically wherever she went, was her only response, aside from a tantalizing "You'll see!"

Franny folded the bicycle suit of "blue repellent cloth, bound in leather all around and consisting of five pieces—jacket, skirt, bloomers, leggins, and cap," and laid it in the trunk beside the plain black Henrietta skirt, washable linen crash walking suit, double-cape macintosh, over-gaiters, corduroy leggins, and other strange purchases, and Kerry could contain herself no longer: "Franny! Either I'm crazy or you are! And since you're the one making these far-fetched purchases, I think it's you. I can't stand it! What are you doing? Where are you going, if going you are? Certainly these things are not for use in Toronto. You'll have to tell me," she threatened, "or I'm not going with you again. And Aunt Charlotte won't let you go alone."

"The bicycle suit, Kerry? It comes as near to riding clothes as I can get and not wear trousers. Sidesaddle is out of the question. You've read the Duchess of Somerset's memoirs, how the sight of her riding sidesaddle, exposing her woollen petticoats, caused two mule teams so much alarm that to pacify them and prevent the wagons from leaving the trail, she had to conceal herself behind some bushes until they had passed. If one is to fork a horse—"

"Fork a horse?" Kerry asked feebly. This was worse than she had imagined! "Franny! You're sicker than I thought!"

"But I'm perfectly well, Kerry!" And Franny whirled across the bedroom in as graceful and useless a demonstration as could be imagined. Falling on the bed, she waited until she had regained her breath. Then, sitting up, she said, with a twinkle, "Are you prepared for a surprise? Perhaps a shock?"

"Depends," Kerry said briefly, hoping, rather desperately by now, that this secret was good and sensible and that the change in Franny was a healthy one, a permanent one. But *bloomers?*

Franny was fumbling in a drawer, withdrawing a packet of letters, tied—of all things—with a blue ribbon!

"Franny! Don't tell me you're in love again!" Kerry was more than a little concerned now. Not again could she stand the heartbreak that Franny—as dear to her as a sister—had already experienced, taking her almost to her deathbed.

"Listen, dear. Listen, and don't talk for a few moments." The old, gentle Franny was speaking. In a few words she explained that in the magazine Kerry had left with her—as well as many newspapers she had perused—there were numerous advertisements for a wife. Lonely homesteaders were desperate for female companionship and wrote appeals for a wife; bachelors across the West, with no prospects in their community, had written; organizations set up for the purpose had written, extolling the virtues of such a life and urging a response from females interested in "adventure, satisfaction, and true love."

"Franny—you didn't—"

"Shh, dear, and listen. No, I didn't answer them, though I was tempted. You don't know, Kerry, how lonely and desperate I've been, and how completely hopeless about my future. So, I wrote my own letter, you'd call it an advertisement, I suppose."

"You wrote—"

"Newspapers, magazines—Winnipeg *Free Press, Western Producer,* and others—those that were most likely to be received and read in the West. The great and glorious West, Kerry! Where things are happening! Where there's *life!*" The near-invalid Franny was replaced for the moment by none other than a fiery fanatic.

"Here," she said, taking a deep breath and settling down, "see for yourself what I said."

Silently Kerry took the paper, followed the pointing finger, and read, "'Single woman, financially independent and with a pioneer spirit, desires correspondence with interested male, age 25–35, serious intentions in mind. Would prefer a gentleman with some education and polish, and whose dreams, along with mine, will bring satisfaction and fulfillment.'" One further line included the request that mail be sent in care of B. Gideon.

"Gideon has been getting answers—there's been no lack of answers—and Gladdy has been bringing them to me and mailing mine. You mustn't blame either of them. I threatened them with murder and mayhem if they told!"

"And that stack represents the responses?"

"Yes, and I've read them carefully. Out of them all, I selected one, and we've corresponded several times. My last letter, Kerry, informed him of my decision."

"Decision?" Kerry asked half fearfully. "What decision, Franny?"

"I've decided to pack up and go to Saskatchewan. That's why the clothes, which I deem fit for the frontier; that's what all the secrecy has been about. I'm going West, Kerry!"

"To marry this . . . clod?"

"Kerry!" Franny said reproachfully. "You don't even know him! He's a man of some culture, who, like me, wants adventure and isn't afraid to go after it. He hasn't asked me to marry him, as yet, but I know it's coming. I want to see him, get to know him. So I'm not totally foolish after all!"

"'Thy tacklings are loosed'!" The remote Scripture, which Kerry had never needed before, was a cry from her heart.

Franny tried to laugh, as she so often had across the years when Kerry used Scripture indiscriminately. But the laugh was of short duration, for Kerry's face, so dear to Franny, was filled with a mix of pain and bitterness.

"Dear Kerry, trust me," Franny said, putting out her hand in a small gesture of comfort. "I've written him and told him I'm coming. I'll be on my way just as soon as I can get matters arranged about the transfer of funds—I'm so stupid about banking—and take care of a few matters here and do a bit more shopping . . . it's been such fun, Kerry. You can't believe how alive I feel."

"But a trip that far! Franny, you're attempting too much—"

"Nonsense! See how well and strong I am!" And Franny laughingly flexed a slender arm.

"Not really, Franny!" Kerry cried, hating above everything to confess her concerns. Franny's health, always precarious, was exhibiting the same symptoms it had when Señor Garibaldi was in the picture; they were false then, and she feared they were false now. Kerry knew, if Franny did not, that Franny's lungs were involved; she knew that the family doctor was gravely concerned over this flare-up of vitality and vigor. Was it, he wondered, eating away her remaining strength?

"The last thing you need is to be worked to death on some homestead! And it's too soon! It hasn't been all that long since you were flat on your back—sick, very, very sick! You need time to prove that this burst of well-being is real and lasting, and not a temporary thing!"

"Real and lasting, or temporary," Franny said quietly—a Franny not heard from before—"it's my chance for a life. Don't try and talk me out of it, Kerry. I'm determined; my plans are made, and I'm going just as soon as I'm sure Connor Dougal has my letter advising him of my decision."

"Connor Dougal—is that what you know about him—his name? With others to choose from, what made this one attractive, enough so that you'd pledge your life and, I suppose, your love? Or does that come later?" Kerry was very close to tears, and all in a desperate attempt to discourage Franny from the mind-boggling plans she was making.

Ignoring Kerry's words and her tears, Franny rustled around and drew out a snapshot. It was unprofessional in quality, obviously taken with a small camera and somewhat indistinct, but the man's face was clear enough. His hat was pushed back, and one lock of hair fell over his brow in attractive disarray. Kerry could find no fault with the square, rugged face, the cleft chin, the open expression.

"How can you be sure this is his picture? How do you know if this is really . . . what's his name?" Kerry hadn't really forgotten the name, nor would she ever. Franny had sung it like a paean of praise—*Connor Dougal!*

"I've read what he has to say, and it grips me," Franny answered now, finally on the defensive. "And I know this much—he's a homesteader in the Saskatchewan Territory. Doesn't that awaken something in you—something that longs for new horizons?"

Kerry's opinion of far horizons was very narrow at the moment. "I suppose," she said hollowly, "you've sent him your picture, too."

"Not yet. I want to have a new one taken, now that I look so much healthier—better. But I did send him a gift."

"A gift? What—"

"I sent him," Franny's eyes were very bright, "my father's vest chain."

"Oh, Franny! The only thing you have of his! You can remember it shining across his vest and the little charm dangling from it—a small compass, wasn't it? You played with that charm when he held you on his lap! You've told me so, and what a special memory it is! How could you—"

"It was the only masculine thing I had, and I sent it happily. I feel good knowing Connor Dougal—don't you just love that name—is wearing it."

"A farmer, Franny! How often have you seen a vest chain on a bib overall?"

"When he dresses up, I mean, of course," Franny amended patiently.

Kerry, finally, was silent. What was there to say? Franny sounded very, very sure of herself.

"And so," Franny was saying, "do you know how I finally made my choice among these responses? It was Connor Dougal's address, the name of his town . . . community . . . where he lives. It's *Bliss*, Kerry—*Bliss*. Could anything go wrong, with a delightful and promising name like that? I believe it's an omen!"

16

What a hodgepodge they were, what a conglomeration of nationalities. From most corners of the world they came—all seeking a homestead.

"Keep Canada British" was the cry. But the gates were open, and like a mighty, rushing stream, they could not be stanched. Wanted or not, welcome or not—they came.

English settlers were pursued with some vigor. Contacted through a London office, every adult over twenty-one who signed on for western Canada was paid a bonus. Bonuses were also paid to Frenchmen, Dutchmen, Belgians, Scandinavians, and Germans.

Not so blessed, not so sought after—the Hungarians, Russians, Ukrainians, Poles. But they came. They took what was left, whether it was poplar or swamp, paid their ten dollar filing fee, got in their buggies, and drove the muddy roads to 160 acres that they could call their own. And, most generally, made a go of it. "Foreigners," they were called, while the favored races were termed "white." Their arrival by the thousands caused bitter debate in Parliament. "Canada is a dumping ground for the refuse of every country in the world," one member was reported to have said rashly. But they were a quiet and industrious people. They were a hardworking people. Freedom was a prize to be treasured. Independence was a goal to be gained. They would, literally, earn the respect of their neighbors and the world in general, becoming Canadians along the way.

Before the railway, these settlers, choosing the Northwest, were outfitted in Red River and trailed in by cart, by boat, or by portage. Luxuries were not feasible to transport, and most homesteaders suffered unspeakable deprivation, simply "making do" on what the land provided.

On the open plains, unless lumber could be brought in, a soddy—turves from their own land, cut and piled, bricklike—was the only alternative for a home. Many people had a great aversion to them because it was generally thought they attracted fleas and bedbugs; certainly they were a plague to be reckoned with. In the sod hut's favor—warm in winter, cool in summer, or at least warmer and cooler than a tar paper shack on the open prairie. For those who sought out the bush and accepted the backbreaking task of clearing five acres a year for three years, a log cabin, chinked and sealed, would be home.

The bush wasn't friendly, it didn't give ground easily. On the prairie it was just plow, and sow, perhaps chop a few willow roots; in the bush it was chop and cut all day, and for many days out of the year. In spite of that, there were those who rejected the prairie with its unending horizon and terrifying loneliness and chose the green and near-impenetrable bush. But prairie or bush, the land was pocked with sloughs, sloughs, and more sloughs, and overhead was a sky whose vastness was beyond expressing or grasping. Prairie or bush—the venturesome and visionary dared; the stubborn and desperate endured.

Connor Dougal had chosen the bush. Five years of backbreaking toil had seen the clearing of twenty acres for planting; another dozen acres cleared for pasture but with their stumps not yet grubbed out; a garden spot, a farmyard dotted with several small buildings, and a house that was little more than a cabin.

Connor Dougal was a landowner, a man contented with his accomplishments thus far and with a dream and a plan to bring it to fruition.

Gregor Slovinski, his neighbor in one direction, though older than Connor, was more lately come. His bush was giving way, slowly but surely, under the mighty swings of his axe. For pure physical accomplishments, no one could compete with the mountainous "foreigner." He was too good-natured to create trouble or to react with violence to teasing—most of it being in fun anyway. And he was too big and strong to be picked on seriously.

Between the neighbors, a bond of friendship had developed. Both were bachelors, both were homesteaders and were clean-living, clean-talking males. Both were believers, having been brought to salvation in Jesus Christ by the young, green, but earnest pastor, Parker Jones.

Parker Jones had been in Bliss two years. But in that time, a remarkable change had taken place in two of the district's most eligible bachelors—Gregor Slovinski and Connor Dougal. Steady, dependable Connor, and powerful Gregor—an unlikely pair but brothers in Christ. They found occasions to help one another, to eat together, to travel to town together, to attend church services in Bliss together. To pray together.

As for marriage—perhaps because of their new faith and the principles each was attempting to live by—their contemplation of it was cautious, careful, Christian.

They discussed it at times, and usually in the presence of their minister and friend, Parker Jones, who was himself unmarried. Each man usually had advice to give the others, less eager to take advice himself. A good deal of teasing, chaffing, and kidding marked their times together.

Many a lonely evening was passed in what each thought was good company.

"You, at least," Connor Dougal pointed out to his pastor one evening after chores as the three sat around his table, discussing this ever-interesting topic and sipping coffee as black as the inside of the pot from which it was poured, "have hopes in that direction. You nabbed onto the best prospect in the district."

"Nabbed is hardly the word," Parker Jones amended with a smile. "But you're right about one thing—Molly is the best."

"Then why, for heaven's sake, are you skirmishing around about marriage and settling down? You might consider being a better example to us, right, Gregor?"

"Yah. You bedder vatch out, my frien'. Here you haff two poor bohunks who iss looking for such a vun as Miss Molly Morrison," rumbled Gregor, giving Parker Jones a sly poke in the ribs that almost toppled him from his chair.

"I'm praying about it, you two! There's a time and a season for all things—"

"Yah, yah, ve know—a time to be born, a time to plant, a time to laugh, a time to luff, a time to hate—vy does it say dere's a time to hate, Parker? Issen dat a bad ting?"

"How about," added Connor, " 'whosoever hateth his brother is a murderer'?"

As so often happened when these three got together, a discussion broke out. This time it was over "hating" and its meaning, as opposed to "esteem less," which Parker Jones brought forward as a better rendering of the passage that says if a man comes to Christ, he cannot be a disciple unless he hates his father, mother, brethren, sisters, and even his own life.

"Esteem less, eh? That makes sense. You see why we need you, Gregor and I? But, Parker—this talk of quitting the church, now where did that come from? And how about Molly? What does she think of this? And how does she fit into this picture—would she be happy away from Bliss and her family? Her old Mam—her grandmother—is not long for this world."

Parker Jones sighed. In need of a confidant, he had shared, in a dark moment, his feelings of insecurity regarding his call to the ministry, the size of the task, and his poor showing (he thought) as a pastor. The recent death of Henley Baldwin, for instance, had shaken him considerably. Not that Henley, a believer, hadn't made it to heaven and his eternal rest, but that he, as pastor, hadn't made Henley's apparently miserable life easier, happier.

"It would have taken a miracle for that," Connor Dougal said. "The odds were against his happiness, what with Della's personality and all. What a brabbler!"

"Now vait a minute," Gregor said. "Brabbler? Vos iss? Maybe she vas yust sick to det' of the homesteat. Ve know dat many vomen break down, some die even, and many yust fade away. She's a mighty . . . ah, spiff voman."

"Spiff! That's a new one. I'm not sure Della'd go for that," laughed Connor, while Gregor puffed and huffed until the color of his cheeks was almost one with his cinnamon-tinted hair and beard.

"She needs our understanding, I'm sure of that," the pastor said, wondering at the same time if he could practice what he preached.

"That poor kid Dudley. He's stuck here for sure." A concerned Connor shook his head. "I think, from what I can make out, Tilda Hooper has made the decision to look elsewhere. That puts one more back on the list of available females, Gregor. It's a mighty skimpy list—Molly already spoken for, Matilda looking the Felker lad's way, and Gramma Jurgenson."

All three bachelors grinned, though it was a serious topic.

"You forgot one, Connor. And dat's Della Baldwin."

"A fate worse than death," muttered Connor Dougal.

The three men, bachelors all and wishing otherwise, gloomily contemplated their options and, except for Parker Jones, found the future hopeless insofar as marriage was concerned.

"Ah well," Connor said, "let's be grateful for small blessings—anyone want more coffee?"

His compatriots groaned and extended their cups.

Franny's cheeks had gone from blazing red to chalk white, all within a few moments after the reading of a letter.

Ever since Fanny had revealed her "secret" to Kerry, her plans had been an open book, and she had shared any correspondence with her freely, with excitement. Proud, she was, proud of her spirit of independence, proud of her ability to make and carry out her plans, proud of the surge of strength that came with each day's challenge. And proud of the connection with the good-looking man in the small photo.

She had been waiting impatiently for Connor Dougal's response to her letter telling him that she was prepared to make the trip to Saskatchewan. He would not only confirm her decision as being right and proper but would give instructions about just what day of the week would be best to arrive and where she should disembark. Her supposition was that Prince Albert was the nearest station; Bliss, she understood, for all its beauty and promise, was not on the railway line. He would have looked into accommodations for her, whether in the more distant Prince Albert or in the hamlet of Bliss, where she would be comfortable until their plans could be finalized and, glory be! the wedding take place. Yes, it was important to hear from Connor Dougal.

Franny and Kerry were together in Franny's room, repacking for the umpteenth time, rearranging, removing the questionable, adding anything that had been purchased lately and deemed to be indispensable to life in the bush, on a homestead, in a log house. Connor Dougal, Franny said, had written descriptively of his bush home. That letter had been one of several she had happily shared with Kerry.

My house has become my pride and joy, as it is one of the finest in the community. Much thought has gone into making it comfortable, as well as pleasing to the eye. Most homes here are of log, rather crude and even makeshift, certainly not to be considered a long-term dwelling. And certainly not proper for a lady! It is set in a grove of poplars, yet with enough clearing so that it is filled with light. It has been my pleasure to add plenty of windows, something that is often lacking in hastily built shacks. You, if you care to, may want to add rugs to the floor in place of the huge bear skin that is currently before the fireplace. It makes for comfortable, casual lolling about of an evening. As I relax there and dream, after a long day's work, it is of having you at my side, the firelight on your face and bringing a gleam into your eyes that only I can satisfy.

Franny read in a low voice, coloring daintily before the final sentence was through. Folding the letter again, she clasped it to her breast, and her eyes did indeed, even now, have an unaccustomed gleam in them.

Kerry wanted to cry out to her, "Franny, how can you be sure he's telling the truth? How do you know he isn't a charlatan after your money?" Wanting to cry out, she kept silent; the days of questions, reproach, and warning were all in the past. Franny had defended Connor Dougal staunchly and had insisted, moreover, on her right to make her own decisions. "After all," she said, "I'm twenty-four years old, an adult by anybody's reckoning."

"Yes, but love is blind, Franny! How can you love someone you haven't even seen, haven't talked to—"

"I've 'talked' to him, Kerry. By mail and more intimately than I've ever talked to anyone. Except you," she amended hastily, seeing the reproach in Kerry's eyes. "But," she added, "it's on a different level . . . it's different altogether, Kerry, when your heart is involved. It's a sort of . . . sweet intimacy." Franny dropped her eyes as she hesitated over the final revelation.

"Sweet intimacy—when he's a thousand and more miles away and you're here?" Kerry had all but exploded. But this was in the days before she learned to keep her thoughts to herself and to refrain from responses that hurt and sometimes aggravated her dear Franny. *But oh,* she gritted to herself, *that I could go and confront this deceiver!*

That Franny's heart was involved was never the question—it did indeed seem to be. The problem—to Kerry and to Aunt Charlotte, who of course had to be let in on the plans—was the trustworthiness of the stranger at the other end of the relationship.

"At least let me send Gladdy along with you," Aunt Charlotte pleaded, but to no avail. "It's not proper for a lady—particularly a young lady—to travel all alone."

"No, Aunt Charlotte, though I thank you. This is my responsibility and mine alone. I've made the decision independently and will carry it out by myself. I plan to stay there, to live there, to make a life for myself there, and what would Gladdy do then? Come back, of course, but—by herself?"

And so the problem went round and round, and it was Aunt Charlotte, eventually, who gave in. Though not that exactly; Aunt Charlottte was stiff-armed, and by the sweet and tender person of the usually pliable, obedient Frances. Franny was obdurate, fixed, set in her determination, and no amount of persuasion or threat changed her mind.

Stubborn, Charlotte called it, and for perhaps the first time since Frances had come to live at Maxwell Manor, she found her instructions ignored. It was galling, to say the least; maddening in the extreme.

Together the girls were examining the bicycle suit and the bloomers, a subject of much dissention in the newspapers and at all female gatherings. That it was actually a reappearance for bloomers, some knew, recalling that they had first appeared in the 1860s. At that time, Mrs. Bloomer's "bifurcated nether garment" caused great outrage on sight, and few women wore them twice. Now here they were again, a menace that would not go away. Perhaps, with the furor in the press and the denunciation from many pulpits, they would do just that, but to date they appeared to be doing the exact opposite, as women, like Franny, boldly declared their individualism and purchased them.

The bicycle, until now considered a boy's or man's possession, and for the reason of transportation, had dropped part of the frame so that women cyclists could be accommodated. In so doing it became a thing of evil. "It is undoubtedly the bicycle that is giving the nineties a reputation for gaiety," one columnist wrote, which hurt its sale not a whit. There was no doubt about it—the two-wheeled monster challenged churches, contributed to the emancipation of women, and revolutionized manners. That her beloved Frances should lend her influence in that direction greatly grieved propriety-bound Charlotte.

Charlotte was out of the room, however, and Kerry, with the streak of fun that had always identified her, declared her intention of trying on the outrageous garment. She and Franny were in the midst of this distraction, laughing as they tugged the bloomers into place, when Gladdy appeared, holding aloft *the letter*.

"Oh, do give it to me!" squealed the excited Franny, and the teasing Gladdy dropped it into her outstretched hands. Reluctantly Gladdy turned and left, having other things to do and catching on quickly that Miss Franny was not going to read the epistle while she was in the room.

Franny tore open the familiar envelope. Her eager eyes scanned the page in silence, a half-smile on her tenderly curved lips. The smile vanished, her eyes widened, her hand trembled. Her face blazed scarlet and waned to white. She staggered.

Kerry saw the transformation, her own thoughts going from interest to dismay. If it had not been for her outstretched hand, her arm quickly going around the sagging body, Franny would have crumpled into a heap on the floor.

Indeed, Franny was in a half-swoon; it seemed she was barely breathing, and what breath she had was ragged and shallow. Greatly alarmed, Kerry half carried, half dragged her to the bed, letting her fall across it. She removed Franny's slippers, swung her feet up, and thrust a pillow under her head. From her nerveless fingers the letter fluttered to the floor. Kneeling, Kerry gathered it to her, her eyes swiftly scanning the brief paragraph.

Dear Miss Bentley: [How stilted, how impersonal! How revealing!]

It has been pleasant corresponding with you. I trust you have benefited from my descriptions of, and introductions to, the bush. Indeed it is a place of great attraction. But as a place to live, not so. You will be forever grateful that you have not experienced it firsthand. Indeed I do you a great favor by courteously but insistently discouraging you from any further thoughts westward.

If any words of mine have misled you, you may know it has been unintentional.

Wishing you the best, I remain,
yr. obdnt. servant,
Connor Dougal

18

Reading material, in the bush, was treasured, passed from hand to hand, read and reread—especially during the long winter months--until it fell apart and was used to start someone's morning fire, if the fire had by some misfortune gone out during the night.

Dudley never knew, nor did he care, where the old material on the Cariboo Trail came from; obviously someone had hoarded it and felt it was worthy of sharing. And so several newspaper copies—*The Cariboo Sentinel, British Columbian, Colonist,* and others, as well as R. Byron Johnson's *Very Far West Indeed*—ended up in his possession, having made the rounds, stirring the heart of the adventurous, the dreamer, and the desperate.

Dudley was desperate, feeling as caught as a rabbit in a trap. That desperation had made him a dreamer. Seeing no way out of his present situation yet never settling for it, his plans became wilder and more unattainable as time passed. His dreams rarely touched on reality. There was—he sometimes felt with despair—no hope.

The Cariboo was the maddest, perhaps the biggest, gold hunt to convulse the West, and the sandbars and creeks along the Fraser River had yielded an estimated $50 million worth of gold before it panned out. But what gripped Dudley was more than the gold—it was the free lifestyle, the fever that gripped the hearts of those thousands who came. Surely, somewhere, there was a challenge for him! A challenge that would take him away from the farm, away from the routine of barn-cleaning, horse-curry-ing, egg-gathering, cow-milking, manure-pitching that marked his winter days. Away from home . . . away from the sight of Matilda and Bert Felker together . . . away from Ma and her eternal guardianship of his every move.

Perhaps Della, knowing her son better than he realized, suspected the discontent, suspicioned the dreams, and supposed the inevitable—escape.

With the snow—soft but deadly—beating soundlessly against the windowpanes, with the fire in the heater roaring and Dudley seated across its width from her, Della's sharp eyes noted her son's fascination with what he was reading. Having glanced at the papers and being familiar with the contents, she followed his thoughts with remarkable accuracy.

"Gorges five thousand feet deep," she said into the silence. "Box canyons of perpendicular red rock. Boiling with rapids and whirlpools. That's the Fraser for you."

Dudley started, his rapt attention interrupted by his mother's grim words.

Cariboo country, which Dudley found fascinating—a twenty-two-mile-wide plateau slashed by the Fraser River, beginning its flow at Buffalo Dung Lake (a name Della chose to ignore)—was the source of the most vivid stories that ever came out of any venture of man. Dudley had been immersed in an account of the intrepid prospectors and with them "battled the currents in wooden bateaux lashed like pontoon rafts, six abreast to carry mules and Newfoundland dogs," and with them removed his boots and attempted to climb the trench cliffs barefoot. Reading on, he forsook that group and aligned himself instead with the wiser men who strapped hundred-pound packs of "Cariboo turkey" (bacon) and "Cariboo strawberries" (beans) to their dogs and mules and took the Indian trails along the bank.

"Think of it, Ma . . . Mum! Billy Barker—you've heard of him, Barkerville is named after him—hit a lode that had nuggets as big as hen's eggs!"

"And died a pauper in the Old Men's Home in Victoria."

"A baroness in England arranged with the Bishop of London to send over a 'bride ship.' Did you ever hear the like, Ma?" Dudley asked admiringly. "The *Colonist* identifies them as 'sixty maidens meditating matrimony—ages from fourteen to uncertain.' All of them found mates, Ma, after walking down that gangplank into the midst of all those whiskery, eager faces." Dudley actually chortled at the picture this conjured up.

"Maybe one of them married 'Cariboo' Cameron," Della said quenchingly. "His wife, you may recall, died, and 'Cariboo' paid big prices for men to help take her body to the coast. He pickled her in alcohol in a lead-lined box, put the box on a toboggan, and dragged it to New Westminster for shipment. He finally got her to Ontario all right and buried her there. And what happened to 'Cariboo' and his millions? Died penniless. No, my boy, you are better off with the farm, dying in your own bed—"

Della stopped abruptly with a sudden remembrance of Henley dying in a scarred school desk during a church service in a small schoolhouse in the bush. Dudley, also remembering, added silently, *yes, and he died penniless, and never had any adventure getting that way.*

"Well," he plunged ahead, "if the Cariboo Trail is out, there's always the Peace River country."

"Not open," his mother said, and she dismissed the subject as being unworthy of discussion.

"Maybe not," Dudley continued doggedly, "but it will be. As the prairies and the bush fill up, there's going to be a spilling out into these more rugged, remote areas. One of these days the government will open roads back in there—"

"The latitude is too high for farming."

"No, it's not, Ma! Gregor was there before he settled down here, and—"

"Why didn't he stay there, the foreigner!"

Dudley explained patiently, "He thought about it. In fact, somewhere over there he did some trapping. But without the railway, you can't get furs out that easily. I think he made arrangements with someone there to buy some land . . . he had cash, maybe still does, I don't know. Anyway, he liked that country."

"The more fool, he."

The conversation languished there, as it always did when Dudley revealed any hint of his desire to get out . . . to get away.

The following afternoon, between dinner and supper, under a lowering sky and an ominous silence that often presaged a snowstorm, Dudley made his slow way, through snowbanks and along snow-rutted roads, to the quarter section that was Gregor Slovinski's property.

"Hello-o-o!" he called, receiving no answer to his knock on the cabin door but noting the smoke from the stovepipe.

The door to the small log barn was thrust open, and Gregor's palely pink hair, topped with a lopsided cap, appeared.

"Hello, yourself. Go on in and make yourself at home! I'm coming."

Dudley waited on the small stoop, and soon Gregor was at his side, stamping the snow from his felt boots, sweeping the encrustation of ice and snow from Dudley's legs and feet, smiling a white-toothed greeting, and urging his company into his home.

Gregor's cabin was small and crowded but not offensively smelly or messy. The atmosphere, always closed in at this time of the year, was redolent with wood smoke, bacon grease, and a carbolic odor that could only come from medicated soap.

Gregor pulled off his cap, removed his gloves and coat, and invited Dudley to do likewise. He motioned his guest toward the one and only comfortable chair—a scarred wooden rocker; then he pulled an enamel coffeepot forward from the back of the range top and reached for a couple of cups. Flinching at the black brew, Dudley sipped cautiously.

"How iss eferyting going?" Gregor inquired when the man and the youth were seated at the side of the stove, the only reasonable spot in any busy home to relax and be comfortable.

"Pretty good, I guess," Dudley answered in a tight voice, and Gregor looked at the younger man with a question in his narrowed eyes.

He suspected this was not a casual visit. No one, in the dead of winter, had sufficient reason—outside of an emergency or sheer desperation in the face of loneliness—to trek somewhere through bad weather just to sit. It was done, but always with a purpose.

So they talked about feed, cows going dry, hens freezing. They talked about being isolated and snowbound; they talked about loneliness. They talked about the future.

"Yah," Gregor confirmed, "dis iss da place for me. Lonely or not, I got me a goot place. Besides, I tink I yust luff Bliss. You?"

"Oh, Bliss is all right. But I dunno . . . it's not the only place on earth, is it?"

Gregor's light-colored eyebrows lifted. "Nah," he agreed. "I guess dere's udder places. You tinking about any special place?"

"Well, don't you get, ah, lonely for that place of yours in the Peace River country? On the Parsnip, wasn't it?"

"It's yust timberland. Nah, I'm bedder off here."

Silence.

Gregor gulped his coffee, and Dudley was glad Ma wasn't around to hear it. The fire snapped and popped.

Silence.

A clock ticked clearly, and Dudley's eyes were drawn to the sound.

On a shelf on the wall sat an incongruous item, made more so because of the cabin's masculine look and smell and the massive size and prodigious strength of the man who owned it. It was a clock, no larger than six inches high and five inches wide. The case was made to resemble a basket and was cast in bronze. It had a handle of twisted brass, and from the open top of the basket two tiny brass kittens peeped out, one looking down at the clock dial, the other with a paw raised, batting at something unseen. Dudley was mesmerized. What was the story behind this girlish item?

Gregor watched his guest for the moment. Then, quietly, he explained.

"Dat belonged to my Marta. My vife. She iss buried in da old coundry and our liddle dodder vit her."

Suddenly Dudley's portrayal of being a landowner and adult vanished. Although past his nineteeth birthday, he was as gauche and dumbstruck as any ten-year-old.

"I didn't know," he mumbled, going fiery red. "I'm sorry."

"I's vy I'm here, I guess you'd say," Gregor continued. "Dere was nodding for me over dere anymore. So I vent to da Peace country . . . too lonely. And den I come here, to Bliss. Here I like; here I gonna stay."

After an uncomfortable silence on Dudley's part, he finally spoke, trying to make his voice natural and probably failing, for Gregor's sharp eyes studied the young man's face, learning more than words alone implied. "Well, then, if you're going to stay in Bliss, maybe you want to get rid of your property in the Peace country." Casual, so casual.

"I tink aboud it, sometimes, yah."

"Well, listen."

And Gregor did so while Dudley proposed a most amazing offer.

"I own half interest in our place," Dudley explained in a rush of words, as though they were pent up and ready to burst the dam that had held them back. "I want to get away . . . start new somewhere else. You own a place in the Peace country and don't need it, maybe don't want it. It's just sitting there waiting to be tamed. Could we make some kind of trade? Maybe with a little cash thrown in, on your part, or some arrangement for payments because of my place being proved up and in pretty good shape? Whaddya say, Gregor? Eh? Eh?"

Dudley was pale now, his few remaining blemishes standing out like bare spots in a field of snow. His words, once started, tripped over themselves, and he studied the face of the older man with blazing, eager eyes.

What he had suggested was incredible. Or was it? Gregor, like all homesteaders, planned to farm more than his original quarter-section. But to obtain more land, unless he sold and moved, he would have acreage that was separated from his homestead, perhaps by a great distance, making it next to impossible to work both places. The Baldwin place was the fourth quarter in his own section.

Gregor drew a deep breath; there was one insurmountable problem. Or was there?

"Della—your mudder. Vat does she say? Haff you talked mit her aboud it?"

Dudley's slender shoulders sagged. "No."

"Vould she agree, do ya tink?"

"No. Never."

"Vell den—"

"Listen, Gregor—"

A desperate Dudley laid out his case: He had to get away, start on his own, be his own man. Gregor nodded. "I own half the homestead," Dudley explained. "I can sell it, or trade it. Or just let it sit idle!" And now Dudley's voice was a tightly worded threat: *Just let it sit!*

"It's blackmail, I suppose, of a sort," Dudley admitted. "Ma can't work our place alone, and if I leave it sit, she's sunk! She'll have to agree, if I stick to my decision. She'll be glad to agree—either to have someone work it on shares or buy it outright."

"Vat if she don't?"

"She doesn't have to agree, Gregor. That's my land, or half of everything is, and I can sell or trade it. She'll have to go along with it. She won't have any choice."

"If I don't do it, Dudley, vill you fin' somcone else?" Gregor asked quietly.

"Absolutely! I'm getting out of here!"

Perhaps Gregor thought compassionately of the widow with an uncaring, ruthless partner. Perhaps he saw the arrangement a true godsend. Perhaps, having prayed about additional land, he had a feeling this might be God's answer.

"Tell you vat—I'll tink aboud it some more. How's dat?"

"You will? Honest?" Again the young man sounded like a child. Laying out his offer had been easier than he had anticipated. It was, after all the planning and explaining, too good to be true. Dudley found himself trembling, partly from relief, partly from anxiety that it wouldn't work out after all.

"Gif me a liddle vile, yah? Ve'll see vat ve can vork oud." After that amazing demonstration of his grasp of the English language, Gregor subsided.

Dudley's back straightened. His breath, as quickened as though he had been in a race or, more likely, a tough fight, returned to normal. His rapid heartbeat slowed.

"Gimme some of that coffee," he said, holding out his cup.

Dr. Blake came out of the sickroom looking very grave. Very grave indeed. Charlotte and Kerry were awaiting him in the parlor, and it was there Gladdy led the dignified man of medicine. There with a sigh he seated himself, at Charlotte's invitation.

With two faces turned toward him—one lined and pale and obviously greatly concerned; the other young and pale, and just as concerned—his usual brisk demeanor gentled, and with sympathy he said, "It's not what you wish to hear, ladies. Not at all, I'm afraid."

"I knew it!" the young woman muttered half aloud, her pale face clouding with the feelings that darkened it. Her fingers were threaded into a knot in her lap, and her lips, usually full and full of fun, were as twisted as her fingers, and the agony in each was clear to be seen.

"Yes," Charlotte said sadly, "hoping for good news, I've been braced for bad. The evidence before our eyes is overwhelming. Nothing we do seems to help—not palatable food, which Mrs. Finch has worked so faithfully to provide, not loving encouragement, not even the mild scolds I've administered for her own good. Nothing has reached her; it's as if she's shut away in a cocoon of suffering and won't, perhaps can't, come out. We've tried humor, music, reading to her—though it was all pretty poor stuff, I'm afraid. We couldn't reach past the barrier. The barrier," she finished bitterly, "that cruelty erected."

Kerry spoke up. "I don't know if it was so much cruelty as carelessness. And that's what puts me in a rage! That . . . that *man*, that *creature*, just so carelessly tossed her aside, as if she didn't matter! I've heard of men who consider women nothing more than playthings! It's as if he were playing with her. His careless unconcern for her feelings was the cruelest blow of all. Now it seems that blow was a deathblow! Something in her died; it's as if she doesn't want to have help . . . doesn't care anymore."

"That's true; she isn't cooperating in any way," Dr. Blake confirmed. "She just lies there, silent, and growing weaker by the hour."

"Those bright cheeks—they're not a good sign, it seems to me," Charlotte offered. "And though her face is pale otherwise, her eyes glitter. But it's an unhealthy glitter."

"Too bright of eye, too brilliant of cheek," Dr. Blake agreed. "It's not the bloom of health. You knew, of course—have known for years—that her lungs are involved. Her hopes, her excitement about a new life, infused her with an energy that was false. But this blow she suffered—it has swept away all pretense at normalcy. She's sunk back, and ever further back, into what we call—"

"Pining sickness," Kerry supplied abruptly.

"I beg your pardon?" Dr. Blake said, startled.

In response, Kerry quoted a Scripture learned long ago and hidden in her heart ever since, a portion of the Bible that seemed to her to be sadly fitting now: "'I have cut off like a weaver my life: he will cut me off with pining sickness.'"

"That's Bible, Doctor," Charlotte explained. "Kerry has this way of resorting to Scripture when greatly moved, or when nothing else will do—"

"Pining sickness?" the good doctor repeated. "I never heard it explained like that, but I believe she's described it very well."

"The question is," Charlotte faltered, "can one die of pining sickness?"

"I never heard it diagnosed as the cause of death," Dr. Blake said thoughtfully, "but pining . . . grieving . . . can take the heart out of recovery. But the really fatal thing, you must remember, is the disease that's eating at her lungs. I know of no cure." The doctor spoke heavily but honestly.

"Tell me, Doctor, could she have gotten well if she had gone West? Could that have worked a cure?" Kerry spoke tersely, as if much depended on the answer. "If so," she continued, wrath building, "Connor Dougal—never will I forget that name!—is personally to blame for Franny's illness, and I'll hold him responsible if she dies!"

"We'll never know, of course, whether carrying out her plans, going West, might have worked a cure. But certainly it could have lengthened her days. Contentment is a great healer." The doctor's voice trailed away. It was supposition, pure supposition, and he was, after all, a man of science.

"And her recovery now depends on her incentive to live and get well," he added finally. "The human will is a marvelous thing, a powerful thing, more so than we understand. Someday we'll be better trained to handle these body/mind illnesses. Until that day, we do the best we can. And the best we can do now is to make Frances comfortable, care for her tenderly, and be prepared for the . . . inevitable."

The inevitable. It had an ominous, a final sound. Kerry could not settle for it.

Back to the sickroom Kerry went to do what she could, though half sick herself with the despair that ate at her heart. Having little or no memory of her mother and many unpleasant memories of her father, Kerry deemed Frances the dearest person in the world to her, and now she was pining away before Kerry's eyes.

As Kerry sat by the sleeping invalid, waiting for—she knew not what, memories thronged her mind, memories that took her back to the day of her introduction to Maxwell Manor and Frances Bentley.

Even in those days Franny had not been well. But she had rallied and strengthened, and ten years had passed during which she enjoyed fairly good health. Recalling those early days and her own precocious ways, Kerry smiled—sitting there by the sickbed—thinking of her own childish ignorance, shyness, and boldness. Her boldness, then as perhaps now, was ever a means of covering up the shyness.

There was no other way she could account for the courage that had prompted the first rush of verses as she met the Maxwell household, and Franny in particular. A classic example was her effort to describe her immediate fascination with Franny, calling forth soulful descriptions such as, "Thou hast ravished my heart with one of thine eyes."

From her sickbed Franny had squeezed Kerry's hand and laughed her delicious little laugh, captivated by this refreshing child. Never had the small Kerry had such an appreciative audience.

Kerry remembered now that she had followed up that particular quotation with a question, asking, "Why did she ravish him with *one* eye? What do you suppose was wrong with the other eye? Once I had a pink eye, and I could hardly keep it open. Do you think the bride had a pink eye? Whatever it was, the bridegroom loved her anyway. Do you know he thought her hair was like a flock of goats? I'm sure he meant something nice, don't you? Maybe he just didn't have a good 'magination."

"Well, little one," Franny had said through a mist of tears, "you have enough 'magination for all of us."

"I 'magined sometimes that Papa married Miss Perley or maybe some beautiful lady who was much kinder, and we got us a house, and there was a garden, and a cow to milk, and chickens to give us eggs. Once when we were in our ears in the rent, Papa boiled eggs for our supper in a can in the fireplace."

Here Kerry had paused and asked her inevitable question after she had said things too wise and too wonderful for her own understanding: "How could we be in our own ears, do you think?"

"I think you mean 'arrears,' Kerry. That means you were behind in paying your rent."

"Oh that," she had answered with relief. "I thought it was something like the pink eye, only in the ears. I only had a pink eye one time, but we were often in our ears—a-rrears. It seemed to make Mrs. Peabody crabby, so I suppose it was a bad thing."

"You won't have to worry about things like that anymore, wee Kerry. Uncle Sebastian and Aunt Charlotte will take care of you from now on. It's the hope of all of us that you'll be very happy with us. We'll be great friends, you and I."

"I had a friend. Her name is Cordelia. She called me bad names; sometimes she called me a lumpy toad. Once it kindled my wrath, and I called her 'ye generation of vipers.'"

That was when—on the very first day at Maxwell Manor—Franny had put her arms around the small girl and hugged her close. Remembering, Kerry's purple-black eyes filled with tears, reminding her that Franny, seeing Kerry's tear-filled eyes for the first time, had said they looked like "pansies in a spring shower." Franny had brought the starving little heart love, acceptance, and understanding.

The flooding memories were too much. Sitting at the bedside of this dear one, Kerry's eyes brimmed, and the tears—of remembrance, of happiness, of pain—ran over.

Perhaps it was her small sniff; perhaps it was because of her movement to capture a dainty handkerchief from her skirt pocket that roused the sick girl. But Kerry felt her free hand clasped in slim fingers and now, as in earlier days, a flood of warmth and protection swept over her. Franny and Maxwell Manor had been her safe haven.

"Oh, darling—you're awake," she responded now, blinking through tears.

"Mustn't cry, Kerry . . . not worth it. Remember . . . remember always . . . that you've brought me, all of us . . . much happiness. Never change, Kerry."

Kerry's tears were flowing in earnest now. "Please, Franny, get well again! Just think about getting well and strong again! Please, dear. . . ."

Franny's frail hand gave Kerry's a little shake. "Aunt Charlotte," she whispered. "Please get Aunt Charlotte . . . I need to see her . . . alone."

Kerry flew to find her aunt, and for the remainder of the day, the sickroom was off limits. Kerry didn't know what went on there, but early in the evening Gladdy came to get her, whispering, with tears, "Your aunt says you are to come. You and your uncle—I'll go get him." And Gladdy sped off, her hair flouncing madly and her tears flowing freely and making a path through the freckles, those that remained since childhood and would remain with her always.

At the midnight hour it was all over. Franny was at rest, forever at rest.

Gladdy helped a weeping Kerry from the room, their tears and sobs mingling. Straightening herself, supporting herself with one hand on the wall in the hallway, Kerry spoke through stiff lips:

"That man—that Connor Dougal—I'll find him if it's the last thing I do, and I'll make him pay!"

It was a vow that sustained her through the next few days, through the heart-wrenching drama of the funeral, through the dark days that followed.

K eren," Charlotte said, and her nostrils flared and her nose tip pinked—a double ... no, a triple whammy. Not only the flaring nostrils and the pinking nose but the use of her full name should have alerted Kerry to the opposition she was up against. And normally she would have paid strict attention to the signs of disapproval.

"Keren!" Charlotte said again, adding another powerful missile to her arsenal of weapons: It was her tone of voice—like a clap of thunder on a pleasant day, like the snap of a whip on a defenseless back, like doomsday to a condemned creature.

Not for years had Kerry heard Aunt Charlotte's voice resound with such terrible possibilities for disfavor and discipline as it did now.

"*Keren!* You are to put such foolish nonsense out of your head *this instant!*"

And though Kerry quaked—Aunt Charlotte was a formidable opponent—she was not shaken from her position.

"Oh, Aunt Charlotte! Please see it my way! Please ... my mind is made up, you see."

"Well, just unmake it!" Charlotte snapped. "You are not, by any stretch of the imagination—and you've always had more than your share—going to this outlandish place named Bliss but probably meaning misery! If I have to lock you in your room, you're not going, and that's all there is to it!"

Lock her in her room indeed! Kerry—young, strong, vital—looked at Aunt Charlotte's stooped figure, too heavy, too flaccid, too infirm to follow through on her threat, and felt that a pert "You and who else?" would be an appropriate answer.

Kerry had never been a sassy child, and she wouldn't be a smart-aleck adult. Aunt Charlotte had been too good to her, too kind, to hurt her feelings. Kerry feared it would be upsetting, even traumatizing, to Aunt Charlotte when she realized that all her threats, her pleadings, her arguments, would make no difference in her niece's decision.

And so she answered as gently as she could while still standing firm.

"Aunt Charlotte, I didn't even mention it to you until all my hesitations had been settled and my mind made up. I didn't arrive at this decision easily. But it wasn't long after Franny's death that I came to the awareness that I would never have any peace until I made that false wretch—that Connor Dougal—pay for what he did to her. I can't rest until I do."

"But that's terrible, Kerry! It's retaliation, it's revenge, and you of all people should know what God thinks of that! He won't smile on such an endeavor!"

"It's an eye for an eye and a tooth for a tooth as far as I'm concerned. That's certainly scriptural."

"But it's not what Jesus taught! He said if someone smites you on the cheek, turn the other cheek also!"

"Why, Aunt, you surprise me; I didn't know you knew any Scripture." During all the years of Kerry's references to the Bible, no one had ever challenged her before. This wasn't surprising, seeing that no member of the family attended church except for the traditional Easter morning service. No, Scripture quoting was the prerogative of Kerry alone. How odd to have her own method thrown back in her face.

Charlotte had the grace to flush; she was well aware that in the area of religious training she had been sadly lacking where the girls were concerned.

"That's not to say I don't read the Bible," she said defensively. "And," she added pointedly, "the New Testament is clear on loving and forgiving."

"Are you asking me to forgive that man, Aunt Charlotte? He hasn't even asked for forgiveness, has he? In fact, that creature doesn't even know the damage he's caused. Well, I'm going to see that he knows. I plan to see that he suffers for it." Kerry was coldly steadfast in her awful purpose.

"No good can come of it, Kerry! Not to him certainly; nor to you."

"Ah yes! It'll do me a world of good to see that man hurt as Franny was hurt. It makes me burn whenever I think of his callousness and the unspeakable effect it has had on all of us, Franny in particular. Why should he get away with it?"

"And just how do you plan to carry out this nefarious scheme?" Aunt Charlotte asked with a sigh, capitulating like a burst bubble. She knew her Kerry; Kerry would never have brought her mad scheme this far if she didn't intend to carry it through.

"That's a little nebulous right now," Kerry admitted. "But before I get there I'll have a plan, you may be sure, and when I get to this Bliss place, I'll put it into action."

"Like what, Kerry? Tear his eyes out? Spit in his face? Denounce him as a rounder and a cad?"

"It'll have to be something painful," Kerry said decisively. "I wish I were a man in times like this! Obviously I can't inflict physical damage. I'll have to do it in another way. But he'll know it when it happens, and he'll know why."

"And then what?" Charlotte asked quietly.

Kerry hesitated. "I don't exactly know. I suppose I'll come back here—if you'll have me."

"Silly, silly girl, even to ask. This is your home; nothing you can do will change that."

"Thank you, Aunt Charlotte," Kerry said a little unsteadily. "You know how I feel about you and Uncle and how much I love Maxwell Manor—it's been a real home to me."

"So when will you be leaving this loved home?"

Kerry sighed; it was a heavy burden she had taken upon herself. "Just as soon as all the snow is gone, and that's not going to be long. I'll get there at the very beginning of spring, and it will give me several months before snow flies again, when I'll need to get out. If I don't, I may not make it until another spring. Can you imagine a worse fate than to be stuck in a backwoods place by the ridiculous name of Bliss for an entire winter? So as soon as carriages roll freely and there's no danger of the train being held up anywhere, I'll be on my way."

"Alone, Kerry? Now here I really must be adamant. It just isn't done!"

"There are always people going West; perhaps I can latch onto some such group or family."

The improbability of this eased Charlotte's mind; it could take a long time. Unless, of course, Kerry, like Franny, turned to the newspaper for help.

The idea had indeed occurred to Kerry. In fact it was only a few days later as she was poring over the Personals in the various newspapers and magazines Gideon purchased for her that her solution came. And from an unexpected source.

Kerry was on the rug in her room, her dark hair escaping the pins that held it up and back and curling in cloudy wisps around her face. A face that, even in early womanhood, retained some of its early waiflike delicacy. Her eyes were blue-black in concentration; her slender body was bent in graceful abandon over the papers spread before her.

Her absorption was broken by a pair of sturdy shoes that came into her line of vision. Gladdy, feather duster under one arm, was standing beside her.

"Whatcher doin'?" Gladdy asked cheekily in the old, long-abandoned manner of speech and the result of the now-absent Miss Beery's severe insistence on proper speech.

Kerry sat back on her heels, futilely brushing back her straying curls with one hand and giving the hem of Gladdy's uniform a twitch with the other.

"Whatcher think?" Kerry replied, just as cheekily, happy for an interruption and the chance to change her cramped position.

With the camaraderie that marked their relationship, Gladdy folded her slim length and settled on the floor beside Kerry, duster laid aside, her eyes going to the heap of papers and the tablet that was singularly free of notations.

"No luck?" she asked, while her cornflower blue eyes swept the disarray for clues of some success in the search.

Kerry sighed. "Not yet. Maybe tomorrow's batch. . . ."

Kerry was discouraged. If many more days passed and no chaperone was turned up, she might, in a foolhardy move, decide to start out on her own, ignoring protocol and Aunt Charlotte.

But she knew it wouldn't be wise. Besides—*it just wasn't done!*

Except for a few seasons spent at Uncle Sebastian's summer cottage, Toronto was her world, her safe world. And the Territories weren't called the Wild West for nothing. Many and lurid were the stories and accounts drifting back to civilization, as alarming as they were attractive.

One woman, in an account Kerry well remembered, reported her first glimpse of the raw settlement where she would be living: "I leaned my elbows on the wooden table in the dirt hut, buried my face in my hands, and sobbed aloud, 'My God, help me to cleave to thee.' I could not help it. I felt so lonely, so homesick, so isolated."

This was the life the homesteaders faced, those who dared leave the populated areas. To strike off into the endless, rolling miles of prairie and beyond took colossal courage—or ignorance. To take a wife, or expect one to follow after, was incredibly audacious. That a woman would consent to go in response to such an invitation was even more mind-numbing.

But, Kerry rationalized, Bliss can't be all that bad. Not anymore. Surely the worst days are over. If Connor Dougal's letters—she had read all of them, going through Franny's things—were to be believed, his house was comfortable and attractive in its bush setting, his crops were thriving, his future was challenging. Why then should doubts nibble away at the edge of her mind?

But whatever the hardships, Kerry was determined to confront them. The trouble was confronting them alone.

And so she heard Gladdy's next words with more excitement than surprise, though she was indeed surprised.

"I've been thinking—" Gladdy began casually.

"Oh, oh!"

"I'm serious! It's this: I want to go West with you."

"Gladdy! Don't even suggest such a thing if you don't mean it!"

"I mean it. I did a lot of thinking before I mentioned it. It's like this, Kerry—my life is going nowhere. Being a maid is not my idea of the way to invest one's time and energy. There's only one life to live, and I don't intend to spend all mine dusting and cleaning someone else's house. I'm two years older than you are. That doesn't make me ancient, but it makes me, well, troubled at times as I look around and wonder where I'm going. All my sisters were married before this. I don't even meet any eligible fellas except maybe a delivery boy or two. This trip, with you, is the only ray of light I've seen on a long, dark horizon. And, Kerry, I've got enough money to pay my own way. I've saved nearly everything I've made for ten years. It'll be an investment!"

That Gladdy was restless, Kerry knew. They were friends, sharing intimacies, sharing dreams. They had talked about it: Gladdy tied into service as surely as if she were still in the old country; Kerry bound by protocol that bade her wait until some knight in shining armor came along and swept her from Maxwell Manor into another such abode.

Her hand went out to Gladdy, who clasped it in a pledge that was to carry them many miles through trials and tribulations not imagined by either of them. Babes in the woods they were.

And that's what Uncle Sebastian called them. With a shake of his head he conferred that title upon them and withdrew to his study and the comfort of his books and papers. Aunt Charlotte was more outspoken in her denunciation of the plan and less easily appeased. To lose her niece *and* her maid—it was enough to give one palpitations of the heart!

Half swooning, Aunt Charlotte submitted to Kerry's ministrations as she fanned her face, rubbed her hands, and tenderly brushed back her hair. When she was recovered and finally convinced of the departure of Kerry and Gladdy, she sat up sensibly and helped lay plans.

"Money," she said. "You'll have to have money. But fortunately that's no problem anymore." She made reference to the announcement Sebastian had made not many weeks ago concerning Franny's estate, which had been left to Kerry. While it was not enormous, it was not insignificant. "If you have money, you can hire a great many things done that penniless people find so difficult, even degrading. Clothes. You can go through Franny's wardrobe; some of it can be shared with Gladys." And Charlotte was off on suggestions regarding things necessary, and useless; sensible, and ridiculous; desirable, and far-fetched.

Her greatest fear, it seemed, was their health, her wildest recommendation, what to do to take care of it. Where in their luggage—would they pack, and would they ever use—blood builder, mosquito deterrent, nerve steadier, brain cleaner, electrifying liniment, eye water, worm cakes, rat killer, and slippery elm lozenges?

Eventually the buying was accomplished, the packing completed. The time schedules were checked, the necessary banking done. It remained only for the snow to melt and the weather to moderate.

The departure of Kerry and Gladdy was accompanied by many tears, many instructions, and many inquiries into what they had and what they had forgotten. Finally the two were seated in the family carriage with Gideon at the reins. He had his instructions not to leave them until they were safely entrained; he was to see that their luggage accompanied them, to inform the conductor that here were young ladies in need of his tender and special care, and to slip a sizeable bill into his palm at the same time.

Finally, the train carriage vibrating beneath them, seated together with numerous bags around and above them, their color as high as their spirits, Kerry and Gladdy waved good-bye to Gideon from the window. Gladdy threw caution to the winds and, in view of her liberation, blew the staid and proper Gideon a kiss, thereby coloring his cheeks the shade of a ripe plum.

Hardly had they glanced around at their traveling companions, removed their capes and shawls and settled back, than Kerry said, "Here's the plan. I've got it all worked out but didn't dare mention it until we were underway."

"You mean you've finally figured out what you'll do?"

"I'm going to make that bushman fall in love with me, Gladdy. I'll do whatever it takes to make him fall in love with me, head over heels in love with me, even ask me to marry him. And then, Gladdy—I'll laugh in his face!"

K erry and Gladdy rode a packed train. The gap between Ontario and British Columbia had been bridged, and although
the trickle had a small beginning, it would soon increase to a roar
of immigration. Here, in the vast West, the immigrant would
become a homesteader, on 160 acres he could call his own, and
for only a ten-dollar filing fee. The great migration had begun.

In the beginning, most of them trekked in by wagon. The
prairie schooner became the final means of completing the long
journey, a journey that had begun across the ocean in a distant
part of the globe. By prairie schooner or wagon or Red River
cart, they came. They were, almost to a man, fleeing poverty,
oppression, enforced servitude to king, czar, landowner. No man
was consigned to be a serf in Canada.

Hundreds of immigrants would draw rein, finally, at a piece
of land that was wild and untouched, and they would begin the
lifelong task of wresting home and livelihood from soil that had
never known the bite of a plow or echoed to the swing of an axe.
Eventually, arriving by train, they would climb out of a cramped
colonist car at a railway shack, with no friend or family to greet

them and no one to direct them about where to go or what to do next. Their gear was unloaded and left at the side of the track, and the train—an encroacher in the wilderness of grass or bush—seemed in a hurry to escape, wheezing quickly away to the horizon and out of sight, leaving only silence and loneliness. At times the pure, lilting song of a bird jarred shocked senses to the grim reality of their predicament. They were cast—totally and irrevocably—on their own devices.

Some newcomers knew how to tackle the situation, knew how to farm, had a few skills for building, for caring for animals, hunting for food. But thousands did not, never having put hoe in garden or milk in pail. The suffocating heat of summer was unexpected and the hammering blizzards of winters so cold they could snap barbed wire. Still they came, to walk their own land, to live their dream or, in many cases, watch helplessly as it shriveled and died along with their crop.

The Indians had come; the fur traders and explorers had come; and now it was the time of the settlers. Tiny settlements began to appear in the vast expanse of the prairie and the green tangle of the bush. A trickle of wheat began to make its way to the railway, a trickle that was to cascade into a flood and earn for the prairie provinces the title of bread basket of the world.

Kerry's and Gladdy's tickets said Prince Albert, Saskatchewan, though Saskatchewan was not to become a province for several years. Prince Albert—the heart of the bush and the end of the line. First the prairie, then the bush, then the forests. And beyond—ice and snow and tundra.

As their train crept across the prairie, Kerry and Gladdy could see an occasional lump or mound of sod that broke the ceaselessly flowing sea of grass. It was identified as the abode of humans by the ribbon of smoke rising from a tin stovepipe. Even Gladdy, raised in poverty in the slums of London, shuddered.

"Like field mice," she said, shivering, "or badgers in their hole. At least we had company in our misery. Where is there a store? a school? a *neighbor?*"

"I thought you were prepared to be a pioneer," Kerry teased.

"I am," Gladdy defended stoutly, "only please—not on the prairie!"

"Look at the company you'd have," Kerry said, pointing out the jackrabbits that flourished in countless numbers.

"You'd have them in your cook pot. And like as not, be glad of them," someone said, overhearing the conversation. "Letters from my brother refer to rabbit stew all the time. Rabbit stew, oatmeal, and in an emergency, bannock."

Gladdy squared her narrow shoulders. "Whatever . . . wherever," she maintained. "Somewhere I'll find what I'm looking for. And I'll recognize it, and I'll settle there and be happy."

"I believe you mean it," Kerry said. "But first, you have to help me with my plan. Remember, that's why we came."

"Aren't you going to make the West your home?" the friendly traveler inquired, eyebrows lifting.

"Absolutely not!" Then, lapsing as she did on occasion, she quoted, to Gladdy's amusement and the stranger's perplexity, "'For want and famine they were solitary; fleeing into the wilderness in former time desolate and waste: who cut up mallows by the bushes, and juniper roots for their meat.'"

"Oh, I don't think junipers are indigenous to the area. And mallows . . . ?"

Nevertheless, Kerry had made her point—no wilderness for her.

But her outlook about the West changed when at last the prairie was behind them and greenery surrounded them, swept past them, all but enfolded them like a green shroud. And would have, if it wasn't kept cut back from the track. Alongside, cordwood lay piled, six-foot lengths of poplar and birch—grist for the engine's firebox. Now from time to time a small clearing appeared and in it a cabin.

"I wonder," Kerry said thoughtfully, "if the bush, closing one in like it does, wouldn't be as hard to live with as the grass that goes on forever."

"Well, you don't have to worry about that," Gladdy reminded her. "You'll only be here—until fall, is it? What if your plan doesn't work out by then?"

"I'm prepared to stay until it does," Kerry said doggedly. "But it won't take that long. Have you forgotten, Gladdy, how scarce marriageable women are here? And those letters of that Connor Dougal are very revealing—he's lonely, all right. And ready."

"Maybe not, Kerry. Look how he backed out of his arrangement with Franny. That doesn't look like he's very eager, does it? I think he was just toying with her. One can be very safe—from a distance. When it looked like she was going to come and take him up on the relationship, he was scared off."

"It would be risky, being pledged to someone you've never seen. And he never had a picture of Franny. That's how come I feel perfectly safe. In all his letters to her I never saw a reference to me, or to you, and only one brief mention of Aunt Charlotte. We'll be total strangers to him."

The girls had lowered their voices, and the friendly traveler beside them had taken herself off to the end of the car and to the kettle boiling there on the stove.

The colonist car was simply that: a car carrying colonists across Canada. To the dismay of the girls, most everyone was sick. They had disembarked from a nightmare of a sea voyage underfed or poorly fed and stepped immediately onto a train, with no time for recuperation. Consequently there was dreadful coughing, considerable vomiting, with children wailing, adults whey-faced and peaked.

Kerry and Gladdy were grateful for the large hamper of food Aunt Charlotte had insisted on sending and for the wonderful supply Mrs. Finch had prepared—chicken, bread, raw carrots, pickles, cheese, cookies, cake. When the train stopped long enough to allow the passengers to get off and stretch their legs, there were vendors selling various things, and the girls purchased fresh milk, apples, chocolate, even hard-boiled eggs. Eventually ragged Indians appeared, selling crafts they had made—arrowheads, feathered gewgaws—which Kerry and Gladdy avoided, not scornfully but with pity. For these were ragged, underfed, sad beings who seemed to feel no hope for anything better.

It was a long, tiresome trip. The seats made of wicker were hard and served as both living and sleeping quarters. Each car bore the name of a Canadian animal; Kerry and Gladdy traveled in Caribou, and when they detrained, this name helped them locate the proper car again with a minimum of time and effort.

For those folks who needed to prepare their meals, one big stove at the end of the car served everyone. Here they warmed milk for the babies, boiled water for tea, attempted to fry eggs and potatoes, made bannock. The stove was also the only source of heat, and Kerry and Gladdy, most of the time happy to be away from the ruckus and the odors of that area, suffered from the cold at night and on certain days when winter, slow in passing, brought the temperature low again.

At night babies cried, mothers shushed, men snored, the ailing coughed, and someone chunked wood or coal into the stove every once in a while. The farther they traveled, the more room they had, as family after family said their good-byes and were helped off the car. For some this was in the middle of the night, and the girls, peering out of the window, could see no sign of a station or a person or even a light. Dumped ignominiously on the prairie or in the heart of the bush, families were left to sink or swim, survive or perish, on their own. Sad to say, many perished.

It was late in the day when they chuffed into Prince Albert. Here a crowd of spectators had gathered, some to meet travelers, most to be entertained. The arrival of a train was always of interest, coming as it did from the "outside" and reminiscent of places and people quickly becoming just a memory.

Prince Albert, named for the queen's dead consort, was founded in 1866 by the Reverend James Nisbet, who came from Ontario to establish a mission among the Cree Indians. It was situated on the North Saskatchewan River, and the area's rich earth and abundant resources quickly attracted settlers; it became a center for river freight travel and a hub for the railroad. Rolling grainfields appeared as the lush forests yielded slowly to the homesteaders' need to clear five acres a year for three years; the sloughs and meadows watered and pastured the settlers' horses and cattle; the trees provided building material for cabins and barns.

"Smell that?" Kerry breathed, stepping down from the odorous car onto the platform. It was a mix of invigorating air, new-budded trees, wood smoke, and pine. Even the smoke from the stack of the train could not mask the freshness. Kerry breathed so deeply and so often, she felt giddy.

"Now this is more like it!" Gladdy exclaimed, glancing around. "It is quite civilized. For a frontier, that is. I can see several stores, and that looks like a lawyer's sign . . . and there's some kind of mill over there on the hillside—"

"Can you see a hotel, Miss Bright Eyes?" Kerry was staring up at the bowl of a sky that seemed to defy description for color and size.

"Oh, say, young man—" Gladdy was calling in her new voice as mistress of herself and director of her own life, "over here, if you please!"

A towheaded youth, cap askew, boots clattering on the station platform's planks, galloped their way, a grin of willing cooperation on his freckled face. "Yes, ma'am?"

"Can you tell us, my good lad, if there's such a thing as a hotel in this, er, city?"

"Yes, ma'am."

"Yes, ma'am, you can tell us, or yes, ma'am, there is?"

"Yes, ma'am, I can tell you, and yes, ma'am, there is—and it's right up Main Street. In fact you have your choice—"

"Take us to the one that you would want your sister to stay in if she needed a room."

"Ain't got no sister."

"Your mother . . . your aunt, anybody you feel responsible for," Gladdy explained patiently, obviously enjoying the role of being in charge. "Now these are our things, here, and here, and over there."

"I'll get the wagon, miss," the young man said, still grinning but a little more respectfully now to Gladdy's satisfaction and Kerry's amusement.

With their goods and chattels loaded and Kerry and Gladdy seated on the high spring seat of the wagon, the young man standing in front with the reins in his hands, they bounced their way up a very rutted street toward town.

"Wait!" Gladdy ordered, and the driver hauled back on the reins with a surprised look on his face. Kerry's face was as surprised as the lad's.

"Look, up that side street—isn't that a boarding house? We'd be better off there, Kerry, if there's room. It would be more home-like, and we could probably take meals there, too. How about that place, young man?"

"If'n you want to, we'll drive there and ask." So saying, he turned the wagon and in a matter of moments hauled it to a halt in front of a large, three-story house, well-built, freshly painted, and with crisp curtains at every window.

"Pilgrim Boarding House for Men," was the sign's discreet disclosure. The young man's grin widened.

Perhaps it was the grin; at any rate Gladdy said, "Hold this rig still, young man. I want to get out."

Kerry looked on in amazement as Gladdy clambered down, smoothed her hair, straightened her skirts, and marched up the walk to the front door. There she knocked, and Kerry watched while Gladdy engaged in a brief conversation with an aproned woman.

"'The stranger did not lodge in the street; but I opened my doors to the traveler,'" Kerry murmured, quoting the ancient Job, while the young man's freckled face grew puzzled, a reaction

Kerry was prepared for, having conjured it up in many faces across the years of Scripture quoting.

To Kerry's surprise, Gladdy was counting money out into the landlady's open palm.

"Well, what are you gawkin' at?" she demanded as soon as she had marched back to the rig. "Get out and come in."

"How did you do it?" the lad Gus asked, obviously awed. "That's for men only."

Gladdy only sniffed. Kerry refrained from asking at the moment, but Gladdy could see the question in her eyes. When Gus opened the tailgate and began carrying their bags toward the open front door, Gladdy explained.

"I offered to work in the kitchen. She's short of help right now. That way, we can have the hired girl's room on the third floor. I don't imagine you'll refuse the lodgings, will you?" Gladdy gave Kerry a keen look.

"Not at all," Kerry said quickly, remembering her roots and the boarding house of her early years. Life had made a circle, it seemed.

As she paid off the young man, Kerry asked, "Gus . . . do you know the community of Bliss?"

"Heard of it—it's east a' here about nine miles."

"Would you be available to take me out there say, day after tomorrow? In," she added hastily, "a buggy?"

"Could," Gus answered, laconically. "Will, too, if you say so."

Arrangements were settled, drayage costs paid, and Kerry followed Gladdy toward the boarding house and a climb of two long flights of stairs to the small room under the eaves. Here Gladdy was already making her "nest," removing her hat and gloves, opening bags, laying out certain items, preparing to wash in the enamel basin that was all, obviously, a hired girl rated. Having been a "hired girl," most of her life, Gladdy was right at home.

"Not bad," Gladdy said, "considering."

"Considering?"

"Considering that I have gone back into servitude." And Gladdy made a small grimace.

"I paid Mrs. Pilgrim for a week's rent and for two meals a day during that period. I'll work out the rest. You can pay me your share—in cash." Gladdy was a sharp businesswoman. "It's nice and clean, at any rate. And I'm used to the climb, you may remember. . . ."

Kerry was paying no attention to her traveling companion and roommate; rather, she stepped to the low window, bent, and peered out. The window faced east. Out there, about nine miles away, was a false-hearted blackguard, unaware of the fate that awaited him.

"First step accomplished," she said half aloud, with satisfaction. "Step number two coming up day after tomorrow. It shouldn't take more than six or seven steps, and it will be *fait accompli*. Connor Dougal, enjoy your last few carefree days!"

Aside from Gladdy's chores, which dealt mainly with the preparation and serving of meals, Kerry and Gladdy were free, the day following their arrival, to get themselves and their clothes in order. Rinsing her hair for the third time, Kerry remarked, "I feel like I'll never get all the smoke out! Some of those men in that car smoked like chimneys. Ugh! And any time anyone opened a window to try and get fresh air—"

"Or throw up!"

"—smoke from the engine came in, even cinders."

"We wiped dirty smudges from our faces more than once."

"Yes, and our handkerchiefs may never be white again. Have you talked with Mrs. Pilgrim about using her tubs and lines and doing some laundry?"

"It's a good thing water is abundant; this is a land of waters— blue, blue waters. You've used enough of it on your hair alone to bring on a drought! Yes, I've made arrangements with our land-lady, and when I finish my morning chores tomorrow, I'll do up our laundry while you take yourself off to this . . . place of Bliss."

"If there's one thing it's not," Kerry said darkly, "it's blissful. At least as far as I'm concerned. I don't expect to get any fun out of the ordeal. But satisfaction? You can be sure of it!"

Then, like an orator breaking into impassioned speech, she delivered feelingly, "'What indignation, yea, what fear, yea, what vehement desire, yea, what zeal, yea, what revenge!'"

Gladdy's reaction surprised both of them. Not a church girl by any means, still Gladdy said, uneasily, "Are you sure you always quote these amazing verses at the proper time and give them the proper meaning?"

"They're just words, Gladdy, wonderfully expressive words, nothing more."

"I suppose so," Gladdy said. "Well," she continued eventually, "how will you go about this vengeance? Travel to Bliss, ask for this Connor Dougal, and go confront him? And then what?"

"I'd like to smite him hip and thigh, but I suppose that wouldn't do. I'm not big enough for one thing. Secondly, it would be over too soon. No. That man," she brooded, "is going to suffer."

Gladdy sighed. Now that they were here and it was all so beautiful, so unspoiled by man, it did seem a shame to sully it.

"First of all," Kerry said, "I'll find a place in Bliss where we can board for a while, if that's possible in such a small burg. We'll move out there, and then take it day by day."

Making their plans, the girls took turns combing out each other's curls: Kerry's still thick and dark and curly, worn tidily and fashionably up but always prone to small curls slipping out of control and ringing a face that even in early adulthood retained a certain pixielike quality; Gladdy's still bushlike, curly as frazzled wool from a lamb's back and violently red, an unusual head of hair that got fascinated attention wherever she went. Now, freshly washed, it sprang up like a tumbleweed and heartily resisted every effort to tame it.

"Leave it be," Gladdy said eventually with resignation. "I'm doomed to go through life looking like a mop-head. It's a cross to be born."

For an hour that afternoon the girls wandered over the town and were pleased to find several general stores, at least two hotels, a druggist, a couple of hardware stores, most all of them located on River Street. There were other stores specializing in novelties; there was a boot and shoe store in combination with a furniture store; there were two dentists, a watchmaker, four lawyers, sign painters, several schools, a newspaper office, sawmill, flour mill, and more.

The "Palace Saloon of the North West," known to local citizens as "Woodbine Billiard Parlour," invited all to "come where the woodbine twineth and the whangdoode mourneth for her young." Interest greatly piqued, still the girls scurried past the place of entertainment, which they were certain would not have been given a stamp of approval by Aunt Charlotte. Even here, decency and order must prevail.

At the appointed time, Gus pulled up to the boarding house in a shiny one-horse phaeton. The rig was their best, he solemnly informed Kerry as she prepared to step aboard. She could have told him that it was "hung very low, the bottom step being but fifteen inches from the ground." She could have pointed out its "black and gleaming body," its gear "dark Brewster green with suitable gold stripe."

Being Kerry, she couldn't refrain, finally, from "This phaeton comes with 'whip socket, Brussels carpet, anti-rattlers, and shafts.'"

Gus was indignant. Any blind man would know it came with a whip socket and shafts! But the anti-rattlers and Brussels carpet? He was impressed in spite of himself and slid Kerry a speculative glance out of the corner of his eye, then said cautiously, "And the horse? What can you tell me about the horse?"

"I'm ignorant about horses," Kerry admitted. "All I know is that this one is . . ."

About to identify the sex of the horse, she caught herself, colored richly, and finished lamely, "that it's red."

"Roan," he said firmly. Then, his self-confidence somewhat restored, he shook the reins, clucked in a businesslike manner, turned the rig, and they were off.

"We'll keep a good pace—a *spanking* pace," he said with aplomb, "and get there by noon. Did you bring a lunch?"

Kerry looked properly abashed. "I never thought of it," she confessed. Never before had she been so far from civilization but that services were available.

With his manhood and superiority now fully restored, Gus could afford to be kind. "You can have some of mine. Ma fixed a couple'a san'wiches and stuck in some cake. We'll get some milk offa somebody, maybe buy it at the store. That is, if Bliss has a store."

Bliss had a store. But its wonders were not revealed until Kerry had absorbed the glories of a ride in springtime bush. She was exhilarated by the fresh breeze, noting again its fragrance. Unpolluted by any act of man, sky and land and water and awakening greenery combined to produce a potpourri so distinct that it would remain forever the mark of the bush in Kerry's mind.

"I love the breeze," she rejoiced, removing her hat and allowing the wind to have free play with her hair.

"Wind—it's the most persistent element of our weather," Gus said, perhaps quoting someone wiser and better informed than he. "Even hot summer days are made pretty comfortable by the breezes we generally get. But winter—that's another story!"

"Bad, eh?"

"Below-zero weather can become almost unbearable when a strong wind blows, I can vouch for that for sure. I've had frozen cheeks, frozen nose, frozen toes. Enjoy this while you can."

And with these words of warning and admonition, Gus gave himself to other descriptions of the land, its weather, its birds, its wildlife, its sloughs sparkling and rippling in the sun and breeze.

I believe, Kerry concluded almost immediately, *that I could come to love this land, this wild land, this untamed land.*

But people were doing their best to tame it. Clearings appeared in the bush with some regularity, and the sounds of human presence and influence were heard—the chopping of an axe, the lowing of a cow, the far, faint cackle of a hen. And from time to time a man or woman crossed a farmyard, looked toward the passing rig, and waved.

"Now," Gus said eventually, "from here on I think it's called Bliss, though we're still a few miles from the town—hamlet, I guess you'd say. The district round about is also known as Bliss."

Breaking out of the enveloping curtain of green—such a fresh, new, tender green—they came directly upon a clearing with a few buildings. It appeared as if Bliss had one street only, with a few small buildings on either side of that street, on wandering lanes.

At one end of the hamlet was a building that was obviously the schoolhouse. Identified first by the teeter-totters and swings in the yard, it was made of lumber and painted white, with a row of three windows down each side; a neat, serviceable building. The only other significant thing about it was the cordwood stacked nearby, obviously awaiting a sawing day to ready logs for burning in the heater that must be tucked inside the building, below the stovepipe. Wires attached the stovepipe to the roof, anchoring it against the winter gales Gus had mentioned.

"Now what?" Gus asked, slowing the trotting horse.

Be decisive, Kerry told herself. "The general store—that's where I want to go."

Her voice may have sounded decisive, but her heart was pounding and her mouth felt dry. Finally, actually here in Bliss and on the field of battle, she felt very unsure of herself. Only grim determination to avenge Franny's death kept her going.

Alighting, Kerry entered the general store. Smelling of sawdust, leather, spices, and coffee, it had one long counter down the side and in the corner a walled-off area with a small front opening that was the post office. The beanpole of a man behind the counter looked up from serving the one woman present and watched as Kerry made her way toward him.

His head dipped. "Hello, ma'am," he said. "Name's Barnabas Peale . . . called Barn by all and sundry round about here. What can I do for you?"

Lodging—that came first. "Mr. Barn . . . Mr. Peale," Kerry began, stumbling a little. She wished she had turned toward the store's supplies first, giving herself time to come up with a sensible reason for being here.

"I'm Keren Ferne," she finally managed, "and I want . . . that is, I need to inquire about lodging. Is there a place where I . . . my companion and I, might stay for a few days?"

Barn Peale's eyes went to the phaeton just outside the door and the young man sitting in it. "Your friend, ma'am?" he asked politely, turning eyes like a sad bloodhound's her way. In them she could read reproach.

Kerry answered quickly, "Oh, not the lad in the rig. No, no. My companion is a female, as I am."

Kerry found herself blushing furiously, feeling herself so blundering, so stuttering, that it was no wonder the storekeeper's eyes remained gloomily suspicious.

"Well, now," he drawled, studying the situation thoughtfully.

"Land's sake, Barn!" The woman spoke for the first time. She too had watched Kerry's approach, watched keenly during the short conversation, and seemed to have made up her mind. "You know right well that my place is the only one that could oblige! You trying to do me out of some business?"

Barn looked sheepish. "Well, no," he began, "I was just bein' keerful—"

The woman tutted, turned toward Kerry, put out her hand, and said, "I'm Ida Figbert. Yes," she added, her eyes twinkling, "Figbert. You don't forget that once you've heard it. But you can call me Ida. What do you have in mind, dearie?"

Kerry could have kissed her, so relieved was she. Smiling gratefully, she took the work-worn hand that was extended to her in a grip that managed, in spite of calluses, to be gentle.

"My traveling companion and I," she repeated, "are interested in lodgings for a while, I don't know precisely how long—"

Barn opened his mouth as if to blurt "In *Bliss?*"

Mrs. Figbert was before him. "I have a 'stopping house' on an acre of land behind the store. 'Twas my husband, Jack, that built this store in the first place, and we lived back there, as I still do. Jack was carried off with the influenza three years ago, and I sold the store to Barnabas here and kept the house. I needed some way to have an income—I had two girls to provide for, both married now—and with no other accommodations between Duck Lake and Prince Albert, it seemed like a good idea to open a stopping house. And we do get a fair amount of traffic through here. People want to rest and clean up a bit before going on into P.A., Prince Albert, that is."

With that much information quickly imparted, Ida Figbert paused for breath, her bright eyes looking up at Kerry. If she was an advertisement of her lodgings, they must be satisfactory, for she looked content and well fed. Her clothes were of the calico, homemade vintage, and wash-worn. But clean; Aunt Charlotte would approve.

Since it seemed to be the only possibility of meeting her needs and she could see no reason to hesitate, Kerry was quick to say, "It sounds just fine, Mrs. Figbert," changing it to "Ida," at the little lady's reminder.

"My friend is in Prince Albert, and I need to get back there tonight," Kerry continued. "We could pack up and get out here in a couple of days, if that suits you."

Ida Figbert was pointedly silent while giving the interested Barn a patient look. He took the hint and shambled out of hearing, but regretfully—why anyone would want to lodge in Bliss, of all places, and for a matter of weeks, maybe longer, was a puzzle and a curiosity.

"I am sure you have your reasons, dearie," Ida said conspiratorially. "No need to spread them around. You are safe with Ida Figbert."

She counted out some money, laid it on the counter, picked up her basket, and turned to go. "See you, Barn," she called. "Come, my dear, you'll be needing your dinner, and there's no other place to get it. We can talk while we eat. You can see the room, and we can talk about prices."

Ida Figbert's entrance into the picture was so encouraging that Kerry found herself relaxing, feeling that plans would work out fine, just fine.

She was so certain of it, in fact, that as she followed this new acquaintance around back and across a grassy plot of ground, she couldn't refrain from quoting, with a definite lilt to her voice, "'The blessing of her that was ready to perish came upon me: and I caused the widow's heart to sing for joy.'"

Ida looked up with surprised eyes. "Well, yes, it makes me happy. But—her that was ready to perish?" she questioned, blinking a bit.

"Well, *him*, actually. You see . . ." and Kerry found herself once again, as in days of long ago, explaining that it was quite proper to suppose, in the Bible, that *him* included *her*.

Ida Figbert appeared a little confused by it all. Nevertheless, she rallied and said admiringly, "It's a fine Christian woman you are, it's plain to see."

"Oh, no," Kerry said quickly. "It's not that at all. You see, as a child I learned all these more or less disconnected bits of Scripture. . . ."

She faltered, unwilling to douse the approval in Ida's eyes. It was obvious she had presented herself in a way that was far from the truth. A fine Christian? Wasn't everyone? Everyone, that is, aside from lawbreakers, drunkards, and such, including that wretch Connor Dougal! Oh, he was a low, despicable person!

172

"And it's a wonderful memory you have!" Ida was compli-
menting. "Now here's my place, as you can see from the sign on
the fence."

IDA'S STOPPING PLACE, the sign read, and they opened
the gate and walked down the path to the house, around the side,
and to the stoop of a lean-to, obviously the customary entrance.
Out back was a log barn and what appeared to be a chicken coop.

Gus, following, tied the horse to the fence, opened his lunch
under a nearby poplar where, shortly, Ida brought him a mason
jar filled with milk. Thereafter, he dozed, his cap over his face.

Besides the lean-to, which was the kitchen, the main body of
the log house was divided into an area that was dining and living room combined and two small rooms that were obviously
bedrooms.

Ida bustled around making tea and serving up two bowls of
the stew that was simmering on the range along with slices of
excellent bread. She and Kerry sat at the round table in the "room"
and talked.

"Yes, you'll find stopping places here and there," she explained
in answer to Kerry's question. "You'd be surprised how eager
women are to sleep somewhere other than in the open or under
a wagon. I put the women in that room," and she pointed, "and
the men have to make do in the barn; they don't seem to mind.
But I make it plain that I want no smoking out there!

"I charge twenty-five cents per person for supper and the same
for breakfast. Folks seem to find that reasonable. Oh, and twenty-
five cents for the bed. For each person," she added. "Now you
and your friend can have that room and take your meals here,
even do your laundry and take your baths and all, for a dollar a
day. Each, that is. That seem fair to you?"

Kerry hastened to assure her that it was and that they would
take her up on her offer. "You see," she explained, thinking fast
before the inevitable question put her on the spot, "I am looking
for some property around here, an investment, you might say."
There, that would give her time to execute her revenge on Con-

nor Dougal and also explain any roaming of the area she might do, including a visit to the Dougal homestead now and again.

Ida Figbert was repeating, slowly, as though the idea were incomprehensible to her, "Invest . . . Bliss. . . ."

"Is there a better area?" Kerry asked, realizing her reason for an extended stay sounded weak and counting on Ida's love for Bliss to make the idea acceptable.

"Oh, no, none better. You'll like Bliss, I'm sure. But—are you planning on staying here permanently? Settling here?"

"Time will tell," Kerry answered airily, and silence fell.

"Well," Ida finally offered cheerily, "it'll be nice having a fine Christian like you to join in the worship at church."

"Church?" Kerry asked feebly. "I didn't see a church—"

"We worship in the schoolhouse. No use having a building sit empty over the weekend, is there? Parker Jones, our minister, will be so happy to hear you are moving in."

"Parker Jones . . . happy . . ." Kerry faltered, growing alarmed.

"I'll invite him over first thing so he can meet you. I'm sure he'll agree that you'll make a wonderful teacher for the Bible class!"

Kerry was aghast. Aunt Charlotte had always warned her that this indiscriminate quoting of Scripture would catch up with her someday. This, obviously, was the day.

"You'll be here in good time to get settled," Ida rattled on, "and go to church with us next Sunday. Won't Parker Jones be pleased! And Connor! Connor has been filling in as teacher of the adult class but admits he's green at it, having been a Christian a very brief time. You'll be in his class Sunday."

Connor Dougal teacher of a Sunday school class? All the better! *Lo,* she said to herself, *how are the mighty fallen!*

I da Figbert was disappointed, on Sunday morning, to learn that
her lodgers—newly moved in, with the help of the gangling
Gus—were not to accompany her to Sunday school.

"Oh, too bad!" she mourned. "You would be such a blessing,
Keren, what with your knowledge of Scripture. And you, too, of
course, Gladys," she added hastily. "No doubt you would con-
tribute much to us all."

"I'm afraid not," Gladdy said with a smile, as much a "hea-
then" as Kerry where spiritual things were concerned.

Though skipping the class, the girls had firm intentions of
attending the church service. There, as at no other time or place,
they would have an opportunity to meet the people of the community, Connor Dougal in particular. Ida had assured them that
barring some emergency on the homestead—the birth of a calf,
perhaps—Connor was sure to be there.

"Parker Jones, our pastor, met with him and Gregor Slovinski in Bible study every week a couple of years ago. Long winter
evenings are mighty lonely and all the more so for bachelors living by themselves, and Parker Jones wouldn't be past using it as

175

an inducement to get together. They met at either Connor's homestead, or Gregor's, or at the parsonage. They ate supper together—can't you just see the three of them clearing up and doing the dishes!—and then Parker Jones opened the Word and they talked and discussed for hours. Before winter was over, Connor and Gregor were convinced of the truth of what they were reading and studying and accepted Christ as their Savior. Isn't that wonderful?" Ida's face glowed as she reported this victory.

"Wonderful," piped Gladdy agreeably.

Kerry, tight-lipped, said nothing. As little as she knew about being a Christian, still it seemed that anyone making such a claim would never be a deceiver. Hypocrites, however, she had heard of, and Connor Dougal must be the ultimate in that hateful category. As Elihu to Job, she muttered, "the hypocrites in heart heap up wrath" and counted her wrath heaped high indeed.

"We'll come along in time for the morning church service," was what she said.

Ida tripped off alone toward the end of town and the school/church building. She carried her Bible and her quarterly and $1.40 in tithe, the amount owing from the first week's board paid by her lodgers. How happily she would drop it in the offering plate! There were times when Pastor Jones's pay was skimpy indeed. It was, she supposed, the main reason he delayed getting married. Bliss's own Molly Morrison was clearly in love with him, and he—serious, conscientious dear man that he was—put off taking the step that would give him a "helpmeet" and his congregation a queen in their parsonage. That their "parsonage" was just a small log domicile set on an acre of land donated for that purpose mattered not at all. Molly—capable, sweet, dear girl that she was—would turn the wee log house into a home, given an opportunity.

News of Kerry's and Gladdy's presence in Bliss had infiltrated the community. No one could understand why two single, apparently financially independent young women would look Bliss-ward, with the entire West beckoning. But hadn't they, the people of Bliss, had a choice also? And hadn't they made that choice the beautiful and bountiful Bliss? This generous description of Bliss was hastily amended. That it was beautiful, no one questioned, but Bliss's bounty was capricious. How the vagaries of the weather tried the soul of the homesteader! It bent their frames permanently, roughened their hands, toughened the complexions of their women, and, some years, tightened the belts of everyone dependent on the land for their very sustenance. Late June and early August frosts were not unheard of, and in the best of times the frost-free period as far north as Prince Albert was just over one hundred days. Every year was a gamble; they were all pawns to the whims of the weather.

Kerry and Gladdy, with Aunt Charlotte's guidance, had bought and packed clothing that they felt was serviceable, muted as to fashion or decoration or uniqueness. Still, they felt like peacocks among prairie chickens as they made their entrance that first Sunday morning. Perhaps it was the newness of their ensembles and the fact that neither girl felt quite natural in them; perhaps it was that, simple in cut and style though the garments were, they were cut from excellent material and sewn with great skill. Their figured moire and grosgrain skirts, though black in color, were rustle lined and velvet bound, and each featured a four-yard sweep, a width that was restrained—according to their Toronto seamstress—but of splendid proportions in the eyes of the good women of Bliss. Gladdy's jacket, of gray covert cloth and quite the finest she had ever owned, fitted her slim form perfectly, and she couldn't resist walking like a queen while wearing it. Kerry's short, flaring cape, "Havana" in color, trimmed with jet and lined with silk serge, was eye-catching. Their hats were small according to fashion but featured folded ribbons, loops of lace and plume and discreet rosettes. Looking around at the tired headgear of the Bliss women, Kerry determined to rip some of these decorations off before another Sunday rolled around.

The congregation was milling around, visiting, choosing seats, greeting one another, but all shifting and talking ceased when the girls stepped inside the door. The young men of the district, in their assigned cloakroom area, backed up out of the way until the coat hooks on the wall behind jabbed them unmercifully.

Ida Figbert bustled forward to greet them. Taking each girl by an elbow, she ushered them forward, skirting the heater that reigned majestically summer and winter, up to a double desk. Here they were introduced to the people who flocked around. Without exception they were smiled upon, their hands were clasped warmly, the few words of greeting were spoken heartily and honestly.

"Brother Jones," the happy Ida was beckoning, "come meet the newcomers."

In a dark suit already somewhat dated, white shirt with cuffs and collar beginning to show wear, the pastor of this group of believers stepped forward to smile, shake hands, and welcome Kerry and Gladdy to their midst. Not a large man, there was about Parker Jones a restraint, a neatness, a quietness of demeanor that each girl found tremendously appealing. Without trying, the man of God witnessed to the grace of God.

Taking his place at the front of the room, Parker Jones, by his very presence, commanded attention. "Let us come into the Lord's presence with thanksgiving in our hearts," he said, and he bent his head in an opening prayer.

Kerry was so enthralled with the uniqueness of the place, the gathering and the meeting, that she missed the announcement of the first hymn. It was hard to believe that in a matter of days she had been transplanted from civilization to the rudeness of the frontier. She watched with some amusement the faded little lady who played the small organ, accompanying the singers, her hips churning with vigor, driving her feet like pistons as she pumped forth the melody.

"Oh, glorious hope of perfect love!" they sang, with spirit if not with harmony:

> It lifts me up to things above;
> It bears on eagles' wings.

It gives my ravished soul a taste,
And makes me for some moments feast
With Jesus' priests and kings,
With Jesus' priests and kings.

With conviction they sang it. With full confidence they feasted with Jesus' priests and kings. In their patched, outdated Sunday best, they feasted. With their garners empty of store after a long winter, they feasted. With their cellars yielding only a few of last summer's withered potatoes, they feasted.

And Kerry, in her "Very Knobby" cape, her "Vici Kid" button shoes, and her "Sweet Creations" hat, hungered. With her purse on her arm filled with more money than these people saw in a year of hard work, she hungered. Hungered and wondered why and for what.

Was it strange then that the man of God, who had prayed earnestly and long over today's message, would take his Bible and read Luke 1:53—"'He hath filled the hungry with good things; and the rich he hath sent empty away.'"

These people, these poor people, these hungry people, God had filled with good things. Parker Jones understood it; Parker Jones described it. Parker Jones offered it—the satisfying portion in Matthew 5: "'Blessed are they which do hunger and thirst after righteousness,'" he said, "'for they shall be filled.'"

They sang, "'Fill me now, fill me now; Jesus come and fill me now. Fill me with Thy hallowed presence; Come, O come and fill me now.'" They sang, and a broken sinner made his way to the small, rough bench that had been brought in and set at the front of the room for this very purpose. It became, under his tears and prayers, an altar, and when he stood up, to the hearty "amens" of the congregation, his face was wreathed in smiles. "Jesus saves me," he proclaimed, and not a soul doubted it. Not understanding, Kerry believed him.

Saved. It was a funny word. It was a tantalizing word, a word that was to fix itself in Kerry's mind and in her heart, until the one should understand it and the other believe it.

Folks who hadn't had an opportunity to get acquainted at the opening of the service came around now, shyly for the most part, always warm and welcoming. Heads nodded agreeably, names were given, kind voices murmured words of greeting, smiles were sincere.

But when one name was spoken, all else faded away. The light from the window was blocked momentarily by a tall figure, his elbow held firmly by Ida Figbert as he was propelled forward.

"Keren . . . Gladys . . . this is Connor Dougal."

Kerry's smile stayed in place—fixed. For that she was to be ever thankful, because her heart turned to ice. All thoughts of hungering and thirsting and the need for "good things" fled in a breath; here was reality, and it wore the casual clothes that suited it so well, that spoke of a gentleman, that cried "good taste" without slavishness and that emphasized masculinity without bravado.

For a moment Kerry's eyes met Connor Dougal's. If the man's straight glance meant anything, if the pleasant smile meant anything, if the well-spoken words meant anything, here was a foe of considerable stature. Kerry was prepared for a bumbling backwoodsman, yet here was self-assurance and poise. She was prepared for a man of little wit, yet here was a keen-eyed, thoughtful man; prepared for an oaf who could entertain himself at a woman's expense without concern, yet here was a man of some charm and the grace not to emphasize it.

Putting out her gloved hand, Kerry was surprised to have it clasped—swallowed—in a hand that was accustomed to hard work, but understood courtesy. Here was a voice with some culture; the introduction was acknowledged in manner suited to the finest drawing room.

Ah, she said to herself, *but this man is clever. It will make winning, and the working at it, all the more stimulating.* Something in her heart thrilled at the quality of the man and the challenge he presented. She hadn't guessed it would be an exciting game as well as a satisfactory one. Seeing his masculinity, his demeanor, she reveled in the victory that would bring him down. For, looking around, she knew her competition was nonexistent. She was counting heavily on the fact that this man was of an age to want . . . need, a wife, and here she appeared as though out of the blue, perhaps—would he believe?—an answer to prayer!

"Miss Ferne," someone was saying, a someone with midnight black hair almost as uncontrollable as Gladdy's, "I'd like to invite you and your friend to take Sunday dinner with us. We're always prepared for a full table. Reverend Jones—Parker, that is—usually eats with us every Sunday noon, as well as others. It would give us an opportunity to get acquainted. And perhaps we can help you in your search for . . . a homestead, is it? Ida has shared with us that much of your purpose here in Bliss."

About to refuse the invitation, Kerry noticed that Connor Dougal was making his way out of the room with Parker Jones, and she was struck by the realization that he was to be included in the invitation. When better to begin her campaign? To warm up to him innocently, in good company, to flirt discreetly, and do it all this first day! With luck Franny would be avenged and she and Gladdy out of here before snowfall.

"Why, thank you," she said to the young woman, a little older than she, a little taller, and of vivid coloring. "Molly Morrison," the pleasant speaker was saying by means of introduction.

Molly Morrison. Ah, Parker Jones's intended, or so Ida Figbert had hoped and had relayed to Kerry. She would be a good match for the minister. Well-spoken, lovely, she would grace a parsonage whether in downtown Toronto or backwoods Saskatchewan.

"I can't speak for Gladdy—Gladys, that is," Kerry said. But Gladdy, who was chatting easily with new friends, was quick to accept, and so the arrangements were made.

Kerry and Gladdy rode in the Morrison wagon with Molly's father and mother, Angus and Mary, while Molly and Parker Jones rode with Molly's brother Cameron and his soon-to-be wife Margo. Following were two buggies with the additional guests, Connor Dougal and Gregor Slovinski. Angus Morrison, a gray-haired, large and sturdy Scot, explained again to the girls how Connor and Gregor had been discipled personally by Parker Jones and what a joy it was to see these rugged men of the north bow to the plans and purposes of God in their lives.

Keeping her plan in mind, and its inevitable outcome of humiliation and embarrassment for Connor Dougal when he was unmasked, Kerry could almost feel regret for the sake of these good people who so admired the false-hearted man in their midst. But she hardened herself immediately. When the community learned what a beast he had been, how cruelly careless of another's feelings, they would realize she had no choice. This false reputation that the man was building for himself, how frail it was, after all.

He buildeth his house as a moth, Kerry said to herself with bitter satisfaction, and she savored the Scripture and the thought.

There was one more member of the family to meet: Kezzie Skye, well-loved grandmother whom they all called "Mam." Herself a new Christian, her joy fairly radiated from her, her joy and her peace. Kerry sensed a story here and hoped her stay would be long enough to include the hearing of it.

Mam was too frail to suffer the jouncing trip to church but well enough to keep the range stocked with wood, and when the group reached home the oven dinner was done to perfection. Kerry, with some embarrassment, realized how little she knew of housework, having lived "upstairs" at Maxwell Manor and having received no training of any sort in her earlier years in lodgings with her father.

Gladdy, however, was in her element and busied herself immediately, setting the table, making gravy, slicing bread. What a wife she would make for some pioneer, Kerry thought with admiration. What would become of Gladdy when Kerry left? It would require some serious consideration on Kerry's part, for the frazzle-headed young woman was dear to her.

Seated at the vast table, Kerry and Gladdy bowed their heads over a meal for the first time in their lives and felt the food was all the better for the blessing Angus Morrison pronounced and the thanks he expressed.

Kerry found herself seated next to Connor Dougal, and conversation, due to his easy persistence, flowed naturally.

"I, too, came across country but much more uncomfortably, I imagine. You see, I've been here over the three years necessary to prove up my land, and that means I made the trip before the railway came through. I came by prairie schooner. Now Gregor," and Connor included the man who sat across the table and who smiled as he listened, "hasn't been here as long as I have. He went farther north first, to the Peace River country. His homestead backs on mine—"

"Your homestead backs on mine," Gregor said peaceably with a thick accent.

Everyone laughed as though at an old joke, and Connor amended, "We're back-to-back."

"Lissen, Miss Kerry," the big man said seriously, leaning across the table, "'ve understan' you may be lookin' at property here in Bliss. Yah?"

Kerry hesitated. Strange, how difficult it was to talk sensibly about her nefarious plan while she was surrounded by these people, these people who so freely offered friendship and fellowship. The Scripture *There were giants in the earth in those days* came to mind, and she felt it suited the men and women of the bush—of average size physically but of indomitable will and unquenchable determination. But qualms could not be countenanced! Buying or at least looking at property was indeed the scheme she had mentioned as a way of explaining her purpose in the community, and she would pursue it now.

"Yes, that's right," she answered, confirming her half-formed plan. "I've had some funds willed to me, and I feel this may be a good investment. But I'm in no hurry; we're well and comfortably settled at the stopping place, and I can take my time about any decision. Do you know of any homestead that's for sale?"

Gregor Slovinski cleared his throat, shuffled his feet, and spoke after a moment's hesitation.

"I don' know if it iss goot for me to say, but d' young man Tutley Baldwin iss vanting to sell his half of dat homestead. Perhaps ve shouldn't talk aboud it anywhere else. I'm not sure his mudder knows."

But apparently the folks at the table had suspicioned this, and no one looked too surprised.

"If you're interested, Kerry, it would be worth looking into," Angus Morrison said. "But, Gregor, it was my impression you wanted additional land yourself."

"I been tinkin' aboud it," the massive man said, his beard and hair bright in a ray of sunlight coming through the window, "but dere are problems in it for me dat might not exist for a voman. Vat you tink?" Gregor looked around the circle questioningly.

"You're right," several murmured. "Yes, it would be better if a woman partnered with Della," said another.

"Well, I'll look into it," Kerry said. "Now, Connor," they were all on a first-name basis by now, "tell me about Bliss and why I should consider making this area my home. If indeed I should."

It was a subject dear to the man's heart, obviously, and he was an excellent example of the contentment Bliss could give. Contentment and satisfaction, the satisfaction that comes with hard work well done. The satisfaction that comes with taking something that is nothing and transforming it into something worthwhile.

When the rhubarb pie smothered in thick cream had been served and devoured, when Mam and Mary, never strong since the shipboard birth of her child years before, had been put down for naps, the table was cleared, the dishes done, and the farm toured, the day drew toward evening and chore time.

"I'll take the girls home," Connor offered, and he did so, offering further opportunity for Kerry to continue her interested questions, to feign fascination with Connor's remarks, to glance at him from under half-lowered eyelashes and, finally, to grant him a lingering handclasp and a tantalizingly meaningful farewell at the stopping place gate. Gladdy sat, during the ride, as one hypnotized, eyes fixed on the far horizon, saying little.

Walking from the gate to the door, Kerry turned to wave a handkerchief of farewell to the man Connor Dougal who was, indeed, watching. With a small smile of satisfaction she turned to Gladdy's face, expressionless in the dimming light.

"Well?" she asked.

"Well, what?"

"Well, how did it go, of course?" she asked a trifle impatiently.

"Charmingly, just charmingly," a low-voiced Gladdy said. "And perfectly hateful!"

M a," Dudley began, his use of the shortened title an indication of the courage he was mustering.

Della turned from the dishpan, her eyes disapproving. But
Dudley, holding on to his small victory, kept his eyes on a point
somewhere over her shoulder. This was, after all, new ground.

"Sit down, Mum," he said, softening a little, knowing full well
the blow he was about to give his mother would have her reeling. It was a mark of his determination and his new and developing manhood that made such a confrontation possible at all.
But could he carry it through?

I have to! he thought desperately, as though struggling for his
breath, perhaps his very life.

"Sit down?" Della asked, wary now.

"Yes, please."

Della dried her hands on her apron and sat, leaning her elbows
on the table's oilcloth and fixing suspicious eyes on her son. Dudley wasn't proving to be as amenable as she had hoped. What was
he up to? Marriage? He was far too young—not yet twenty—

and, hopefully, she could bludgeon, by force of will, such an impractical idea out of his head!

"Those young women that have just arrived in Bliss—" he began.

For a moment Della was indeed alarmed. Marriage with one of these outsiders? Totally ridiculous. Then, certain that they weren't fools, she breathed more easily.

"What about them?"

"They, or at least one of them, is interested in investing in property—"

"In Bliss?"

Dudley sighed. "And Ma . . . I'm going to go talk to her about my half of the homestead."

Della's eyes were as large as sauce dishes. "What?"

"It's mine to dispose of any way I want," Dudley managed, before his mother's full wrath descended in sound and fury on his senses.

Dudley closed his eyes, gripped his hands, bowed his head, and let the waves of vituperation flow over him. When it seemed Della was out of breath, he spoke.

"I'll thank you to be decent to her when she comes—"

"Comes? Here? Are you totally out of your mind?"

"It won't do any good to go on about it, Ma. I've made up my mind. I'm getting out of here, starting somewhere else. And I'm excited about it, Ma. Surely I deserve my chance, just as Pa did. If it isn't this girl, someone else will come along sooner or later, maybe buy me out, maybe work the farm and send me part of the proceeds when harvest is done. It's bound to happen. At any rate, Ma, I'm going to town now and see if this Keren Ferne will come and look the situation over."

"Bring her!" Della said briefly. "Go on, bring her. We'll see, won't we?" She rose to her feet, went back to her dishpan, thrust in her hands, adding, "See this dishwater? That young miss never touched dishwater! Go tell her all about it—or get her, and I'll tell her!"

Very shortly, Dudley was knocking at the Figbert door. When Ida opened it, she heard with surprise the young man Dudley's inquiry. "Is the young lady here who was at church yesterday? The one who mentioned being interested in a place?"

"That'd be Miss Ferne. Yes, she's here. Come on in, Dudley."

Ida led the way to the "room" and said, "Keren, Gladys—" and the girls looked up from the letters they were writing. "This is Dudley Baldwin. I guess he wants to talk to you about something." And with that, Ida went back to her work in the kitchen.

"Sit down, Mr. Baldwin," Kerry said kindly.

"Dudley—it's Dudley, ma'am." Dudley called her ma'am though she wasn't as old as he; but to him there was something regal about her that called forth this title of respect. "I heard about you being interested in an investment in Bliss. I have property I want to sell, ma'am. It's my pa's homestead, a quarter section about two miles from town. Buildings are all up, crop's in, things are going pretty well as far as I can see."

"Why do you wish to sell?" Kerry asked, as if she were accustomed to buying property, and making suitable inquiries of this person that was not much older than she, but who was, she supposed, infinitely more business-wise.

"Time for me to move on, ma'am," Dudley explained, as if he were accustomed to selling property and moving on.

"I see. Mmmmm," Kerry hmmmed blankly. Where to go from here in this spurious scheme to further her plans? "I see," she repeated.

"Perhaps," Gladdy interjected quietly, having had her say regarding Kerry's revengeful attitude and wishing only to get it over and done with and herself away from Bliss, "we should see this property. Is that what you have in mind, Mr.—that is, Dudley?"

"Yes, ma'am." Dudley turned his attention to the other young miss in the room and found himself fascinated. First by the bluest eyes he had ever seen, including Kezzie Skye's, and then by the most amazing hair anyone could imagine. He was tongue-tied before such glories.

"Well then," Gladdy said as naturally as she could under such a gaze, "let us put on our hats and accompany the man."

Man. Dudley's status, until now bordering on change and in a state of flux—adolescent one moment, adult the next—made a dramatic leap. Never again, forever, would Dudley be considered anything but the man he had just been proclaimed. As though knighted by the queen herself, the mantle of adulthood settled on him, felt itself comfortable, and routed forever the youth who had been in uneasy residence.

Kerry supposed, having deliberately gotten herself into this fix, that she should carry through. Rising, she and Gladdy prepared themselves for the buggy ride and soon were on their way.

"I need to explain," Dudley said as they approached what appeared to be a well-developed working farm, "that only half the farm is mine. The other half belongs to my mother. She might, when she sees I'm really getting rid of my share, consider letting her half go, too."

Before Kerry had time to assimilate what this might mean, they were helped down and ushered into the whitewashed log house, small but adequate and clearly as neat as a pin.

"Mother," Dudley said, "this is Miss Keren Ferne. And this—Gladdy McBean." Why he hadn't said "Gladys" he didn't understand; it was as though he had already committed himself to intimacy with this glorious creature.

"Miss Ferne is interested in looking at the place, with an eye to investing. In my half of the farm, Mother, unless you would consider letting your half go. I know," he finished doggedly, his eyes fixing his mother's with a surprising firmness, "your folks back in Iowa write that they would love to have you there with them now that Pa's gone."

Della snorted most indelicately. "You're out of your mind, young lady, if you imagine you can survive the realities of the bush. This is no play-pretty and no tea party for children!"

Kerry's first reaction was one of distaste for the ill-bred response of the woman. The second was a feeling of relief. *Ah,* she thought, *here's a woman who is going to make it difficult, even impossible, to do any business. Thank goodness!* Not really wanting to carry out her avowed purpose, Kerry was happy for the means of escape.

Nevertheless, the charade should be carried out. "If you'll lead on, Mr. Baldwin," she said clearly, while Della glowered in the background, "I'll be happy to consider what you have to offer." Following a stiff-backed Dudley, she glanced at the house, went through the barns, listened to his description of the acres under cultivation, and more.

The ride back to the stopping place was a quiet one. Getting out of the rig and turning toward the house, Kerry felt that she should be definite about the outcome of the visit to the farm, thus bringing to an end any false hopes Dudley might be harboring.

"I'm afraid it's not quite what I had in mind," she offered, halting but definite.

If she had been concerned for Dudley's reaction, she changed her mind when she realized he was paying her little or no attention. Dudley's eyes were fixed, in what could only be described as awe, on Gladdy. She, in turn, was absorbed with staightening her windblown clothing. Intent on her disarranged attire, Gladdy failed to see Dudley's hand as it reached toward her hesitantly, tentatively, lightly touching the hair that had blossomed out of her hat into a tumble of curl and color. Quickly he pulled back when she turned and lifted her head.

But Kerry saw.

With Gladdy passing on into the house and Dudley standing beside the rig, his cap in his hands, his face a study—if ever love was seen to bud and blossom, Kerry had a ringside seat.

With a handshake and a word of thanks to Dudley, she followed Gladdy with this certain realization: There is no need to worry about her when I leave. Her future is outside, standing dumbstruck beside a worn buggy, a cap twisting in his hands, a light as of the dawning on his thin face.

190

"Well, what do you know," she murmured.

"I know," Gladdy said crisply, "that his mother is not about to sell. If that man is set on getting away and starting over, he'll have to do it independently. And I believe," she added thoughtfully, "he's just the man to do it. Peace River country? Sounds like heaven, the way he says it."

———

As soon as chores were over, Dudley washed himself, combed his hair, put his cap on his head, and prepared to leave the house.

"And where do you think you're going?" Della asked, her hands once again in the ever-familiar dishwater, this time washing the milk pail and strainer.

"Just out, Mum. I won't be too late." With that, the new Dudley went out quietly and walked down the road toward Gregor Slovinski's place, even finding the peace of mind to whistle a bit as he went, dreaming a new dream.

"Hello, dere," Gregor greeted. "Yust the fella I vas hoping to see. Come on in."

Dudley stepped past the big man and felt himself—at a little less than six feet to Gregor's six-foot-eight—almost insignificant in comparison. Only his newfound self-confidence, so magically given and so treasured, kept him from feeling like a kitten in the presence of a wild boar. Gregor's speech, however, was gentle enough, rather like the purr of a great cat, rumbling in his vast chest and issuing out from some hidden source in the lionlike mane of beard and hair, which seemed all of a piece.

Once seated, Dudley regained his threatened composure; it took courage to pursue his course of action, with so many odds against him.

"Vell, vas iss?" Gregor resonated, at the identical time Dudley was saying, "What did you want to see me about?" Both stopped in unison, both laughed heartily.

"You first," Gregor commanded, and when Gregor commanded, lesser men obeyed. Dudley smiled, not intimidated, for

Gregor was truly a gentle giant, insomuch as anyone knew. Thus far. There was always the fearsome possibility that Gregor might decide to try out that magnificent strength, and then what?

"I'm here, Gregor," Dudley began, and he couldn't keep a trace of desperation from his voice, "to ask if you've come to any conclusion about taking over my land—buying, or if that's out of the question, working it on shares. I just need enough cash to—" Dudley paused, swallowed, and plunged in, "to get me away from here. I want to start out on my own. I think you already know that. Surely you can understand, Gregor. You had that chance, my pa had that chance, Connor had that chance. It isn't as if there's not plenty of wilderness yet, calling out for homesteaders. I want to be one of them!"

Dudley breathed deeply, calming himself. "Now then," he said, "you know what I have on my mind. Now tell me—what did you want to see me about?"

"Da same ting," Gregor said, and Dudley's head lifted, his eyes searching the big man's blue ones. Blue, bright blue, but not as blue as the eyes of Gladdy McBean.

"What do you mean, Gregor?" he asked, holding his breath. Good news could be his undoing, so accustomed had he become, these last three years, to life's harsh blows and painful disappointments. He braced himself but whether against bad news or for good news was unclear.

"I'm tinking," Gregor continued, "dat I vill say yah! How vould dat be, Tutley?"

"Tutley" was holding onto his newly acquired manhood with all his might and main. But inside he was jigging a wild fandango of pure joy. His face must have reflected his relief, for Gregor's broad, whiskery face took on a look of compassion.

"Yah," he said, "ve vill work it oud. You can be on your vay long before da snow, in time to find someblace and get seddled before vinter."

The remainder of the evening was spent working out plans, writing up an agreement, which Gregor pretended to understand

and which he signed trustingly, and deciding how and when the news should be broken to Dudley's mother.

"Don' you vorry none aboud her," Gregor said earnestly. "I'll see dat she don' need anyting, like vood and vater, and all dat stuff. Maybe it vill do her good to be alone, yah? It mide make a new voman of her." And Gregor roared a great laugh at his own expense, but it was not an unkind laugh, and Dudley felt . . . knew he was leaving his mother in good and capable hands.

Part of the arrangement was that Dudley would go to the Peace River country and look over Gregor's land there. If he liked it, further arrangements could be made that included a trade of property. Dudley was quite confident that he would find exactly what he wanted at the wild and rugged Peace River. His joy, as he walked home, was boundless.

One thing remained. Dudley, in the grip of a newfound confidence—which had been confirmed beyond his wildest dreams in his talk with Gregor—could believe that it, too, would work out.

But before that—his mother had to be faced.

<hr />

Della raged, Della roared, Della wept, Della flung herself about. Della begged. It was almost more than Dudley could take. But somehow, a quiet resolve had settled into his innermost being. It was, in fact, as though a lifeline had been flung to him and, threatened with drowning, he clung to it as though life itself were at stake. And perhaps it was. It was slow death for all his dreams were he to stay in Bliss, subject to his mother's demands and commands. He came from each session, each scene, shaken and trembling but resolute, and he went ahead with his plans.

As for the wily Gregor, he avoided confronting Della, putting it off until she should have accepted the deal as done. When finally he met her as she came from the chicken house and he from the barn, her face froze into a mask of—what? Scorn? Dismay? Fury? All that, he supposed.

And yet, being Gregor, he was able to doff his worn, tweedy cap, hold it against his broad chest, and say softly, "Good day, Missus. Did you know dere is a nest in da haymow? I heard a chiggen cackling up dere."

With a sniff Della's chin went up, and she swept past him, or tried to. With her exaggerated flounce, her skirt snagged on the wire of the chicken run. Looking down at it, her hands engaged in hefting the egg basket, she was indecisive, for the moment, about how to proceed.

With the agility and grace of movement that some large men demonstrate, Gregor stepped around her, bent his big frame, and worked the material free. If he was more deliberate than was necessary, and if he was filled with the pure joy of having her thus at the mercy of circumstances, no one was there to judge. Della may have suspected it, however, for her face grew redder and redder, and her voice spluttered when, free at last, she managed "Thank you, I'm sure!" and fled the scene. About halfway to the house she seemed to collect herself, hesitated, and swerved toward the barn and the aforementioned nest in the mow.

Behind her, Gregor watched in silence, smiling ever so slightly when she made the decision to heed what he had told her. It was a small beginning.

⌁

At the stopping place, Ida Figbert knocked on the bedroom door and called, "Gladys, someone to see you."

To Gladdy's surprise and to the confirming of Kerry's suspicions, it was Dudley Baldwin. Standing just inside the kitchen door, cap in hand, he had eyes only for Gladdy McBean.

"Dudley!" she said, surprised. "Was it Kerry you wanted to see?"

"No, ma'am, that is, Gladdy. I wonder if you'd do me the honor," and his pale, thin face flared red, "of taking a ride with me."

"Me, Dudley? Are you sure you mean me?"

The more she questioned, the more certain he became. "You, ma'am, that is, Gladdy," he repeated, his voice firming remarkably.

"Ride?" she said, amazingly thickheaded. "Ride . . . where?"

"Just ride," Dudley said. "You know—ride out together."

If Gladdy hadn't caught on before, the level, half bold look Dudley fixed on her should have informed her. And did, eventually.

When at last she had a glimmer of light on the subject of "riding out" (first cousin to "stepping out," she supposed), her cheeks flamed. She breathed a faint "Just a minute" and escaped.

Back in their room, with the curious eyes of Kerry fixed on her blushing face, she stammered, "He . . . Dudley, wants me to take a ride with him! Isn't that funny? He wants to go out . . . riding with me!" And she tried to laugh but managed only tears.

Kerry hastened to put her arms around her, and together they wept a little and eventually laughed a little, but at themselves.

"Silly goose that you are," Kerry said tenderly. "And why wouldn't he? Here, tidy your hair and put your hat on. Though I have an idea he'd just as soon you left your hair loose and free."

With these confusing words in her ears, Gladdy was helped out of the room by Kerry, herded toward the door and outside. Kerry watched through the window as Dudley helped her into the rig, took his place beside her, called "Hup" in a no-nonsense voice, flourished the reins, and curveted off down the road.

◦———◦

Although what happened on that ride was too personal and too precious to share in its entirety, Kerry and Gladdy were good enough friends for the bare bones to be told. Dudley had driven to a spot beside a lake of blue, blue waters, and with the warm spring sun beating down and the blessing of birdsong raining upon them from all sides, had laid bare his heart.

He told her of his plans to move, to leave Bliss for the wilderness beyond. He told her enough about his mother for her to grasp his need and his desperation. He shared his dream of starting over as a homesteader in a new place; he described the probable difficulties of such a move.

"I'm young," he said, "but no younger than thousands of men before me. I'm not green, as many have been, having helped on the farm all my life. I'm not heading out into the unknown, exactly." And he told her of Gregor's tract in the north, and she heard again the singing words "Peace River country."

"This is the hard part," he told her, but with enough courage to turn toward her and look her in the eye. Deliberately, he continued, but humbly. "I don't want to go alone. A man needs a wife. I wonder if you'd dare take a chance on me, Gladdy McBean, and come with me. I know it seems short notice, but others do it and make it work. I can't promise much, but I can promise I'll be good to you and look after you the best I can. And . . . I think . . . I think I can promise to love you . . . forever."

The neglected child who hadn't felt loved since she left the slums of London and perhaps not then, the little maid who once said she never saw any eligible men except delivery boys, the young woman who had thrown security away for the dangers of the West and an unknown future—should she hesitate now that she was offered a home of her own, a future to work toward, and a love for all time?

Dudley, straight and strong and purposeful, was waiting for an answer. "What do you say, Gladdy McBean?"

Most of this Gladdy relayed to her friend Kerry, in bits and pieces, and between tears and laughter.

"And of course you said—" Kerry prompted at the culmination of this story of the wooing of Gladdy McBean.

"I didn't have to say a word," Gladdy said, rosy-cheeked. "I guess my face spoke for me."

The truth of the matter was that it had indeed spoken volumes, and an elated Dudley had pressed those same rosy-hued cheeks into his rough shirt, looking blindly over Gladdy's dear head at his future, a future that, for the first time, had all the earmarks of his dreams and more. Bending his head, he kissed her, and it was as sweet to both of them as the seeking honeybees around them could have desired.

And Kerry—would her plans and schemes bring the same light of joy and satisfaction into her eyes? She wondered. For the first time, she wondered.

The remainder of the week was marked by an occurrence of great import to Kerry's plans; it came about quite naturally. Almost as if it were meant to be, she exulted, and furthering tremendously her scheme to cultivate, capture, and unmask Connor Dougal.

Because some of their luggage had been left in Prince Albert until such time as Kerry felt their stay in Bliss should be permanent enough to warrant carting it out, there were various items she and Gladdy lacked. Needing stationery to continue her written saga of the trip to Aunt Charlotte—who had demanded of her a promise to keep faithfully in touch—Kerry had put on her hat and gloves, picked up her purse, and turned her well-shod feet toward the Bliss store.

How magnificent the sky, how wide and wild the land—*"He stretcheth out the north over the empty place."* And here was she, along with a few other puny mortals, nothing more than an ant for significance in the vastness of God's creation. Shaking off the strange, even frightening, revelation, she strode with purpose toward the store. Ants indeed!

Entering the building, she came from an inner place of hushed reverence and unusual introspection to the restless scurryings to and fro of people harried by the need to store up garner. And more—to store it while the sun shone and the snow and cold had reluctantly withdrawn for a time. Soon they would roar back, recharged and ferocious and bent on mischief.

"Hello, Miss Ferne."

"Good morning, Miss Ferne."

It seemed the shoppers had all been in the church service and knew her, though she found it difficult to recall a single face. And then that one face came into her line of vision, and a remembered voice spoke, "Hello again, Kerry."

It was Connor Dougal. Kerry could only explain her bounding pulse to the satisfaction of coming face-to-face with her opponent.

And what a worthy opponent he was! The little picture he had sent Franny, which was even now tucked in the purse she carried, hadn't done him justice. It hadn't shown how tall he was and had only hinted at the broadness of his shoulders; it hadn't revealed the glints in his earth-colored hair or the depth in his gray eyes; it hadn't caught him smiling or captured the warmth of his voice. It had been a colorless likeness and not a live, breathing, vigorous male creature. Half panicky at her turn of thoughts, Kerry recognized the trap into which she had been enticed—*"It bindeth me about as the collar of my coat"*—and made an attempt at rational thinking.

"Connor! What brings you to town on a busy weekday morning?" she asked and found it not difficult to pretend interest, not impossible to smile fetchingly, though unskilled in the art.

"I'm on my way to Prince Albert, actually. Just stopped for mail; thought reading it might shorten the long miles for me. For a few moments I can lose myself to the bush and be back home in Scotland with the family gathered round."

"Yes, of course," she said, her mind working furiously. She would go with him! What an opportunity; perhaps a God-given opportunity, though she knew little or nothing of prayer and wasn't certain that God cared one way or another about her quest for revenge. If He did, He probably wished her well and the hypocrite Connor, his comeuppance.

"Do you suppose," she said, with her sweetest smile, "that I could go with you? Gladdy and I left some of our baggage there because at the time we were not certain just how long we'd be in Bliss. Now that it looks as if we'll be here at least for a while longer—"

"I say," Connor Dougal interrupted, "you're not thinking of leaving us any time soon, are you? You haven't really experienced bush life, and we haven't had a chance to get acquainted. There's the picnic coming up and a few things that might be interesting, even if it is the busy time of the year."

"I'll stay, of course, if it is . . . important enough to do so." And Kerry, to her own shame, lifted a wide-eyed look—which she intended to contain a hidden message—toward the man whom she in her heart blamed for Franny's death, and for whom she had no other plans than to make him pay.

"We'll have to see that there is such a reason," Connor Dougal replied, quietly and quite seriously, and Kerry's already misbehaving heart seemed to skip a beat. How well her plan was working! "And a trip to Prince Albert might be the place to start," Connor concluded.

How simple it was, after all! Here, in the bush, where women were as scarce as hen's teeth, the whole process of getting acquainted—doing it by speaking stilted phrases, going through the motions of Victorian protocol and chaperoned all the while—was dispensed with. Men, like this rugged individual standing before her now, went to the heart of the matter at hand. With chores to do daily and the crop to be brought in before winter, there was no time for dallying. People either made up their mind and married or struggled on alone. Connor Dougal, if he were interested, would waste no time and would expect no coy teasing about the matter. All the better for her plan to be finalized, over and done with before more time was wasted.

All these thoughts raced through her mind as the brief interchange of conversation took place. In spite of heightened color and quickened breath, *things are going nicely,* Kerry assured herself and turned to go briefly to the stopping place.

"I'm going to Prince Albert with—you know who!" she advised the questioning Gladdy, to be rewarded by a somber look and a shake of the tousled head.

Gladdy had made herself abundantly clear on the subject of revenge. "Forgive and forget," had been her advice. "The business of living here in the bush is serious; there's no time and no energy to waste on something that can't be helped or changed." And Kerry had frowned.

"Get your ticket," Gladdy advised now, "and make your plans to leave. If my wedding is delaying you, there's no need. It will come off as planned, and Dudley and I will be on our way before summer is over."

Kerry's eyes glittered. "No way am I leaving until that man knows what he did and how Franny and all of us suffered. No. He's going to suffer accordingly, and then and only then will I leave."

"And leave happily, I suppose?" Gladdy said. "Leave ruin behind you and be happy about it? Forget it, Kerry, I implore you!"

"You're happy. Let me be happy in my own way," Kerry retorted, then picked up a jacket and purse and turned to leave.

Connor was waiting in the wagon at the gate. Leaping down he helped Kerry put a foot on the hub of the wheel, then swing herself up and over and into the rig. Side by side they sat on the spring seat, riding through scenery as lovely as one might dream up but with the fragrance of the bush to add reality.

"I don't believe one has a sense of smell in dreams," Kerry remarked, drawing into her lungs the remarkable mix of flowers, rain-drenched greenery, and much more, all contributing to the uniqueness that was the bush. "If one could bottle this fragrance and sell it, one would be a rich person."

"You've said it well," Connor Dougal replied. "I'm rich, having it to myself. But I like to think of the fragrance of the bush as the essence of milk and honey. You know the Scripture, I'm sure—'He hath brought us into this place, and hath given us this land, even a land that floweth with milk and honey.' Could anything be better than that?"

Scripture, being quoted to her? First thing she knew, he would be testifying to her. But this was no time to carp over such annoyances; this was the time to make hay while the sun shone, she thought, pleased with the bucolic observation.

Riding along with the object of her intentions, Kerry was thrilled to her toes with this golden opportunity to exploit the loneliness of this bachelor, winning for herself and for Franny a great victory.

Therefore, she said, "There is more, so much more, to this place than the fragrance. Tell me of your dreams for your place . . . for yourself."

Connor looked pensive for a moment. "My homestead is my pride and joy, I suppose you'd say. One is bound to be tremendously gratified when land that was overgrown and overrun yields to axe and sickle and grub hoe, when a field is finally planted and a crop harvested. You hold your threshed grain in the palm of your hand, and it looks like pure gold. Your first lettuce for the season, after a long winter, is as beautiful in your eyes as emeralds. Wild fruit, like pin cherries and strawberries, glows like rubies. But there, I grow maudlin in my desire to make you see the benefits and blessings of the bush. If you stayed," he added, far more serious now, "becoming a full-time resident, you'd need to rely on all the womanhood and strength of character that you have, just to stick out the winters."

"I'm sure, if the inducement were sufficient," Kerry said, trying not to speak too archly in her desire to win his attention, "no woman would mind paying the cost, whatever it might be. I'm sure I wouldn't mind. The attraction of the city seems small in comparison to," and she flung out an arm dramatically, "all this."

The trip was shortened by their interest in each other's stories. Connor listened with sympathy to Kerry's true account of her early years of deprivation, her rescue by an aunt, and the subsequent happy years. Once or twice she had to catch herself sharply from some reference that would include Franny, or Maxwell Manor, or Aunt Charlotte. She heard the account of his emigration and the hard years of back-breaking labor that had brought him to this day, a landowner and accepted part of the thriving community of Bliss.

Upon reaching Prince Albert, Kerry was dropped off at Pilgrim Boarding House for Men, where she was greeted cheerily, served tea and leftovers from the noon dinner hour, and urged to rest until time to leave. Then, with the remainder of her baggage loaded onto the wagon and the afternoon sun slipping on down toward the horizon, Kerry and Connor began the homeward trek. Happily for them, the year had begun its lengthening of days, allowing for a long evening of light in which to cover the distance home.

It was as a warm dusk settled over the bush, when the birds were muting their daytime chorus to an evening sonata, after the glorious sunset had made conversation, for a while, an interruption, that Connor became serious.

"Kerry," he said in a tone of voice she had never heard before from any man, at any time, for any reason. Ignorant as she was, and inexperienced, she recognized it for what it was.

"Yes, Connor," she said softly and explained her rapid heartbeat as anticipation for the playing of the game.

And what a game it was! Almost she could imagine it was real, that she was indeed receiving her first serious attention from a man. She found it natural to let herself revel, in the dimming light, in a sensation as of a warm, enticing, cloudy shawl wrapping itself around her, warming her in its soft webs.

And yet Connor, for all he said, left some things unsaid.

"I'm what is called a bachelor," he began seriously, yet with a half smile. "And bachelors, everyone thinks, are pathetic creatures. But I've not wanted to ask any woman to share my life until I could offer a roof, a good, substantial roof, over her head and the assurance that the worst is over. I'm ready now to settle down, raise a family, build up my farm, and enjoy to some extent the fruits of my labor. I'd be much happier enjoying them with someone." He didn't say who.

But Kerry knew. How bitterly she knew! Darling Franny had been his choice at one time! It was only with determination and self-control she kept herself from raking at that handsome countenance, screeching out the anger that smouldered in her heart toward him.

Instead, Kerry fixed her eyes—which she knew were great and dark and long-lashed, perhaps her best feature—on Connor's face as he talked, turning to face her occasionally, turning his profile at times as though some things were too intimate to share with ease.

"You must see," he continued, "that it's not possible to have a girl of your caliber, an *available* girl, come to the area, without asking yourself if she might be the one. Whether you'd have a chance."

"Connor," she said softly into the evening's hush, broken only by the creak of leather and the thud of horses' hooves, "you'd have a chance."

She could hear Connor's indrawn breath and felt him relax into the seat beside her. Only then did she realize how intensely he had been speaking.

"Well, then," he said, holding the reins with one hand and putting the other over her own clasped hands, "we'll just take it from there. We'll pray about it and take it from there."

Kerry felt a great wave of disappointment sweep over her. Surely it was because she wanted, above everything, to get this miserable experience out into the open and over. Until Connor Dougal declared love for her, the time for thrusting in the knife had not arrived.

Could the real thing be any sweeter than the remainder of the trip with his hand clasping hers, the moon rising, shedding its gentle light on the scene—two people, alone, moving through the sweet, dark night toward . . . ?

Could the real thing be any sweeter than the tender manner in which, once home, he handed her down from the wagon? Could anything offer more promise than the way his lips came down towards her, lingered, and touched themselves to her forehead? Could anything have held more promise?

"From now on," she exulted later to Gladdy, "I just have to be nice, and gentle, and make myself terribly attractive to him, and he'll be hooked and humiliated and given the heave-ho."

"But, Kerry," a sighing Gladdy replied, "you are naturally nice and gentle and attractive."

"Not to Connor Dougal, I'm not! Or at least not for long!" Kerry answered grimly and wondered why she so dreaded the destroying of his opinion of her. What did she care!

Plenty, her silly heart whispered.

I f you were a praying person," Gladdy said, with great serious-ness, "I'd get you to pray about today's excursion."

Kerry was thrown into turbulence of spirit for a moment. Never had it been said and said so baldly: *If* you were a praying person. She couldn't defend herself; Gladdy had lived with her too long for her to be defensive of her prayer practices, which, aside from "Now I lay me" as a small child, were nonexistent.

Having heard Parker Jones preach, she wondered now how she had been so presumptuous as to suppose she could make her way through the trials and temptations, pitfalls and pressures of life without prayer. And yet, when she tried to pray, she was as one stricken dumb. What did one say when approaching the great God of the universe, the God who *sitteth upon the circle of the earth, and the inhabitants thereof are as grasshoppers?* The God who *thundereth marvelously with his voice?* The Ancient of days, whose throne is *like the fiery flame, and his wheels as burning fire?*

Filled with Scriptures that stirred, troubled, and worried, Kerry had somehow overlooked those that would have comforted, guided, and encouraged.

"Gladdy," she reminded now, "you could pray for yourself, you know," and Gladdy fell into the same ruminative silence as Kerry. With all their studying and reading, something had been significantly overlooked.

"The sooner we get out of this place, the better," Kerry declared. "Your future is set, and you'll be gone soon enough. But me? I'll have to get to work with more determination. And if the outcome astonishes and dismays the people of Bliss, so be it. I'll do my best—or worst—and get myself out of here, never to be seen or heard from again."

But would she? There was something compelling about the place, this place called Bliss. Something on the inside of her called, *Don't go—you'll never find another place like it!* What a turmoil of feelings!

As for Gladdy, she was exalted to a place of pure joy. Hadn't Dudley declared his love for her, and wasn't she even now feeling an answering surge of warmth in her heart toward him? Till death do us part—it was a solemn thought and a sweet one. After years of aloneness, Gladdy *belonged*. She would dare the wilderness itself if Dudley were at her side.

Today, however, she was to go to the Baldwin homestead to help lay serious plans, to add her life savings to Dudley's funds and make lists of things to buy, things to do, things to pack.

Kerry, at a loss to know how to accomplish her own ends quickly, refused the invitation to go along. "No, thank you," she said with fervency. "I know trouble when I see it, and I'm staying away from that Della Baldwin."

Never having driven a rig in her life, Gladdy borrowed Ida's horse and buggy and, stiff as a poker with anxiety, took off down the road. Kerry stood in the yard watching, convulsed with laughter that was tempered by concern. If Gladdy survived, she would try the same thing, perhaps ending up at Connor's place for a cup of tea . . . was that out of the question? She feared it was. If only she could indeed pray, what a prayer she would make! And all directed toward a bitter consummation of Connor Dougal's responsibility in Franny's death. Not quite certain that God would be in sympathy with such a prayer, she remained silent. And strangely dissatisfied.

<hr/>

When Gladdy, perspiring and weak from tenseness, pulled into the Baldwin yard, Dudley was awaiting her. There was a fine glow on his face as he reached for her hand and helped her down.

"Brave girl," he said and, mother or no mother, touched his lips to hers. Each started back, as though a spark had been ignited between them. Staring at each other, silent and awed, neither spoke.

"For heaven's sake, *Dud,* tie up that horse and bring the girl inside!" Della's querulous call rang out from the shadow of the porch.

Walking side by side, carefully not touching, Dudley and Gladdy crossed the yard and entered the house.

"Good morning, Mrs. Baldwin," Gladdy said, obviously still bemused by Mother Nature's explosive confirmation of the feeling developing between herself and her "intended."

"That'll be *your* name, don't forget, if this madcap plan goes through. But then, you're old enough to make up your own mind. If Dudley is bound and determined to go his own way, then I guess it's a good thing he'll have somebody to go along with him." With that, Della seemed to lay aside her objections and went about helping.

Gladdy was surprised and pleased to see the sets of dish towels and pillowcases, the odds and ends of household gear, the canned goods and condiments that Della had laid aside for her son's use in his new venture. "Might as well go prepared," she said offhandedly. "Henley and I were in the same situation once, with much less in the way of goods. We made it, and you can too."

Gladdy was in a daze of mixed feelings: her new association with a husband-to-be; Della's surprising attitude; the wonderful selection of things she and Dudley would have to take with them.

For a girl who had owned nothing all her life in the way of worldly goods, it was a marvel and a wonder.

Before she climbed into the buggy for the return trip to the stopping place, Gregor had arrived on the scene. Gregor was bringing equipment to the Baldwin farm, replacing the items Dudley was taking with him.

———

"That Della surprised me," Gladdy later reported to Kerry. "Perhaps it was seeing all these things in excellent shape that Gregor was bringing to the Baldwin place, or maybe it was finding out that I wasn't quite a pauper and had funds to put toward this venture. But anyway, whatever the reason, she was as nice as anyone could want—"

"'I washed my steps with butter,'" Kerry murmured, and Gladdy frowned.

"Now what is that supposed to mean?"

"I don't interpret them," Kerry said loftily, "I just quote them."

Quite used to these scriptural interruptions, Gladdy sighed and continued. "Back to Della—if you care to listen—Dudley says she can be that way, nice one minute, cutting like a knife the next. I guess I'm glad we'll be out from under all that. Do you know what else she said?" Gladdy blushed a rosy red. "'The worst thing about all this is that you won't be around so I can dandle grandchildren on my knee.'"

"Heavens! What did you say to that?"

"Well, nothing, actually, though I felt like saying 'Don't count your chickens before they're hatched!'" And both girls fell onto the bed, laughing. But it was a joyous laugh. Joyous for Kerry because her friend seemed truly happy; joyous for Gladdy because these blessings were in sight and no longer an impossible dream.

———

Dudley and Gregor had much to do before Dudley should be free to leave. They were making the Baldwin wagon into a covered wagon or prairie schooner; they were sorting harness and tools, deciding what the home place could do without and what Dudley should take. He would take the team of horses, a cow and her calf, and the dog.

They were turning a small shed, or granary, on the Baldwin place into a shack for Gregor. The two homesteads were part of the same section and could be reached by a track between the properties, but there would be times when movement between the two would be impossible due to the dropped temperature or the drifts of snow that tended to pile up when snowstorm followed snowstorm.

Gregor felt he should be near so that Della would feel secure until she became accustomed to living alone. So he supposed— and Dudley agreed—that it would be good to bring his cattle over. In that way, he could milk cows for both households and care for all the stock at the same time. That meant, of course, that this shack would be Gregor's home; the cabin on his homestead would remain vacant most of the time.

"I think," Dudley had confided in Gladdy, "that he wants to have a place where he can go if things get too miserable here. Trouble was—Dad never had that option. It might have cooled Ma down rapidly if he had ever stood up to her or pulled out . . . or *something*."

When Gregor's housing arrangement was explained to Della, she merely sniffed. Gregor and Dudley hid their grins.

Della was turning out to be more of a surprise than anyone would have imagined. Curtains appeared for the shack's windows, then a braided rug. Gregor brought a small, flat-topped heater on which he could heat coffee and food, a bed, and a comfortable wooden rocking chair. A cushion appeared, as if by magic, padding the chair's seat. And, interestingly, it matched the curtains.

"Charming," Connor ventured, having come over to help and staying to admire. Gregor's mighty fist was shaken in Connor's face.

"Hey, back off!" Connor spluttered in mock terror. Even in play, Gregor's strength was formidable. No bearcat would tangle with him, for sure and certain! Would Della?

"Gregor," Connor said, becoming thoughtful, "looks to me as if you're settling in here for the long haul."

"Could be. Could be," Gregor said noncommittally.

Connor pondered the situation. Della had been a widow for three years or so. A handsome woman in her prime, with an abundance of energy, she could very well consider marriage again. Especially with her son absent and the house empty of a male presence.

Connor studied Gregor. No telling exactly how old he was, but surely no more than two or three years younger than Della, if that. Connor had an idea that if Gregor shaved off his beard and cut back his hair, his age might be revealed as far different than anyone suspected; there was considerable gray in the cinnamon-tinted aura that ringed his head.

He had been married years ago and fathered a child. Yes, Gregor had lived, had suffered, had survived. This present challenge was small in comparison, Connor supposed.

"Vat aboud you, my fren'?" Gregor asked, casting a keen if small eye on his friend and interrupting Connor's speculations.

Connor feigned ignorance. "What do you mean?"

How much should he share of his hopes, Connor wondered, his tentative dreams? This man Gregor was the closest friend he had, along with Parker Jones. If they couldn't share personal things with one another, there would be no one else. He knew that Gregor was a praying man, and there was something about this situation with the newcomer Kerry Ferne that had him puzzled, almost uneasy, and it demanded prayer.

Gregor shot Connor another knowing glance. "Don't blay dum wit' me! I mean dat young voman Kerry. Vat you gonna do aboud her? She's only gonna be here a few veeks more, I tink. You gotta vork fast, my fren', if you're inderested. And I tink you're crazy if you're not."

Removing a nail from his mouth and hammering it into the floor they were repairing, Connor's response, from his kneeling position, was muffled.

"You 'tink' too much!" Connor said. "You're too suspicious. But I suppose it's natural, whenever an unattached woman comes around. I admit, Gregor, I'm in deep. But so far, just in my thinking."

Connor sat back on his heels, his disreputable hat pushed onto the back of his head, his forehead creased in a frown, and his eyes thoughtful. "There's something about it all that troubles me. I can't put my finger on it. I'm praying a lot, though, and I wonder if this is some check of the Spirit. Parker Jones assures us the Lord will give wisdom when we ask. I'm asking. I wouldn't want to marry the wrong person; making a mistake that would wreck my entire life, not to mention hers."

"Neder should you let her get away if she's da right vun. An' you ain't got long to make up your min'!"

"Will you help me pray, my friend?"

Gregor assured Connor that he would, adding, "An' you, Connor, how about you praying aboud me and, me an' . . . dis Della arrangement."

And so it was agreed. They parted company, each much more at ease than before, and feeling that, having committed their way to the Lord and trusting in Him, He would bring it to pass.

Kerry and Gladdy had another Sunday dinner at the Morrisons', and not only were Gregor and Connor included, but now Dudley must come, too. With his new status as husband-to-be and his plans to take to the road very soon, trekking even farther north and west, there was a dignity about the young man that had been missing when his life was at loose ends and his dreams hopeless.

Kerry worked her wiles, such as they were, on Connor Dougal. Why was it, she wondered, more frustrated than was called for, that he directed such straight looks at her? Why was there very little laughter and repartee on his part, when he was not a humorless person? Why did she feel that Cupid's bows were falling short of their mark? Half-sick with the sham and the charade, Kerry's feelings dropped to an all-time low.

It's not working! she thought, *and I can't wait around here forever. I guess I'll have to corner him, accuse him and destroy him, and do it ruthlessly!* And it all seemed sadly dissatisfying.

When dinner was over and Mary and Mam were down for their needed Sunday afternoon rest, the young women—Kerry and Gladdy, Molly and Margo—enjoyed the comradeship of doing up the dishes together while the men took themselves off to the shade of a nearby poplar. Even Kerry, who had no previous experience, plunged in and helped.

"Have you had any success in finding a place?" Molly asked.

Kerry shook her head. "No, and I'll not look much longer."

Gladdy glanced at her sharply. Was this trip's purpose, for Kerry, about to come to an end?

"You could take our buggy for a day, if you wish," Molly said, rubbing the dishrag with Fels Naptha and working up a suds, "and drive around the area. Sometimes people don't really know how badly they want to leave until the opportunity presents itself. Cash speaks louder than words in instances like that."

"Thanks, but it isn't a matter of life and death," Kerry explained, not wanting to buy a place by any stretch of the imagination; simply needing an excuse to stay in Bliss.

⟨⟩

"Did it ever occur to you," Gladdy asked later in the privacy of their room at the stopping place, "that you're being as deceitful as Connor Dougal was?"

Kerry flared angrily. "Don't mention my name in the same breath with that pious trickster! It isn't the same thing at all! He deliberately set about to victimize—"

"And you're not?"

"He dropped her like her feelings didn't matter!"

"Won't you, when this is over?"

"She never heard from him again!"

"Will they hear from you? Face it, Kerry. You are deceiving them, and you don't care about their feelings; you'll pull out of here once Connor is unmasked and go off and leave a real mess here for others to handle. Right?"

"It has to be done," Kerry persisted stubbornly, and Gladdy fell silent.

But a little seed had been planted, and try as she would, Kerry couldn't get it out of her mind. The remainder of the day and into the evening she was heavyhearted, restless, torn. At last she threw up her hands, figuratively speaking, in capitulation to what Gladdy had said, and admitted to herself with painful honesty that she was nothing but a miserable fraud, no better than the man she had come to persecute.

With Gladdy already retired for the night, Ida said, "I'm going to my room, Kerry. Will you put out the lamp, please, when you come to bed?" and Kerry, troubled and despairing, went outside, to stand alone in the fragrant night and look up at the stars. Their steadfastness, their quiet, seemed to mock her unquiet spirit.

"'Behold,'" she cried out to them silently, tears on her cheeks, "'for peace I had great bitterness.'"

They twinkled on, they shimmered, distant and silent. Feeling like a speck in comparison, Kerry prayed the first spontaneous prayer of her life, tossing it out into endless whirling space to find its way—she knew not where.

But first it was natural, being Kerry and overwhelmed by heaven's vastness, that a verse of Scripture would come into her mind: "'When I consider thy heavens,'" she murmured brokenly, "'the work of thy fingers, the moon and the stars, which thou hast ordained; what is man, that thou art mindful of him?'"

Then she explained humbly—and it was the little waif Kerry speaking—"O Lord, in your Book, when it says 'him,' I believe it means 'her,' too. Then, O Lord, 'what is woman, that thou art mindful of her?' Please, O Lord," and the cry was a prayer, "be mindful of me!"

The night continued silent, the air continued fragrant, the stars were unchanging. Kerry went inside, prepared herself for bed, blew out the lamp, climbed into bed, closed her eyes, and felt that the dark wasn't as impenetrable as it had seemed before she prayed.

Gregor Slovinski stopped by the Connor Dougal place to drop off the mail he had collected on his trip to the post office. Finding Connor taking a break with a cup of coffee and a cold biscuit, Gregor joined him at the table.

"How's it going?" Connor asked. "I don't see as much of you as I did before you moved. Having the care of two places really doubles your work. Or will, when Dudley is gone. How are you getting along with Della?" Might as well be blunt about it, Connor figured.

"So far, so good," Gregor said, spreading syrup on a biscuit and taking a huge bite out of it. "Vat a voman!"

Connor looked at his friend with surprise, perhaps even awe. "You're kidding, surely! You almost sounded admiring. What would prompt such an evaluation of the brittle and bristly Della?"

"Lissen, my fren'," Gregor said, seriously. "All dat voman needs is prober handling. You godda know da prober vay to vork mit her. Some peeble don't . . . ain't . . ." Gregor was at a loss for the "prober" words to express himself. But he tried. "What I mean iss, she's been left to run vild over peeble all her life. I betcha she done it to her ma and pa; I betcha she done it to her husban'. I betcha it made her unhappy, doin' it! Ever'body needs to know where da boundaries iss. Animals need 'em, shildren need 'em, peeble need 'em. Yah?"

"Well, I knew her husband a little; he died soon after I came. He was a good man by all accounts and very good to Della. But you're right, he didn't stand up to her. As for Dudley, well, kids are taught to respect their elders. Until recently, Dudley has been as tame as a house cat. Seems he's finally getting a backbone, and I'm glad for him. It'll make the difference between a miserable existence as an underdog, or becoming an independent man with a life of his own."

"Dat Gladdy," Gregor said admiringly, between sips of scalding hot coffee, "ain't she somepin'?"

"Dudley's a lucky young man. I predict a good life for them. A hard one, but a good one. When are they leaving, by the way?"

"Two, t'ree weeks. Now, Connor, vat aboud dat udder young voman, Kerry Ferne? Ain't we been prayin'? If you don't get a

216

move on, my fren', she'll be gone. Den vat? You'll be a lonesome old bachelor once more, vit no hopes of anyt'ing bedder."

Connor was silent for a moment. "I know," he said finally. "But it's not right, somehow. I'll just keep praying and waiting, if that's what it takes. Not everyone is as lucky as you, Gregor, to fall into the hands *and lands* of the 'prober' female."

Gregor roared his mighty laugh. "Hah, Hah! Vell, I may be on her lands, my fren', but I ain't in her hands!" And he slapped Connor on the shoulder until Connor's cup slopped its coffee, and the chair on which he was sitting shook and wobbled.

"Easy, you great wooly mammoth!"

"I bedder get back home, or dere von't be no more ubside-down cake for me. Dat would teach me a lesson! Yah!" Gregor grinned, and his huge frame trembled in mock fear of the dreaded Della.

"Upside-down cake! You're turning her *world* upside down! Yah!"

◦━━━◦

"Take your Bibles," the pastor said, "and turn to the first verse of the Gospel according to St. John."

There was a shifting of the congregation as they opened their well-worn Bibles. Rough fingers parted the fragile pages tenderly, locating the proper selection.

"'In the beginning,'" read Parker Jones, "'was the Word, and the Word was with God, and the Word was God.'"

Reading from her neighbor's Bible, Kerry heard the words as thunder in her ears. *The Word was with God, the Word was God.*

What did it mean? Using words from the Bible as she did, having memorized as many of them as she had, still the meaning of *the Word* escaped her.

But Parker Jones was not done.

"The Word was made flesh and dwelt among us," he explained earnestly. "His name was Jesus. He came down and lived among us, and men beheld His glory—"

And women, Pastor. And women! cried the listening Kerry silently, her mind just beginning to recognize and her heart just beginning to behold.

"—the glory that was his as the only Son of the Father, full of grace and truth."

In that instant, in a blinding insight, Kerry understood that she had known the word, but not the *Word.* Acquainting herself with the one, she had overlooked the other. Filling her head with the word, her heart had been barren of the Word. And how barren it was! How starving! Like a flower that has sprouted beside an oasis but has never partaken, she thirsted. Parker Jones was continuing, enlightening her further, and she drank it in.

"John tells us that the world didn't know Him, didn't recognize Him, didn't receive Him. This holds true in our day also. Though we have our churches, our preachers, our Bibles, men and women still live in ignorance of the Word. 'But as many as receive him,'" the voice of the pastor lifted with the good news and Kerry's hopes with it, "'he gives the right to become the children of God—children born not of natural descent, nor of human decision, but born of God.'"

How can it be?

"It's called the new birth," Parker Jones explained, straight to Kerry's heart. "Born again, not of corruptible seed, but of incorruptible, by the *word of God*, which lives and abides for ever."

Parker Jones preached on, and it was good and true, but Kerry was caught up in the marvel of the Word so simply revealed. Phrases and verses tumbled together in her mind, organizing themselves into reality and truth—*the entrance of thy word giveth light . . . thy word have I hid in my heart, that I might not sin against thee . . . there are three that bear record in heaven, the Father, the Word, and the Holy Ghost, and these three are one.*

And "Ye shall know the truth, and the truth shall make you free." Did Parker Jones say it or was it, again, the thunder in her ears? Her ears and her heart?

When Parker Jones gave what he called an "invitation" and explained that the rude front bench was for repentant sinners—should they need to lay their sins and burdens there—Kerry discovered that the sins and burdens of her own poor heart had already lifted and gone, and that by believing in and accepting the Word, she had believed in and accepted Christ.

Perhaps it was her copious tears and her sniffling nose, perhaps it was her lifted head and her trembling smile, but God's people understood and reached for her, arms going around her, hands patting, faces pressed close in similar tears and smiles.

> Peace! peace! wonderful peace,
> Coming down from the Father above!
> Sweep over my spirit forever, I pray,
> In fathomless billows of love.

The third time the congregation sang the song, Kerry had it memorized; her quavering voice joined theirs, and she sang it as a testimony. For here was the peace! She hugged it to her like the treasure it was.

Finally she turned to leave, feeling that she did indeed experience "the peace of God, which passeth all understanding," trusting that it would indeed keep her heart and mind through Christ Jesus.

Smiling brothers and sisters in the Lord passed her along from hand to hand, down the aisle, out the door, to the sunshine beyond.

Peace . . . peace . . . jangle! Waiting for her, meeting her face-to-face—Connor Dougal.

There he stood—Connor Dougal.

There he stood, the man who had shamelessly wooed Franny, breaking her heart and her spirit, and taking her to her grave. There he stood, hat in hand, smiling and more handsome than any man had need to be, a reprobate if ever she saw one.

There he stood, and all of heaven waited, it seemed, for Kerry to move. For her to speak or not speak, to forgive or not forgive, to leave retribution to the Lord or hold stubbornly to her right to it. Having just prayed "Forgive me my debts," would she also pray "as I forgive my debtors"?

Only a second did she hesitate. The Father's forgiving was too sweet to jeopardize, His peace too hardly bought to risk losing. Only a second, but in it Kerry remembered the Scripture, "Let the peace of God rule in your hearts." *Let . . . allow . . . do not hinder or stop the peace.* The choice, it seemed, was up to her. Only a second, but in it Kerry made the decision that put the vengeful spirit from her; she sensed it drop away as surely as a heavy weight might leave her shoulders. Oh, but forgiveness was sweet; sweet to receive, and sweet to give.

With a heart as light as the dandelion thistle floating on the air around her and as happy as the birdsong erupting from the bush, she stepped forward and took Connor's extended hand. New tears, tears of relief and unspeakable joy, welled into her eyes and needed to be stopped before they ran down her cheeks and onto her gown. Her own handkerchief already being sopped, Connor Dougal pulled his large one from his pocket and tenderly mopped the eyes that, in the brilliant noonday sun, shone more purple than black.

"This will be a day of special celebration," Molly Morrison declared at Kerry's elbow. "Remember, our invitation for dinner is a standing one. Today of all days, we want you there with us. You come, too, Connor. And Dudley and Gladdy. Where's Gregor?"

The big man was talking to someone, standing at his horse's head, prepared to leave as soon as Della was in the rig. For the first time, he had brought her to church; Dudley was using the Baldwin rig to pick up Gladdy. Though the walk from the stopping place to the church was short, he relished being with her. Kerry had walked to church with Ida.

Now, standing beside Gregor's buggy, one hand holding her Bible and quarterly and the other pinching her skirt and holding it up out of the way, Della was ready to ascend the one step into the rig. Tapping her foot, Della waited. All of Bliss's congregation noted and waited with bated breath.

Casting a calculating eye toward Gregor Slovinski, Della lifted her voice and called sweetly, "Oh, Mr. Slovinski!"

"Chust a minute, missus," he answered politely, "and ve'll be on our vay." And Gregor returned to his conversation.

That familiar, frosty look and those flaring nostrils might have alerted Gregor to the state of affairs. Perhaps he wasn't looking. Certainly it alerted Dudley, who had been branded *Dud* by Della in an identical situation. It alerted the good folk of Bliss, who could recall hearing Henley scorchingly called *Hen* for the same oversight—not helping Della in or out of the buggy. How would she deal with Gregor Slovinski? They weren't long in finding out.

As though she had a bug on a pin, Della had Gregor where she wanted him—at a disadvantage before the watching eyes of Bliss.

Into the silence, a hushed, waiting silence, Della's voice warbled clear and strong: "Oh, *Slo*, I'm waiting!"

Gregor, all three hundred pounds of him, turned as quickly and lithely as a roused lion. In a split second he was at Della's side.

"You called, missus?" Like a playful lion he roared it, not a foot from Della's face. Startled, she took a step back, dropping the hem of her skirt into the dust, blinking her eyes.

"Yah!" he bellowed joyfully.

Before she could move, he reached for her. His two hamlike hands gripped her around her waist; he gave a mighty heave, and much as a child would toss a rag doll, he swung her up and around, her skirts swirling and her feet flying high into the air. This extraordinary demonstration culminated in Gregor swinging her over the wheel, into the buggy, and onto the buggy seat. The buggy bounced, Della's hat tipped over one eye, and her hair, having escaped its pins in the wild curvet, fell in loose, unaccustomed liberty around her astonished face.

When the buggy had stopped rocking and Gregor had seated himself at Della's side—the expression on his broad face as pleased as though he had taken part in a celebration—a hesitant clapping was heard from the back of the crowd. Within seconds the acclaim swelled into a grand round of applause and a few hurrahs.

"I feel quite certain," Angus Morrison said to Parker Jones, "that we've just witnessed the beginning of a great and mighty miracle. It'll be a long day before she considers belittling Gregor in public again."

"It was a drastic measure," Parker Jones said, awed by the performance, hesitant to approve it, but recognizing its possible therapeutic value. "But I think you may be right. For Della's sake, I hope so. I have a feeling she is in a pit of her own digging and doesn't quite know how to get herself out. Gregor may be just the man to do it. We may yet see a different Della."

"God grant it," Angus said piously, adding more wickedly than he ought, "*and* Gregor."

The congregation, with two stories to relate—one of blessing, perhaps the other also—made their way homeward to dinners that had been left roasting in the oven, a much needed and relished Sunday nap, and the never-ending evening chores and figured it had been a memorable day.

On the way to the Morrison home for Sunday dinner, Parker Jones rode with the family. Dudley took Kerry and Gladdy in his rig, though Connor had invited Kerry to ride with him. Kindly but firmly she had chosen to ride with Dudley.

In his buggy by himself, Connor thought of Gregor and the statement he had made by his amazing reaction to Della's attempt at establishing her authority over him. It didn't exactly seem the Christian thing to do! And yet it was done with such good will, so spontaneously—or was it spontaneous? Connor believed Gregor may have acted with purpose, with the best of intentions. And it might just work. Gregor could well be the very man for the taming of the shrew that was Della Baldwin. Connor regretted that Gregor was missing Sunday dinner with the Morrisons; hopefully Della, with her eyes opened and her thoughts settled, would feed Gregor her oven's roast chicken and vegetables as well as a generous serving of upside-down cake. Upside down! Connor found himself laughing with great good humor at the recollection of Della's first flight through air.

Connor trusted Gregor. Though he would never be a doormat for feet to be wiped on, he was capable of great compassion, sympathy, and gentleness. Moreover, he was a godly man—a combination worthy of any woman's attention. Connor checked his thoughts at this point concerning the future of Gregor and Della, although he had a suspicion of what it might hold.

In Dudley's rig, a wary and uncertain Gladdy watched Kerry secretly from time to time as they made their way to Morrisons and dinner. This step of Kerry's meant the end of her plan for revenge, of that Gladdy was quite sure. Unsympathetic toward it anyway, and having advised Kerry to let bygones be bygones, Gladdy breathed a sigh of relief and felt the coming moment of their separation—she northward, Kerry eastward—would be easier for her if Kerry were free of that terrible need for retaliation. It had happened because of a prayer! Gladdy found it hard to grasp.

Once, catching Gladdy's perplexed eye, Kerry drew a quivering breath and gave her first "testimony": "It's real, Gladdy. And it's . . . oh, so precious." It seemed as if Kerry were about to puddle up again, and Gladdy quickly changed the subject.

Arriving at the farmhouse and climbing down from the rig and joining the others, Kerry's good news was shared again, this time with Kezzie Skye, "Mam" to the entire group, herself so recently forgiven and cleansed of a terrible wrong that had cast a dark shadow on her life for years. Together they rejoiced, and Gladdy and Dudley, watching, felt wretchedly as if they were outside of some blessed circle. And wondered if there was room for two more in it. Wondered, and said nothing.

Wondered and smiled, and ached inside. Talked about their plans to leave, and felt bereft. Held hands under the table, and felt alone. Ate heartily of the roast beef, and felt empty, so empty.

Sitting at the dinner table, side-by-side with Kerry once again, Connor tried, fervently now, to engage her in conversation. Here, at last, was the woman he had looked for and hadn't quite located.

Where, before, there had been a brittle, bright, contrived response on her part, now there was a gentle sincerity. Her great pansy-black eyes turned his way from time to time, and they were guileless, lacking the purpose he had read in them before. Her shining black head tipped attentively in his direction when he spoke, but the little by-play that a man recognizes, the open invitation that had been in her eyes, was missing. Her smile was genuine; there was no flirting.

Here was the woman he had looked for and had not found. Something warm and validating rose in Connor's heart. With any luck—with God's help, he hastily amended—she could be persuaded to stay, could be wooed, and could be won!

But try as Connor would, he could find no answering response from Kerry. The previous interest she had shown in him was missing, and he was puzzled. Why had this morning's experience turned his heart toward her, and hers away from him? For, as the meal wore on, it became very clear indeed that Kerry, though gracious and polite, had removed herself from him in any intimate way. Strange!

But still—because of the morning's spiritual victory—Connor felt convinced that here was a young woman worthy of pursuit. He even dared think that God was in it—after weeks of prayer about it, he could believe that indeed God was in it.

At his side, in answer to an inquiry, Kerry had just stated that she would be leaving in a couple of weeks. He couldn't let any grass grow under his feet, so to speak.

And he made a real effort, only to find, again and again, that the door to anything close and personal with Kerry Ferne was shut. Perhaps locked.

On her part, Kerry was torn by a mix of feelings. Oh, that Connor weren't so attractive to her!

How could she find him attractive—in manner, in speech, in face and figure—when he was a hypocrite at heart? She groaned at her own foolishness. She would be kind to him; she had forgiven him as God required but pursue him any longer? Of course not! She felt sick with shame when she thought about her previous actions. And now, when she had changed and would no longer play at that misbegotten game, he was—if she could read the signs—giving her definite signals of his interest. It was a cruel situation. He had rejected her, for some reason; now she would reject him.

Surprisingly, she was swept by an occasional rising of rage against him. Silently crying out to God for help against this unacceptable attitude, Kerry began to understand what forgiving "seventy times seven" meant. However many times it was required of her, she would do it! So she prayed for grace, smiled on him, hardened her heart against him, and forgave him, all at the same time. No wonder she was sadly torn.

Too bad, too bad, to find a gem of a man and know he was false at the center of his being!

Dudley and Gladdy, across the table, were more quiet than usual. The glad talk of spiritual things—did it make them uncomfortable? Loving Gladdy as she did, Kerry wanted so much to include her and Dudley too in her present joy. A matter for prayer! Already Kerry was learning.

Someone asked that the gravy be passed down the table. Dudley, being closest to the gravy boat, reached for it. His unbuttoned coat fell open as he leaned forward. Shining across his vest, winking golden in the light—swung a chain. A chain with a small round charm dangling from it. A chain with a charm that was a . . . compass.

It was Franny's father's chain and compass.

Kerry had seen it too often and too closely to be mistaken. Dangling across the chest of Dudley Baldwin: the chain and compass that had been the cherished property of Franny Bentley. It was treasured particularly because it had been the only memento Franny had to remind her of her father. It signified Franny's confidence in . . . *someone* in the Canadian bush and had been sent as a token of her trust; it had been a pledge given to an untrustworthy love.

In the moment following the revelation of Dudley's involvement, sight and sound seemed to fade from Kerry's consciousness, and a whirligig of thoughts spun through her head. How did Dudley come by the personal property of Franny Bentley? Had Connor, having dismissed from his mind the idea of marriage, given Franny's gift to Dudley? Or—stabbing her heart with its possibilities—had she falsely accused an innocent man all this time? Finally, should she confront Dudley now, at this moment, and ferret out the truth, or must she sit in stunned silence during the remainder of the meal and afternoon?

She had no choice; her face gave her away.

Sitting across the table from her was the one who knew her best. Gladdy saw the look of shock and dismay on Kerry's face. That face, usually glowing, ardent, even piquant, was bleached of color. Gladdy was alarmed.

"Kerry, what's wrong?" So intense was the edge of fear in Gladdy's voice that everyone heard it. Silence fell around the great table, and all eyes turned—first on Gladdy, then, following her gaze, across the table to Kerry.

Kerry was staring at the bright wink of the handsome gold chain that was stretched across Dudley's middle. So stark and fixed was her gaze that the eyes of one and all turned back across the table, to Dudley.

Dudley was pinned to his chair by the stares of ten people as their eyes focused on a point well below his chin, above his belt, and between the lapels of his coat. His big, bony hand went automatically to his middle, and he gathered the chain and charm into his fist.

"What?" he croaked. "What?"

All eyes shifted to Dudley's face, itself now a sickly white.

Though it lasted but a minute, the silence was electric with meaning. Gladdy was the first to move. She turned toward Dudley, placed her hand over his fist, and loosened his fingers gently. Ten pairs of eyes studied the exposed chain and charm.

Kerry came to the truth in an instant, and it came from the sick face of Dudley and the puzzled face of Connor Dougal. Guilt and shame were written on the thin, shaken countenance of the younger man; innocence and perplexity on the strong, square face of the older man. Connor Dougal did not know! Connor Dougal was innocent. Connor Dougal had never been guilty of the blame she had heaped upon him. Wrongfully heaped upon him.

Kerry was stricken speechless by the revelation, and no one else had the least understanding of what was happening. It was up to Gladdy.

Raising her eyes from the chain and charm, Gladdy looked at Kerry.

"Franny's?" she asked quietly.

Kerry wet her dry lips, swallowed, and nodded, "Franny's. Of course."

Of course! It all made sense at last. How fast her heart beat in that moment, thinking of the morning's precious moment of salvation and what it had saved her *from*. Not the least was her persistent condemnation of a man who was, apparently, innocent of the charges she had leveled at him.

Her joy was tempered quickly by pity—for the shamefaced young man opposite her and the dear, distressed face of Gladdy.

Some day, not too long from now, the concerned friends around the table would be given an explanation. Kerry's wilful part in the story would be told and forgiven. Dudley's part would be told, understood for an adolescent prank that had, nevertheless, terrible results, and he would be forgiven. For the moment, however, the puzzled friends would have to wait and trust.

For Gladdy it would not be so simple.

Gladdy and Dudley excused themselves, left the Morrison home silently, boarded Dudley's rig, and rattled out of the yard and away. What transpired between the recently betrothed pair, or at least part of it, was relayed to Kerry later in the day.

❦

"I knew it was Franny's chain and charm the minute I saw it," Gladdy said to Kerry that evening in their room, "and my heart squeezed up until I thought I couldn't breathe. I didn't know, you see, whether our affection for one another, just beginning to grow, would survive this blow. It was selfish of me, Kerry, but it was all I could think of at the moment.

"We no sooner got away from Morrisons," she continued, "than Dudley pulled the chain off his vest and laid it in my hands. 'Do with it whatever is right,' he said. 'Send it back to the lady who sent it, if you wish. Tell her how sorry I am I was such a . . . a *dud*.' Then, Kerry," Gladdy's voice was sad, "he asked how you and I knew about it, anyway. Can you imagine having to tell him the whole story? The worst moment was when I told him about Franny's death. He seemed like a frozen man, not knowing whether to choke or cry or leap out of the buggy and run away from the sound of my voice. He'll be a long time getting over that, Kerry, if he ever does.

"It wasn't easy to explain our part in it, either." Gladdy's voice was steady, but her eyes were more than a little condemning as she looked at the friend who had set the feet of both of them on the bitter track of revenge. "How can I blame him, when I was part of the scheme?"

Gladdy sighed. "Knowing him a little by now, I think I understand why he did it. It developed out of his poor relationship with his mother and a deep anger toward her. His hopelessness over his future, his adolescence, all were part of it. What happened is, he saw Franny's letter in a magazine and at first it seemed like a lot of fun to answer it. But before he knew it, he got in deeper and deeper. Well, you know, Kerry, as dear as Franny was, she was determined on following through with this and immediately turned serious on him. He got frightened when he realized she was actually going to come out here. He had to break it off, and quickly.

"He cried, Kerry. Have you ever see a grown man cry? It's dreadful. And yet it may have helped him to . . . sort of be cleansed of the awfulness. When he learned that I, personally, knew and loved Franny, he just knew it was all over between us. I think people have thrown him over, disregarded his feelings, most of his life. He feels he isn't much. And here he was, planning a new life and a new beginning, and suddenly it seemed like even that was gone for him. I couldn't let that happen, Kerry. Someone has to give him a chance. I can't throw him over, too.

"Whenever the invitation has been given, at church, he says he feels such conviction that he trembles, but he hasn't been able to respond because it might mean confessing. He's glad, actually, that it has all come out into the open. He says, whatever my feelings are for him, he loves me. I believe he does, Kerry." Gladdy sighed.

"But what about you, Gladdy? It's fine to be loyal and stand by him, but that isn't enough for a life together. How do you feel about him now?"

"Terribly disappointed, I guess. But I do understand, having met his mother and knowing his situation. And then, Kerry . . ."

"And then?"

"I have to practice what I preached to you just the other day. Remember, I told you to forgive and forget. Suddenly I have to face the same thing. But Kerry," Gladdy said weeping, "I don't have the grace that you have."

Kerry stretched her hand to her hurting friend, and as they joined tears and prayers, Gladdy found the grace she needed. Found it, and vowed to encourage Dudley so that he too would find full forgiveness and peace. It was good ground to begin a new life.

"One last thing. How come," Kerry asked, "Dudley had that picture of Connor, and why did he use his name?"

"The picture was taken at his father's funeral. A photographer showed up, looking for a little business, and he and his mother bought the pictures. It was just a freak decision to use it and Connor's name. 'I was all pimply and puny in those days,' he told me. And then he was afraid that if he used his own name, his mother might get hold of a letter. As it was, he intercepted all mail with Franny's return address on it, and no one ever found out. Kerry," Gladdy said directly, "will you forgive Dudley? It was a dreadful thing to do. In a way he's responsible for Franny's death. Will you forgive him? It's important to me."

"I already have, Gladdy. Thank God, I was forgiven first! These Scriptures that I know, they keep popping up, and now they speak to me. It was Jesus who said, 'Judge not, and ye shall not be judged: condemn not, and ye shall not be condemned; forgive, and ye shall be forgiven.' It's that simple. I don't know why I never thought of it before."

"There's no arguing with Scripture." And Gladdy hugged her friend, their tears mingling together.

"I'm glad we'll be leaving here, starting over," Gladdy said. "It'll be so much easier for Dudley to act like a man. I'm going to give him that chance, Kerry. If it kills me to keep my mouth shut and my ideas to myself, I'll do it, and he'll get on his feet and be the head of the household. I need that, and so does he." So spoke the homeless little slum transplant. And so her future stretched out before her.

Back at the Morrisons', with Gladdy and Dudley gone and the air thick with unanswered questions, Kerry had taken a deep breath and said, "All of you—thank you for being such good dear friends. You'll know all about this very soon. I think we should give Gladdy and Dudley a chance to straighten things out first. Now, if you'll excuse me, perhaps I need to leave, too. I need to think and pray and—I need to talk. To you, Connor," she said, making the decision in that moment, and turning directly to him. "I need to talk to you. Would you be so kind as to take me home?"

Difficult though it would be, she needed to explain to Connor her ridiculous posture as a flirt, confess her bitter and revengeful feelings toward him, and ask for forgiveness.

Forgiveness and peace! They were such new gifts; they were to be guarded by all means.

She was graciously excused by the family and Connor quickly consented to drive her home. In the buggy, the horse walking along sedately, the only sound being the rig's creak and the plop of hooves, Kerry's dusky complexion—that went so well with her dark hair and eyes—was drained of color. Connor watched her, concerned.

"I don't know where to start," she faltered.

"First, tell me why it's necessary to tell at all. And why to me?"

"Because it concerns you. You are at the heart and center of it all, why I'm here in the first place, why I—" Kerry's anguish made it difficult to continue. "Why I behaved like such a . . . such an *easy* woman—"

If she had been looking, she'd have seen the little smile that tugged at Connor's mouth. Never would he have described her hesitant attempts to get his attention as the work of an "easy" woman. An inexperienced woman perhaps. An innocent, uncertain girl to be more exact.

"When I'm done," she said, "you'll need to forgive me, if you can."

"I assure you I forgive you now. After all, Kerry, you didn't hurt me in any way. Did you?" His question was gentle. Acquainted with sin, he was also acquainted with forgiveness and its healing qualities. If that were needed, he would gladly cooperate.

"If I haven't hurt you already, I soon would have. And the terrible part is that I would have been glad about it," Kerry admitted, ashamed.

Connor looked puzzled now. "Perhaps you had better tell me," he said.

Where to start?

She turned to her string bag, opened it, and searched until she found it—the picture of Connor Dougal.

"I'll start here," she said, holding it up for him to see. See and frown.

"Where did you get that?" he asked. "I don't believe I've ever seen it."

"It was sent to my dearest friend in all the world, Frances Bentley. She was as dear as a sister to me. I don't suppose that name means a thing to you—"

"Not a thing. I've never heard it before. Never saw the picture, never heard the name."

"Franny corresponded with someone . . . with this man," Kerry held up Connor's picture again.

Connor's eyebrow quirked. He was alert now.

"And," she went on doggedly, "he asked her to marry him—"

"Hold on a minute! This sounds like some fairy story!"

"It's all too terribly real."

"All right. But if it's so troubling, why can't it just be forgotten?"

"Because—now that I know how wrong I was and how innocent you are—I need to ask you . . . with all my heart . . . to forgive me!" Already wept out from the morning's purging, Kerry found a fresh supply somewhere, and again the tears puddled, pooled, and ran. Again Connor's handkerchief was proffered, and again it served its purpose.

"'I have eaten ashes like bread,'" Kerry sniffled, finding the Scripture to be painfully descriptive.

"Come now," Connor said comfortingly, "dry your tears. As near as I can tell, I'm supposed to have done something terrible to this dear friend."

"You, or . . . somebody. But I blamed you. That's why I'm here, Connor—"

As yet Kerry didn't have Dudley's explanation, which would come later through Gladdy, but she knew enough to tell Connor about the letters sent in his name, the proposal, the final rejection, darling Franny's collapse.

"It was Dudley, I suppose," Connor said thoughtfully, "and he sent my picture. It may have been taken at his father's funeral. And the chain and charm—where do they fit in?"

"They were Franny's father's. She sent them to you—to Dudley, as it turns out—as a token of her commitment. She was preparing to come to Bliss. You'd have loved Franny," she finished brokenly.

If Kerry had dared look up, she would have seen an expression on the clean-cut face at her shoulder that would have caused her to catch her breath. When finally Connor spoke, there was such a depth of feeling in his words that Kerry did indeed turn her gaze upward, did catch her breath, did become wonder-eyed.

"Perhaps I can love Franny's friend," he said quietly. "Perhaps she can learn to love me."

The song of a distant meadowlark, winging from Saskatchewan's endless sky, touched the moment with piercing sweetness.

"Perhaps," Kerry whispered, but he heard.

He heard, and his eyes lit with hope and happiness. "Thank You, Lord!" he lifted to that same broad sky, recognizing a wiser and bigger hand than his own in all of this.

Perhaps the sound of the horse's hooves and the turning wheels stirred the surrounding greenery, for a rich paean of song poured forth from the bush's birds, all primed and practiced, it seemed, to celebrate the moment.

"'The time of the singing of birds is come,'" Connor quoted jubilantly, and he drew Kerry's head to a place of rest on his shoulder.

"Song of Solomon, chapter two, verse twelve," Kerry murmured, not a bit surprised that Connor Dougal would describe this special moment with Scripture.

Ruth Glover was born and raised in the Saskatchewan bush country of Canada. As a writer, she has contributed to dozens of publications such as *Decision* and *Home Life*. Ruth and her husband, Hal, a pastor, now live in Oregon.